DARLINE SERVANT

'Patrick, I will not keep a servant who lies to me.'

'No, madam.' He looked down as if studying the carpet.

'What do you think this deserves?'

'I'm willing to be punished, madam.'

'It will be more severe than usual.'

'I'm willing to accept it, madam. Whatever you want to do to me.'

DARLINE DOMINANT

Tania d'Alanis

This book is a work of fiction.
In real life, make sure you practise safe sex.

First published in 1998 by
Nexus
Thames Wharf Studios
Rainville Road
London W6 9HT

Typeset by TW Typesetting, Plymouth, Devon

Printed and bound by
Cox & Wyman Ltd, Reading, Berks

ISBN 0 352 33287 5

Contents

1

A Boy-maid

There was a tap at the door and Lilian came in. 'The young man is here for interview from the agency, madam,' she announced.

The Bare Service Bureau had suggested a boy-maid this time. They supplied domestic staff of all kinds and a speciality was to supply domestic staff who would serve naked on a daily basis; sometimes extending to permanent employment.

'Good morning. I'm Ms Pomeroy.'

The boy bowed and said, 'Good morning, madam.'

'And what is your name?'

'Patrick Lovelace, madam.'

'What a lovely name; it reminds me of the poet. Do sit down.' Patrick seated himself diffidently on the edge of an armchair and Darline sat back and crossed her legs, showing more than a little of her luscious thighs.

'Tell me now, how old are you?'

'Twenty, madam.'

'Have you had any experience of domestic service?'

'No, not really, madam.'

'Then how have you been spending your time up to now?'

'I went to school and then to art school.'

'What did you specialise in at art school?'

'In fashion design, madam.'

'And did you do well at that? What did you major in for the exams?'

'I designed skirts for boys and men, madam.'

Darline pursed her lips and raised her eyebrows. 'I see. Were you noted for anything else in particular?'

'I designed unisex underwear, madam.'

'Mmm, let's go back to your schooling. How did you get on there?'

'I went to a comprehensive school, madam.'

'And did you like it?'

'Not really, madam. I was sensitive and bullied quite a lot. I didn't like football, and I was teased because of that.'

'What were your academic weak points and strong points?'

'I wasn't good at maths; but I was good at art, English and drama.'

'Did you act in any plays?'

'I played Atahualpa in *The Royal Hunt of the Sun*. We had a lovely English and drama teacher, Miss Bennett, and she cast me as Atahualpa. I had to wear a tiny loincloth.'

'Yes, I saw the play some time ago at the National Theatre. Robert Stephens was magnificent as Atahualpa and he also wore a tiny loincloth. Were you cast in any other roles?'

Patrick licked his lips. 'Miss Bennett encouraged us to write a play of our own. Mine was set in classical Rome and it was about a noble lady and her slave. I was the slave and I had to serve her in all sorts of ways. I had to stand ready with a towel and dry her back after her bath. I had to kneel before her and paint her toenails. I had to carry her folding chair when she went out walking. And she made me go naked all the time, even when I attended her outdoors.'

Darline saw Patrick liven up at the thought of it. She felt her nipples stiffen and there was a slight moistening at the delta of her thighs.

'And what was life at home like? How did you get on with your parents?'

'Well, I have to say they were a bit feckless. They just didn't care much.'

'Didn't care about what?'

'Well, they didn't care about my education; I had to really push it to go to art school. They just didn't care.'

2

'Did they ever spank you for naughtiness?'

'No, never.'

'How did you react to the *laissez-faire* attitude of your parents?'

Patrick looked down at the carpet, then slowly raised his eyes. 'I'm sure it was because of that I used to have fantasies. From when I was quite young I used to lie in bed at night and fantasise about being brought up very strictly.'

'Tell me some of the fantasies.'

Darline could see that Patrick was bracing himself to cast off any remaining shyness.

'They were all about being spanked or caned or punished in various ways. At first, until I was eleven, mummy would take me across her knee and take down my shorts and spank me with her bare hand. I used to fantasise that we were rich and lived in a large house with extensive grounds and, from the age of eleven onwards, mummy obtained canes and used to cane me.'

'Describe to me exactly how she did it.'

'For naughtiness or poor lesson work I would be told the previous day that I could expect my caning after breakfast the next morning. I would have the rest of the day and night – and until after breakfast the following morning – to anticipate it. Mummy would have a severe face during breakfast. When we had finished she would dab her lips with a table napkin and I would see them twitching. She would say, "Patrick, we will now go to the schoolroom". I would follow her to the schoolroom where she would tell me to take down my shorts and underwear and lie along a bench. Then she would give me six strokes of the cane.'

'Were there any other fantasies?'

'There were lots. Mummy engaged a tutor for me, a Miss Sonia Birch, and mummy told her that she was to be strict with me. Miss Birch was very attractive and often wore backless dresses and skirts and tops leaving her waist bare. She took over the caning and it was lovely to have it from such a young and attractive woman. There were other

3

fantasies, too. Sometimes we would all three go to the beach. Mummy and Miss Birch would wear bikinis but I would be made to go naked. I was embarrassed at first but soon came to enjoy it.

Darline felt herself intrigued by this pretty young man. She wanted to find out more about him but she had a female model coming for interview shortly. 'Have you any references?' she asked.

'I've got this one from my art-school tutor, madam.' He took a letter from his inside pocket and handed it to her.

Darline read the brief note which said he had done well in his fashion-design studies and that he was of good character.

She said, 'I think I'd like to give you a week's trial. How soon can you move in?'

'Whenever you like, madam. I'm living in the YMCA at the moment. I have a few belongings there.'

'You can move in tomorrow, there is a room you can have.'

Lilian entered and said, 'Madam, the lady model from the agency is here.'

'Thank you, Lilian. Take her to the studio and I'll see her there.' Darline rose and said, 'All right, Patrick, we'll see you tomorrow.'

Darline entered the studio to find the woman looking at a painting on the big studio easel. It featured a naked girl sitting bareback on a rearing horse.

'Good morning. How do you do? I'm Darline Pomeroy.'

'Hello, I'm very pleased to meet you. Trisha Spear.'

'Do sit down.'

Trisha seated herself on an edge of the model's throne and Darline perched herself on a high stool. 'I understand from the agency that you are an experienced model.'

'Yes, I've been doing it for several years.'

'And do you enjoy it?'

'Oh yes, I enjoy taking all my clothes off, I much prefer nude work.'

'Which schools have you worked for recently?'

'Mainly the Slade and Chelsea, and occasionally the Royal Academy. Would you like me to strip off for you to look me over?'

'All right, you can go behind that screen.'

Trisha disappeared behind the screen for a minute or two and emerged naked but for her extremely sexy sandals, earrings, nose ring and jewelled stud in her tummy button. She assumed several poses: arms raised with hands clasped behind her head, hands on hips; one hand cupping a breast and the other extended elegantly.

'Mmmm, I can see you're quite experienced. I like that in a model. I've recently been painting some nudes with horses – I have a private stable yard and a paddock – so I can set up such poses without drawing unwanted attention. Would you be willing to pose outdoors? My elderly groom might see you.'

'Yes, no problem. I've posed outdoors on a fair few occasions.'

'I think I can offer you some work. I'll be in touch as to dates. You may get dressed now.'

Darline sat reading a magazine when Patrick came in to serve coffee. An article on bisexuality in universities had caught her eye.

Patrick bowed attentively and placed the cup of coffee on the small table beside his mistress. He bowed again and was turning to go when Darline said, 'Patrick, don't go, tell me a little more about your home life and your fantasies. I was intrigued, when I interviewed you, about some aspects of your early life. Were any of your fantasies acted out in reality? You said you enjoyed acting in plays.' Darline smiled teasingly at her boy-maid.

'Well, madam, I did start acting some of them out. I had a friend in the fashion class, a girl called Pina, short for Philippina. She used to design the most sexy outfits. One I particularly liked had a black bodice which left the waist bare, and a short skirt made of ruffled black nylon shaped like a bell, leaving nearly all the thighs bare. Pina modelled it in class, wearing shoes with five-inch heels, and they all went wild over it, girls and boys.' Patrick stopped and licked his lips.

'Go on,' Darline said, smiling encouragement.

'Well, Pina and I soon discovered that we shared the same sexual tastes. How we first struck up a friendship was when she saw me reading *Women on Top* during the break one day. It was a lovely September day and I was sitting on the low wall beside the river, just outside the refectory. A lot of them used to sit there in the sun. She put her cup of coffee down on the wall and sat close to me and asked me what I was reading. There was no getting out of it; I showed her the cover of the book.

' "Do you really think women should be on top?" she asked meaningfully. I told her I thought they should, and that was the beginning of it; we became close friends. Before long I asked her to give me a whipping and Pina readily agreed.

'I bought a beautiful whip from an Indian shop. It was a work of art in itself, with a knobbed haft and with the lash tapering in pleated leather to its tip which had a tassel of crimson cord.'

Darline felt herself becoming aroused by the storyteller. 'Go on,' she urged.

'The tricky bit was where and when we could have the session. My mother and father usually went out to the pub on Saturday evenings, so one Saturday night after they had gone out, we went up to my room. Pina wore her special outfit with the black skirt that showed her thighs and the five-inch heels. I stripped naked and we put on a Wagner disc. I knelt and kissed Pina's feet while we waited for the *Ride of the Valkyries* to begin. Then I lay on my bed and Pina began to lash me until my buttocks burned.

'She stopped once and I begged her to go on and she did until she was tired, then she lay on top of me and kissed my back, still holding the whip. At that very moment my parents burst in. My mother screamed and my father raved. They never thought their son would turn out like this. It was absolutely disgraceful. Did we think we could use their home as a kinky sex parlour? And Pina was no better than a tart to do such a thing. Neither of us was welcome any longer and, as soon as I had packed a few things, we left and I found a room at the YMCA.' Patrick was breathing heavily.

'And did you engage in any more flagellation sessions?'

'We thought we never would but we did. It's strange how things turn out sometimes. We both knew a lady who was a mature student and had her own house. Pina told her why I had left home and she was very understanding and said we could come and have sessions at her place. It turned out that she was a dominatrix. She had a lovely house with a large sitting room with an immense pouffe over which I could lie to be whipped by Pina while Zenia sat and looked on. A couple of times Zenia did the whipping. She put Pina and me over the pouffe side by side and lashed us both simultaneously. It was thrilling; and afterwards we kissed and caressed one another with our backsides burning and then we both kissed and thanked Zenia for giving us such pleasure.'

Patrick looked at Darline as if he had perhaps said too much. 'Oh, I'm sorry, madam, perhaps I shouldn't have gone on so long.'

Darline's nipples were now stiff and her clitoris was hard and proud. 'No, don't be silly, I asked you to tell me more. By the way, Patrick, this is the last day of your trial week with me. What do you feel about it; would you like to stay here?'

'Oh yes, madam, I like it here.'

'Well, you have proved fairly satisfactory so far. I'll think about it during the day.'

'Thank you, madam. I hope you decide to keep me on.'

'I have a task for you this morning; I'd like you to hand wash some of my lingerie. I want you to be very careful with them, they are from Maitresse Hilaire of Paris and were very expensive. You may go and collect the items from my room where I have laid them out on the bed. I'd like you to do this next.'

Patrick bowed and went out. Darline looked at his slim figure as he went. He had a tiny waist for a young man, almost girlish. She smiled as she thought of what she would like to do to him. The boy had been brought up in a feckless fashion; no particular guidance or encouragement from his parents! No wonder he had indulged in fantasies of stern treatment and looked to his girl friend for correction. He was right that it was nice for boys and men to be caned by a woman. She had never caned a boy although she had spanked a girl who had previously been in her service. The girl had practically asked for it. The idea of whipping a young man was infinitely attractive. Pina and Zenia were characters! What would her friend, Flavia, the professor of psychiatry, think of them?

Darline had become absorbed in her painting and was enjoying the sensuous drawing of the brush on the canvas, and the smell of oil paint which always made her happy, when there was a timid knock on the door.

At her bidding Patrick entered. He had some moist items of lingerie in his hands. He looked at his mistress and stammered, 'M ... m ... madam. I'm terribly sorry but I'm afraid I've spoilt some of your lingerie.'

Darline looked at the flimsy garments. The stupid boy had attempted to wash several pairs of tiny black knickers along with an expensive roseate negligée and the negligée was now a dirty grey hue with streaks of dirtied rose.

'Oh, you really are impossible. Don't you know, you must never wash black things with delicate pale colours. You've spoilt my beautiful negligée.'

'I'm terribly sorry, madam.'

'Being sorry won't do any good. You are a perfect ninny! You deserve serious punishment – never mind spankings for pleasure.'

'Perhaps, madam, you could stop the cost out of my wages.'

'It would take several weeks for that and you are not going to be with me for several weeks. I have no further use for you; you will leave tomorrow when your trial period ends. You are no better than a half-wit to do a thing like that and spoil something beautiful.'

Patrick went down on his knees. 'Please, madam, don't send me away. I have nowhere to go. They won't have me at home and I can't afford to go to the YMCA. Isn't there anything to be done?'

Darline pressed her lips together. She felt powerful now, with this mild creature on his knees before her. Her lips twitched. 'Is there anything you can suggest?' She could feel the stiffness of her nipples under the painting smock. Sometimes she would paint wearing a smock over her underwear so that she could feel the more sensuous in her kinky black harnessings.

Patrick said, hesitantly, 'Perhaps you could, well, give me a whipping.'

Darline felt herself thrill at the suggestion. She had never before whipped a man. She said, 'Really, this is a bizarre suggestion. No, in any case I have no suitable instrument.'

'Perhaps you could use your riding crop, madam. You told me to treat the leather with saddle soap when I cleaned your shoes. I did so and the lash is beautifully supple.' He was licking his lips.

Darline felt herself beginning to yield. It was such an opportunity. She had often fantasised about whipping men and boys and being spanked or whipped herself by a masterful mistress, someone like Flavia; and Flavia had sometimes spanked her. She had long desired to have Flavia use a whip on her but had been too shy to suggest it.

She found herself saying, 'All right, bring me the crop. No, wait a moment – bring me one of the wraps from my wardrobe; this smock may be restrictive. Bring me the wrap and the crop first and then go to the drawing room.'

The excitement was rising in her now. He deserved it and he wanted it, and she would give it him. In a few moments the boy came in with a black wrap neatly folded and arranged on a tray together with the crop. He bowed low and proffered the items. She took them from him disdainfully and he bowed again and went out. She took off her painting smock and slipped on the wrap, which felt soft and slinky against her skin, over the black underwear. She took the crop and swished it in the air. It was beautifully made in plaited leather over a stiff core, nearly a metre long and tapering to a thin tip, ending in plaited red cord. She had never beaten a horse with it. She had only ever given a lazy or negligent horse a touch of it to show who was mistress. She went to the drawing room, taking her time over it, anticipating what was to come. As she walked in she saw the boy standing in the centre of the room. His eyes widened at the sight of her in the transparent wrap. He looked at the black harnessings on her body under the black silk and then to the crop and then back to her body. She felt deliciously arrogant as she looked at him trembling before her. She made herself take the lead, one could not expect that of this ninny.

Catching sight of a hefty camel saddle in the middle of the room she said, 'I think we'll have you bending over the camel saddle.'

Patrick moved over to the saddle, rather hesitantly, as if uncertain what to do. Darline noticed his hesitation and stamped her foot. 'You are a perfect ninny, aren't you. And you've had experience of being thrashed before so you should know what you have to do. Kneel down and bend your body over the saddle.'

Patrick obeyed and knelt before the camel saddle.

'Now bend your body over it, right over so that your buttocks will be high above the hump of the saddle.' She could feel her erect nipples; she was wearing a bra that let them peep through and they were in contact with the slinky wrap. 'Take down your trousers.'

Patrick unbuckled his belt and dropped his trousers, revealing a tiny pair of black knickers.

'Mmm, I see you have good taste in underwear. That's a small thing in your favour; take those down as well.' Patrick slipped them down to his knees where they made a ring of foamy black.

Darline moved and stood over him. 'I shall give you six strokes this time.'

Darline raised the crop and brought it swinging over in an arc so that it crashed on the boy's body. He gasped. She raised it again and brought it over and down. He was just drawing breath when the next four cuts drew further gasps. Darline lowered the crop. 'You may get up and adjust your clothes.' Patrick got slowly to his feet and pulled up his knickers and trousers.

Darline was the picture of hauteur as she regarded her boy-maid. There was a profound, strange exultation in his face. 'What do you feel now?' she asked.

'Oh, madam, I feel I want to serve you; I feel I want to obey you in everything. I want to stay in your service.'

Patrick went on his knees and, bending, kissed the feet of his mistress. Darline, standing above him, felt like a goddess.

'Get up, you fool. I am prepared to keep you on for a further time of which I shall consider the duration. You may return to your duties.'

The boy got to his feet, bowed, and went out. Darline went back to her studio. She was in a delicious state of sexual excitement as she took off the wrap. Before putting on the painting smock she examined herself in a full-length mirror which she used to see the mirror image of naked models. She had a nice figure and the black harnessings contrasted beautifully with her creamy skin. She felt a yearning for her lover, Flavia, who was in the States in exchange for an American professor. She longed to take Flavia in her arms and kiss her on those luscious lips. Then they would French kiss with their tongues going right in as stiff as phalluses. Then they would explore between one another's thighs.

She took up her palette and brushes and resumed her painting. She suddenly realised that the big hogs-hair brush she held was a phallic instrument, a dildo rod with which to make love to the canvas and apply the linseed-oil-smelling semen seed of the paint. She had made love to her slave a few minutes ago with her riding crop. (Whomsoever you love you chastise well.) She would chastise him out of the strange love she felt for him. She would see if he would be willing to accept further correction.

* * *

11

During the next week there was a remarkable improvement in Patrick's work. He cleaned the baths and toilet pedestals, the bidets and the many rooms. He cleaned Darline's numerous pairs of shoes and boots and oiled her riding crop. He prepared breakfast and the light lunch she required. He did all the washing up, including the washing up after dinner, which was prepared by the heftily built Lilian Brown, who came in daily.

As the days went on Darline started to have strange yearnings. It would be better if Flavia were here to have sex with, but she was not due to return for another month. They had however kept up a passionate correspondence. Darline had written saying that she would like to be spanked by Flavia, to go across her thighs and have her knickers taken down and feel the arousing slaps on her buttocks. But there was another month. She knew that she wanted to whip Patrick again – but she couldn't very well whip him without some pretext. If only he would offend in some small way. But she knew that he was behaving well, in order to keep his job although, she thought, he probably wanted to be punished again.

She pondered the matter which preyed constantly at the back of her mind. What could she do? Was there anything else other than flagellation that would exert her power, her superiority, over him? Something that would not seem too obvious. Then inspiration struck.

The boy was looking rather pale because she confined him to the house all day. It would do him good to have some exercise outdoors. There, that was it, she would make him run round the village green. She lived in the heart of the stockbroker belt; the gin-and-Jag part of Surrey, and the village green had been left in its original state; even the original stocks and whipping post had been preserved. Some of the windows overlooked the green so that she would be able to observe him to make sure he kept running. Sometimes things worked out just right.

A few moments later the boy came in. He was neat and clean. He approached his mistress, bowed and placed a tray of coffee beside her. 'Your coffee, madam,' he said respectfully. He took the coffee pot and efficiently poured coffee and then added cream. He bowed and was about to turn to go.

'Patrick, stay a moment, I want to discuss something with you.'

He turned and looked at her. 'Yes, madam.'

Darline crossed her legs and took a sip of coffee. The skirt she wore was rather short and it rode up slightly, exhibiting an expanse of sumptuous thigh.

'I'm concerned for your welfare and I've noticed that you are rather pale, maybe because your work is all indoors. Perhaps some fresh air and exercise would help. I think it would do you good to jog every morning after you have served me breakfast. An ideal course would be for you to jog round the village green, it's nice and close to the house. What do you think?'

'Well, yes, madam, if you think it would do me good.'

'There, I'm glad you agree. So really the sooner you start the better. You can go out for the first time tomorrow.'

Patrick shuffled his feet. 'There's just one small difficulty, madam, I have no shorts.'

'Oh, good grief, that's no problem. I have some specially designed shorts and tops. They're brief and beautiful.' Darline rose and said, 'Come along to my room with me. I'll look out some things.'

Patrick followed his mistress like the docile dog he was. She opened a drawer and took out several garments in bright yellows, reds and greens and tossed them on the bed. 'A friend, a lady who is in fashion design gave me these. How fortunate for you they are so brief. She intends to create a resurgence in the popularity of hot pants and these are her designs.'

She picked up a scanty garment. 'These may well suit. Being high cut they permit free movement of the thighs. Try them on.'

Patrick stripped to his knickers and pulled on the sleek yellow hot pants.

'Mmm, they fit you very well. In the haunches region you are about the same size as myself. Turn and let me look at you.'

13

The hot pants were so cruelly brief that the curves of the boy's buttocks were visible below the hems. 'Excellent, and yellow is such a noticeable colour, I won't lose sight of you as you jog round the green. Now, let me see if I have a top for you. These tops are for both sexes. They delightfully leave the waist and belly bare; I prefer to call it belly and waist instead of midriff. And this one matches your hot pants. Try this one on.'

Patrick slipped on the chrome yellow top and Darline regarded him.

'Yes, that outfit suits you well. You have such a tiny waist – and a taut young belly to go with it – you would look well in a bikini. There we are. You can start your jogging tomorrow, after you've served me breakfast. All right, you may go. Wear your jogging togs to serve me – then you can go immediately. You had better run on an empty stomach. You can have your own breakfast afterwards.'

Patrick picked up his clothes, bowed and went out.

The next day, Patrick entered with his mistress's breakfast on a tray. It consisted of lemon tea and croissants. He approached her, bowed and placed the tray on a small table beside her. Patrick looked like a slim girl in the hot pants, with his bare waist and long blond hair.

'Good morning, Patrick.'

'Good morning, madam.'

'And how are you this morning, Patrick?'

'I'm very well, thank you, madam.'

'Are you looking forward to your run around the green?'

'Yes, madam.'

'Very well. You may start as soon as you like.'

Patrick bowed and went out.

Darline moved over to a window seat from which she would be able to observe the boy. In a few moments she saw him running down the drive. Two inches of the cheeks of his backside were visible under the openings of the hot pants and, as he crossed the road, a postman grinned and gave a lecherous whistle. Darline thrilled inwardly.

She followed him with her eyes as he started his run along the path round the green. Two workmen were cutting grass beside the path. One of them, catching sight of Patrick, said, 'I like it,' and they both began to laugh. The boy continued his steady jogging. As he put some distance between them Darline followed him through binoculars. He seemed to be fairly fit, seemed to be able to run well. It was only right to make him take some exercise. A tan would suit him, it would contrast with his blond hair.

Two women were coming along the path, pushing buggies. Darline could see the grins on their faces as they caught sight of Patrick. He went on doggedly, pretending not to notice them.

She wondered if she was too cruel to subject him to this. No, she wasn't subjecting him to anything. She was simply making him take some morning exercise for his own good, and he looked lovely in hot pants. Nothing wrong with that. Sometimes men wear backless G-strings or nothing at all. If the yokels felt like laughing, let them. But there was something deliciously sexual and perverse in making him do this; subjecting him to the jibes of the plebeians. And it would toughen him. He was too sensitive by half; much too sensitive for a boy or even a girl. There was a delicious decadence in doing this to him, and he had willingly acquiesced.

She followed him through the binoculars as he went round the curve at the far end of the green. He was now on the home straight. Five youths were lounging against the stocks. They grinned as Patrick approached them. Then suddenly one jumped out and spread his arms in front of Patrick who somehow ducked under one of the youth's arms, and continued. Another lad ran after Patrick and made a rude gesture as if to touch him up from behind, almost reaching the cheeks spilling out of the hot pants. All five ran after him for about a hundred yards and seemed to be jeering at him, then they fell behind and stopped. Weren't such people abominable! They couldn't let something beautiful be itself.

15

As he neared the place where he had to cross the road the two men cutting grass looked up and grinned. Patrick paused to look right and left before crossing. A police car passed and the officers looked closely at Patrick, then drove on.

Darline put down the binoculars and went to her studio. Putting on a smock she started laying out a palette. The images in her mind's eye were erotic and feisty and, as she touched the canvas with the largest hogs-hair brush, she contemplated its shape and thought again how the act of painting was like making love.

There was a knock at the studio door and at her bidding Patrick entered with her light lunch on a tray. He bowed and placed the tray beside her. He was about to go when Darline said, 'Stay a moment, Patrick. Tell me, how did you enjoy your run?'

'Very much, thank you, madam.'

'You weren't bothered by anything?'

'Not really, madam.'

'Not by the villagers?'

'Some grinned and jeered and made remarks but I don't mind.'

'I have an idea. I think I'll accompany you on horseback tomorrow and give you a little moral support; perhaps a little encouragement. Tell Lucan to saddle Tempered Steel and have him ready for me tomorrow.'

Patrick was ready on the forecourt, in his hot pants and top, when Lucan led Tempered Steel round for their mistress to mount, the next day.

The front door opened and Darline came down the steps looking splendid in her riding kit of fawn jodhpurs and red silk shirt, black boots and hard hat. She carried a riding whip and a large red towel. She looked devilishly attractive.

She looked at her boy-maid and said, 'I think we'll have your back bare today. Take off your top.' She smiled impishly. 'I'll give you a little encouragement if you need it.'

16

The boy removed the brief top and stood there bare to the waist, his blond hair blowing a little in the morning breeze.

'Hasn't he a tiny waist, Lucan?' Darline remarked.

The groom grinned at the slim boy standing there in hot pants. He brought Tempered Steel forward to where Darline stood. She took the reins and, inserting a foot into a stirrup, swung up easily into the saddle. 'Let's go,' she said.

They moved off, down the drive, the boy to the right of the horse. Lucan opened the gates for them and they went through and Darline reined in to wait for a gap in the traffic. A man in a Porsche stopped for them and Darline saluted him with her whip as they crossed the road. She felt splendidly arrogant on her horse with her boy beside her. She put her mount into a trot and they set out along the curving path. The two grass cutters were working a little further along the way. They grinned as rider and runner went past but said nothing.

They continued on their way. 'What a lovely morning,' Darline said as she rose easily in the saddle. There was only the sound of skylarks overhead and the creak of saddle leather. Darline was thinking: Shall I give him a stroke of the whip? I'd love to – and he's so submissive it seems he'll take anything. No. Oh, why not? If you want to do something, do it. You have to dare in art and in life and it will be for his own good.

She gave him a light touch of the whip on his back. 'You're slacking a little, Patrick, I'll just encourage you.'

The boy smartened up his pace, raising his knees a little higher. Darline could see a bulge in the front of his pants; the cheek, she thought. I'll teach him. I bring him out to exercise for his own good and he gets excited. I know, I'll give him a light touch every minute, one after each slow count of thirty like they do in art schools for short poses when the model is keeping the time. She counted slowly to thirty and gave him a touch. There was not the slightest mark from the first. She counted again and gave him another touch. There was a look of exultation on his face.

17

Rounding a bend they saw the same two women pushing their buggies. One of them saw Darline administer a stroke to the bare back beside her.

She exclaimed, 'Oh, don't whip the boy like that, miss!'

Darline reined in Tempered Steel and Patrick came to a halt beside her.

'You shouldn't whip the boy like that, miss,' the woman said.

'It's for his own good,' Darline said haughtily. 'It keeps him in the rhythm of going round the track without flagging.'

'What does the boy have to say?'

'I don't mind in the least,' Patrick said. 'It's this lady's way of keeping me up to the mark. Although I appreciate your kindness in thinking of me.'

'Oh, well, I suppose it's all right, then. Sorry to butt in. No offence meant.' The two of them continued on their way.

'I have a surprise treat for you this morning, Patrick. Running makes one sweaty and I thought it might do you good to take a cold dip. You see that spinney of trees. In the centre of it is a pond where they traditionally bathe in the nude. I even thought of bringing a towel along for you. Aren't I kind!' She reined her mount to go along a path between the trees until they came to a clear pond with a smooth sandy bottom.

'There,' Darline said. 'You can take a cooling dip. It's perfectly all right to go in naked, there's an ancient bye-law permitting it. Lots of people bathe naked here.'

The boy slipped off his running shoes and then his hot pants and knickers and waded out into the water.

'Swim to the other side and back,' Darline called. Patrick obeyed, swimming a breast-stroke to the other side and then turning and swimming back.

'There, that was refreshing for you,' Darline said as he waded out. 'I'll help you dry yourself.' She enveloped him in the huge towel and rubbed his back. 'I know,' she said as something caught her eye. Nearby was a wooden receptacle containing some short birch brooms intended for beating out fires. 'I'll give you a Swedish massage: a swishing with one of these. You can lean across that fallen tree trunk. The Swedes certainly knew what they were about when they thought of this method of restoring circulation after a roll in the snow.'

There was a look of excitement in Patrick's eyes as he went and lay along the tree trunk. Darline was thinking: it must be like a great phallus against his body and his genitals. She took up one of the brooms and started to swish him lightly on his back and shoulders, moving systematically down to his buttocks and back again.

'There are no welts from the touches of the whip, but this swishing is bringing up your colour and should soon restore your circulation.'

Darline felt splendid now. She was his masterful mistress and he would do her will. Her nipples were becoming stiff and proud and her vagina felt moist. My God! This is the way it should be.

'There,' she said finally as she replaced the birch broom in its holder. 'Get your knickers and pants on and we'll be on our way.'

Patrick drew on his sleek little knickers and then the hot pants. Darline swung up onto Tempered Steel and they moved off.

'I won't swish you any more this morning,' Darline said. 'You look a perfectly nice colour as you are.'

A couple of youths were lounging by the village stocks. They leered at Patrick in his hot pants but said nothing as rider and runner went past. They turned up the drive and on to the forecourt where Lucan was waiting to take Tempered Steel.

'Give him a good rub down,' Darline ordered. She turned to Patrick and said, 'Have a quick shower and change your clothes and then come to my room to attend to my nails.'

19

2

Painful Lessons

Darline sat in her large luxurious bedroom with her feet on
the footstool before her; she was leafing through a copy of
Apollo. There was a tap at the door and at her bidding
Patrick entered, approached her, and bowed.

'I want you to attend to my toenails. Bring the box of
varnishes.' Patrick went to her dressing table and returned
with the flat box. He knelt before her, opened the lid and
proffered the array of glistening colours.

'Mmm, let me see. Yes, I think we'll have the, no, not
the venom green, no, we'll have our talons shine bright
with the viridian today.'

Patrick took the bottle of viridian and unscrewed the
cap. He placed a tissue under her right foot and, charging
the brush with care, began to paint the toenails, starting
with the big toe. Darline could see that he was thrilled at
his task and was admiring the beautiful feet before him.

'Patrick, there is one matter of some urgency. As I said, I
insist that any servant I employ shall be able to drive. I shall
arrange lessons for you without delay. I am acquainted with
Mrs Ingrid Riding who is director of the Correction School
of Driving. She herself sometimes takes nervous or problem
pupils; I will ask her to handle your case. Be ready for a
lesson tomorrow at eleven. You can take a cold shower
after your run to brace yourself so that you are fresh and
alert for it. I shall not ride with you tomorrow.'

In hot pants and top, leaving his taut belly and tiny waist
bare, Patrick trotted down the drive and across the road

20

onto the green. He carried a backpack with a towel. There was no one around as far as he could see. He always anticipated loutish jeers since being accosted by the five youths on the first morning and, although he was relieved, he admitted that there was a certain thrill in being exposed to the populace in this degrading way.

As he neared the spinney four girls sprang out from behind a rhododendron bush and blocked his path so that he had no choice but to stop.

'Hi,' the tallest girl said. 'I'm Melissa. Let me introduce Sarah, Kirstie and Gala.'

'I'm Patrick.'

'Come into the spinney with us,' Melissa enticed; she was tall and blonde and her manner proclaimed her the leader.

Since that was where he was supposed to go anyway, Patrick went willingly, surrounded by the four girls who chattered like magpies.

'Do you enjoy your jogging?' Melissa asked.

'Yes, I quite enjoy it.'

'We saw you with the lady on horseback yesterday,' Sarah said.

Kirstie grinned. 'Yes, we saw her whip you on your bare back.'

'Don't you mind being whipped in public?' Sarah asked.

'I accept it.'

Gala asked, 'Why did she take you into the spinney?'

'To swim in the pond.' Patrick smiled sheepishly.

Melissa spoke. 'Oh, yes; a lot of people swim in it. Naked swimming is permitted by an ancient bye-law made in the reign of Charles the Second. It was made because a young girl who went to swim naked early in the morning rescued a child which had strayed from its cottage.' Then, smiling curiously, she asked, 'Why do you let her whip you like that?'

Patrick hesitated, obviously undecided what to say. Finally he murmured, 'She's my mistress, I suppose that's why.'

'You're a masochist, aren't you?' Gala grinned at him openly, obviously intrigued.

21

Patrick shuffled his feet and said, 'Yes, I am, I like to be dominated by a woman.'

'How did you develop this taste?' Melissa asked.

'Well, it's difficult, that; I've discussed it with Ms Pomeroy, that's the lady you saw me with, and she thought it was because my parents didn't care much and never punished me. I used to fantasise about being spanked and caned by a strict mother or tutor. Ms Pomeroy thinks that for a parent to be caring is equated with discipline – in other words when a mother loves you she spanks or canes.'

The talk of spankings and canings had created an electric ambience amongst the group.

Patrick, emboldened by his subject, confided, 'I used terribly to want to be treated strictly. I used to fantasise about it endlessly; that's why I'm happy serving Ms Pomeroy. She's quite like a goddess.'

'Jesus! You really are a masochist,' all four girls said, and then laughed at how they had spoken in unison.

'It's lovely to be whipped by a woman,' Patrick mused.

'Mmm,' went the four girls, obviously excited.

Patrick was becoming more confident. 'I feel so carefree when I'm flogged by a lovely woman or when I have to serve her in all sorts of intimate ways. I'd love to give her a massage but that's more than I dare hope for. Ms Pomeroy is lovely, I worship her.'

'Wouldn't you like to have sex with her?' Gala asked.

'Well, no, it wouldn't be proper. You can't have sex with your mistress.'

'My God!' Melissa said. 'You are a total masochist and submissive. What sort of work does she make you do?'

'Cleaning, waiting on her, painting her toenails, cleaning her shoes.'

'Jeez!' Kirstie said. 'Weren't you trained for anything else?'

'I went to art school and trained as a fashion designer. I specialised in skirts for men and underwear for ladies and men.'

'Mmm!' all four girls exclaimed knowingly. 'We're at art school,' they added, smiling.

'Have you ever had sex with a girl?' Melissa asked.

Patrick looked down sheepishly and shuffled his feet in the sand bordering the pond.

'Go on,' Melissa said, 'there's no need to be ashamed if you haven't.'

Patrick was obviously trying to put a bold face on it. 'I – well, I haven't had proper sex, but my girlfriend Pina whipped me once and that started it. The very first time we did it my parents came home early and caught us at it, and I left home. Strangely, Pina's parents were more understanding about it and didn't interfere when we had a session at their house. We also had sessions in the house of a lovely older woman called Zenia, while she looked on, and once she whipped both of us together.'

The atmosphere in the spinney was charged with a strange excitement.

'But you've never had proper sex with Pina or any other girl?' Sarah quizzed him, obviously curious.

'No. By the way, I'd better get on or I'll be late back.'

'And be thrashed again,' Gala remarked with a grin.

'Yes, but I'm supposed to have a cold dip.'

'You'd better have it, then,' Melissa said.

Patrick looked nervously at the four girls. 'Yes, I'd better.'

He slipped off his running shoes and clothes and waded in. He swam to one side, then turned and swam back. When he waded out, he was glistening wet.

'He has a nice figure,' Sarah said.

'Such a tiny waist,' Melissa said, looking tenderly at him.

'Like a slim girl's,' Gala added.

'Thank you,' Patrick said. The girls could sense that he was full of some strange desire.

'Let's help you get dry. Yes, let's. Get his towel,' the girls chorused.

They enveloped him in the towel and all four dried his shivering body.

He looked at them. 'Do you know what Ms Pomeroy did the other day?'

23

'Go on, tell us,' said Melissa.

'She swished me with one of those birch brooms; she said it was to restore my circulation. I went over that tree trunk for it.'

'Would you like us to do it?' Sarah asked and Patrick grinned his assent.

They took hold of him all together and put him over the hefty log.

'Let's pretend he might struggle and try to get out of it,' Melissa said. 'Two of us can hold him while the other two swish him with the birch rods; here, Kirstie, you and I can hold him.'

Melissa held Patrick's slim wrists and Kirstie his ankles. Sarah and Gala seized birch rods and began to alternately swish him from his shoulders to his thighs. He gasped at the sting of the twigs and then began to smile. At last he said, 'Thank you. Please let me go now.'

Sarah said, 'We'd better let him go, or he'll be in trouble.' The two swishers lowered their birches. Patrick got to his feet and regained the slight coverage of his knickers and hot pants and top.

He smiled and said, 'It was good to meet you all.'

'See you,' the girls said.

'See you,' Patrick called back at them.

As he ran up the drive, Lucan emerged from the stable yard and said, 'Madam wants to see you.' He leered suggestively.

Patrick hurried to the drawing room and entered breathlessly. He bowed.

Darline regarded him with well-bred annoyance.

'What is the meaning of this? It is fifty-four minutes since you commenced your run. What have you been doing?'

'I'm afraid I took rather a long time over the swim, madam; the water was so refreshing.'

'So you saw no one else at the spinney?'

He looked down. 'No, madam.'

'Have the courage to look at me, Patrick. You are stating a falsehood. You went into the spinney with four girls. I observed you through binoculars.'

'Yes, madam.'

'Patrick, I will not keep a servant who lies to me.'

'No, madam.' He looked down as if studying the carpet.

'What do you think this deserves?'

'I'm willing to be punished, madam.'

'It will be more severe than usual.'

'I'm willing to accept it, madam. Whatever you decide.'

'I think twelve strokes of a whip will suffice. I have a lovely decorative whip I acquired in France. Unfortunately, I have sprained my painting and whipping hand, so the strokes will be laid on by Lucan. Luckily for you, he is elderly, and will not be able to lay them on hard. But the shame and humiliation of it will do you good. We'll have you strung to a tethering ring in the stable yard; there are some steel rings fixed high for when we drench the horses. You had better have a cold shower before your driving lesson to sharpen your wits. Take this note and hand it to Mrs Riding. You may go now.'

Patrick got into the car beside Ingrid Riding and handed her the envelope. She read the note and said, 'Ms Pomeroy instructs that if your progress is not satisfactory in this lesson, I am to take you to a secluded spot and thrash you. She says that you will learn best through pain. I've never been asked to thrash a learner before. If you are not willing to submit, she will dismiss you. I'm sorry about this. What do you say?'

'I have nowhere else to go and I want to remain in Ms Pomeroy's service. I have no choice but to accept and, if you consider that I merit punishment, I will of course submit.'

Patrick did not do well. He particularly fluffed a three-point turn. Ingrid yelled at him several times but he did not improve. When, a few minutes later, he fluffed an emergency stop for the second time Ingrid said, 'You would have killed someone.' She looked at him and said, 'Are you willing?'

'Do what you like with me.'

'Change seats,' she ordered.

Ingrid took the wheel and drove masterfully to a clearing in Oxshott Woods. They got out and Ingrid said, 'How does Ms Pomeroy punish you?'

Patrick said sheepishly, 'She makes me bare my buttocks and thrashes me with her riding whip.' He licked his lips. He seemed almost to be anticipating what was to come.

'And what sort of position does she put you in for it?'

'She makes me kneel and bend over a camel saddle or stand and bend over a chair. Then I have to take down my trousers and knickers.'

'Well, I have no whip, so I'd better cut a switch.' Ingrid took a knife from the dashboard and cut a flexible ash switch. She examined it and swished it in the air before trimming some projecting twigs and buds.

'We have no saddle or chair so you'd better bend over the bonnet.'

Patrick bent over the front of the car. His hands were trembling as he unbuckled his belt and took down his trousers. They fell to his ankles. Ingrid's eyes widened at the sight of his tiny black knickers with their string sides. Her lips twitched when he lowered them around his calves.

'Ms Pomeroy said in her note that the number of strokes is left to my discretion. I shall not be too severe; I think six will be enough this time. Are you willing to accept six?'

'Yes, ma'am.'

Ingrid felt a bit sorry now that she saw him in this state of disarray, with most of his body bare. He had buttocks like a peach below his tiny waist. But a surge of arrogance was building inside her and she was ready. She raised the switch and as she brought it down and cut her pupil she heard him gasp. He took in a deep breath as she raised it again. A wren chattered its machine gun song in a nearby holly bush. She brought it down harder this time and the boy's gasp was distinctly audible as the wren's chattering ceased. Now the sadistic anger flared in her. She hadn't whipped a man for some time; her husband had been the last recipient – he was a police superintendent who believed in discipline. She brought the switch down and the boy moaned quietly. She could tell he was enjoying himself.

Ingrid raised the switch again. She now felt totally masterful. She brought it down harder still and the boy squeaked like an injured fawn. She raised her switch again, and if the boy made any sound as it connected, it was drowned by the shrieking of jays high in the trees. They seemed to be laughing at the scene. She suddenly felt an urge to flog her husband that evening; she would try to think of a pretext. All men needed it and all secretly wanted it.

She gave him the remaining two cuts, spacing them out, taking her time. Then she tossed the switch aside and regarded the welts on the boy's backside. He remained bent over the bonnet of the car.

'You may get up and adjust your clothes.'

Patrick rose and pulled up his knickers and trousers. He smiled as he buckled his belt.

'No hard feelings?' Ingrid smiled kindly at her pupil.

'No hard feelings.'

'I'll drive us back. You may find it a little painful to sit still.'

They got in and Ingrid put the Fiesta into gear and drove easily along the woodland track.

On a wicked impulse she said, 'You have a nice figure. Such a tiny waist! And you wear sweet little knickers. Oh, I'm sorry. Perhaps I shouldn't have said that. It must have been bad enough being thrashed. It was naughty. Now I deserve a spanking.'

'That's all right. I didn't mind,' Patrick said gently. He shuffled a little in his seat.

'Not stinging too much, I hope?'

'Not too much, thank you. You know about thrashings. You know it stings, then?'

'Mmm, I've whipped my husband and been whipped myself. We all need whippings. If we whipped one another ecstatically instead of making war, the world would be a much better place,' she mused.

'It doesn't sting a lot; just a rather pleasant glow.'

'Would you like to come to my place and I'll put something on it?'

'Not really, thanks.'

'There'll be no one else there,' she persisted.

'No, thanks awfully. You're very kind. But the sting is bearable and I'd better get back. If it's necessary for you to whip me again, or harder maybe, I'll come then. That is, if I may.'

Ingrid brought the car to a halt at Pomeroy Place. Patrick got out and opened the gates and she drove them to the door.

'Oh, just a moment. I have to give you a note for Ms Pomeroy.' She took a pad from the dash, wrote a note, sealed it in an envelope and gave it to her pupil. 'Sure there's no hard feelings?'

'None whatever. Thank you. Thanks for the tuition and for my thrashing, I'm sure I deserved it.'

'See you next time.'

'See you,' he said, and headed towards the house.

When Patrick took in Darline's light lunch he included the envelope from Ingrid on the tray.

As he bowed before leaving Darline said, 'Stay a moment, boy.' She slit the envelope and read the contents, then looked up and said, 'Mrs Riding says that you were particularly negligent on the three-point turn and the emergency stop.'

'I did try, madam.'

'But evidently not hard enough. So she thrashed you?'

'Yes, madam.'

'How many strokes?'

'Six, madam.'

'Where did she do it, as a matter of interest?'

'On my buttocks, madam.'

'No, I mean in what place, what location?'

'I'm sorry, madam. She drove us to a clearing in Oxshott Woods. She cut a switch and made me bend over the bonnet.'

'Was it painful?'

'It stung; but it was over very quickly.'

Darline thought she detected a note of regret in his voice.

'What do you feel about her?'

'I admire her, madam.'

'That I understand and I concur. She is a woman of character. Your whipping will be administered late this afternoon, in the stable yard, following afternoon tea. Bring Lucan to me so that I may direct him.'

There was a knock at the drawing room door and at Darline's bidding Patrick entered followed by the old groom in his fusty breeches and leggings. She regarded them coolly, contrasting the slim boy with the bent old man.

'Lucan, I intend to discipline this boy. Do you agree that you deserve it, Patrick?'

'Yes, madam.'

'And you know what your offence was?'

'Yes, madam.'

'Tell me.'

'I stated a falsehood to you, madam.'

'And you accept my punishment?'

'Yes, madam.'

'Lucan, take this whip and take Patrick to the stable yard and string him to a tethering ring for his punishment. You can tie him with a lunging rope or some such. He is to be stripped to the waist. Prepare him for it and have Lilian let me know when he is ready. I shall come and supervise the whipping myself.'

'I understand, madam,' intoned the old man.

Darline noticed with pleasure that the old man grasped the boy's arm as they went out. She had a sudden voyeuristic urge to observe the scene of the stringing and she went upstairs to her studio which overlooked the yard. She adjusted a Venetian blind so that she could watch without being noticed and peered down into the yard.

Lucan went into the harness room and emerged with a coiled lunging rope. She heard him say, 'Better take your shirt off.' Patrick took it off and Lucan draped it over the lower door of a loose box. 'Hold out your wrists,' the old man said gruffly. He slipped one end of the rope through the steel clip at the other end and pulled it tight around the slim wrists. He slipped the free end through the tethering ring, which was fixed high, then drew the boy up until he was on tiptoe, and secured the loop to a lower ring. He was grinning lasciviously as he pulled the rope tight. Darline almost felt sorry for the boy as she looked down at his semi-nakedness. Lucan then went into the harness room and brought out a tin of saddle soap and a cloth and began to soap and polish the whip, from its stiff haft along the length of the tapering lash. When he was done, he hung the whip on the wall beside Patrick and moved to the kitchen door.

Darline went swiftly down to the drawing room and sat down, crossing her elegant legs.

In a few moments Lilian came in and said, 'Lucan asked me to say that Patrick is ready for his flogging, madam.'

'Thank you, Lilian.' Darline rose and went along a passage and out into the stable yard. Her boy-maid hung there, bare and vulnerable in the afternoon sun. The light created a wonderful effect on his skin. Again she felt sorry at what she was going to do to this helpless and attractive back. But she steeled herself.

'Give him twelve strokes. Don't lay them on too hard but do it slowly and pause between each stroke. No, wait a moment, I'll take down his trousers. We'll have him naked so that you can lay them on straight downwards starting at his shoulders and working down to his buttocks. He won't smart too much in one place then.'

She went up to the boy and unbuckled his belt. Then she unzipped his trousers and lowered them to his ankles. Lucan grinned when he saw the boy's tiny black knickers and watched as Darline slipped them down to the slim calves.

She put her lips close to the boy's profile and said, 'Now, after each stroke I want you to say, "I beg your pardon, madam". Is that understood?'

'Yes, madam.'

'I'm sure you agree that it is appropriate. Do you?'

'Yes, madam.'

30

Darline seated herself on an oak settle and crossed her legs to display her deliciously sexy thighs. She knew that her skirt was really cruelly short for any male onlooker.

'All right, Lucan. Lay them on.'

The groom swung the whip with practised ease and laid the lash across the boy's back and shoulders.

As the whip was drawn back Patrick drew a breath and said, 'I beg your pardon, madam.'

From her seat Darline could see Lilian observing them from the kitchen window. There was a leering grin on her face.

The scene had the feel of a slow ballet or a dream, in which the action is in slow motion.

The old man operated on the boy's back methodically and accurately but not very hard, laying each successive stroke on lower than the last. And after each stroke the boy murmured obediently, 'I beg your pardon, madam.'

By the time Lucan reached the small of the boy's back, the pale skin was crossed with red lines and there was a ridge of puffy skin on either side. After each stroke Patrick made his apology, 'I beg your pardon, madam.'

The gentle whipping descended to the buttocks and, with the last three lashes, the boy exclaimed excitedly when the knotted red tassel at the end of the whip hit his genitals. Lucan lowered the whip and looked at his mistress as if for direction.

'Leave him there for half an hour.'

Lucan nodded and stooped as if to raise the boy's trousers.

'No, leave those down as they are.' Darline rose from the settle and went into the house. She was going to watch from her studio windows. Her nipples felt as stiff as those of a Rodin bronze. She felt depraved and there was moisture between her thighs. What would her friend, Flavia, make of it with her psychological training? Then on impulse she decided to draw the scene.

She found some binoculars and brought his body into close-up. A bee flew into view and buzzed around the naked back for a while and then flew off. Then to Darline's delight a red admiral butterfly flew down and alighted on Patrick's back, just above his left scapula. The contrast of the bright colours of the butterfly and the pale skin was beautiful. Then the butterfly flew down to the boy's genitalia where it alighted on the glans. A tiny drop of lubricant oozed from the end of his penis and the butterfly sipped it with its long proboscis.

Just then, Lucan led out the gelding, Lightning Flash, and tethered him to a ring next to Patrick. He then went back into the harness room. The horse seemed to be quite frisky as a castrated gelding will at times. His great phallus hung loose. Suddenly he pissed long and forcefully, a great stream of yellow-green urine which bounced from the concrete and splashed all over Patrick as he hung there.

Darline dropped her binoculars and hurried down to the stable yard. She filled a bucket from the cold tap and, taking a sponge, began to sponge down the boy's body. She saw him shiver as the cold water streamed down his back. She took a towel and dried his back and legs. Then she saw that her sponging had aroused him and stopped. She untied him and was unsurprised that there was a look of absolute ecstasy on Patrick's face.

Darline was excited and happy at the anticipation of Flavia's return from the United States. It had been a long three months without her, without feeling her body. Darline's joy was such that she was even pleasant to Patrick when he painted her fingernails and toenails an hour before her departure for Heathrow.

She said, quite kindly, 'I hope your back and buttocks did not smart too much from your whipping the other day, Patrick.'

As he knelt, working on her toenails, he just said, 'No, madam.'

'I suppose it did sting for a while, did it?'

'Yes, madam, but not badly.'

She had chosen figure-hugging clothes for going to the airport to meet Flavia. She dressed from the inside out in cruelly minute chocolate-brown knickers and a matching bra which was cut low and daringly revealed the soft curves of her breasts above the scooped top of her off-the-shoulder blouse. She wore brown net stockings held up by a suspender belt that matched the knickers and bra. The ensemble was completed by a tiny mini-skirt which deliciously showed the curves of her netted thighs and her neat round buttocks. She inspected herself in the mirror and examined her back view in another mirror before her departure.

She took the Porsche and, having told Patrick that he was to be on hand in the hall to carry the bags on her return, had him open the gates at the end of the drive. Lucan was the usual gate-opener but he was busy with the horses. She drove along the familiar roads to Heathrow then parked the Porsche and walked to the arrivals area, attracting admiring and censuring glances from women and men as she went. She was indifferent to such attentions, as she was full of anticipation at soon being united with her lover and was yearning to feel her flesh close to her own.

There was a wait of a few minutes and then she caught sight of Flavia pushing a trolley at the other side of the barrier. Darline hurried to meet her as she rounded the barrier and they embraced and kissed lingeringly on the lips.

Darline murmured, 'Oh my darling, it is good to feel you in my arms again.'

Flavia responded tenderly. 'I've missed my loving girl and the feel of her lips. If I decide to go anywhere again I shall have to take you with me.'

'Don't leave me again for so long, my love,' Darline breathed.

'And what sort of time did you have in the States?' Darline asked as she drove the car homewards.

Flavia put a hand on Darline's thigh. 'Oh, darling, I found a rich mine of material among the Californians I studied. I think some of them are even more uninhibited in their kinky behaviour than the English. I have now decided

33

to write a paper on certain aspects of sado-masochism, majoring on the submissiveness of males and how far they will go in their subjection to the female. I may even develop it into a book. And how have you been faring?'

'Very well. I've been busy with my painting and I'm working on a series of nudes posed with horses and sometimes other creatures. Oh, and I must tell you, I have acquired a new maid, a boy-maid this time. He was sent by the Bare Service Bureau.'

'Oh, yes, I know them. And have you found the boy satisfactory?'

'Reasonably so; but I have had to punish him a couple of times.'

'Really, what were his offences?'

'The first occasion was when he spoilt a beautiful negligée he was hand washing. I threatened him with dismissal and he begged me to whip him instead.'

'And did you?'

'Yes, I gave him six strokes on his skin with my riding crop.'

'And what else?'

I made him take a run round the village green and, through binoculars, I watched him talking to some girls and when I quizzed him he lied about it.'

'And what did you do to him?'

'I had Lucan whip him in the stable yard.'

'How many strokes?'

'Twelve.'

'Mmm, not excessive. We all need discipline,' said Flavia.

'We do, darling. I so want to be disciplined at your lovely hands.'

Flavia turned her head and kissed her lover: a gentle brushing of lips on cheek. 'Perhaps the opportunity will present itself.' Flavia smiled enigmatically and Darline thrilled at the words.

As Darline turned in at the gates Lucan left his work of hoeing a flowerbed to open them. He raised his cap as Darline drove in and up to the front doorsteps.

Patrick came down the steps and opened the car door on the driver's side and then went round to open the door to let Flavia out.

Darline walked round the car and said, 'This is Patrick, my fairly new boy-maid. This is Doctor Quayle, Patrick.'

Patrick bowed low to Flavia.

Darline said, 'Patrick, take Doctor Quayle's bags up to the green bedroom. We shall be in the drawing room.'

Darline put an arm around her lover and took her along the hall to the drawing room. Finding themselves alone they turned to one another and embraced and kissed hungrily with open lips.

'My darling, it is so good to hold you again.' Darline's voice conveyed the loneliness she had felt and her present joy. She could feel Flavia's stiff tongue explore her mouth and it was wonderful.

'Do sit down, darling, you must be tired after your journey. It's such a long hop across the Atlantic.'

'I am a little tired. But I have my reward, I'm with you again.'

Flavia seated herself on a settee and Darline sat close beside her. They kissed again on the lips as if they could have eaten one another and then their tongues entwined once more.

'I've missed you so much, darling,' said Darline. 'I feel I want to be good in gratitude to you but I'm tempted to do something naughty so that you will spank me. I must be honest with you, darling. I'd love to be put across your thighs and have my knickers taken down right now and be spanked. I used to love to be spanked by you and feel my backside burning afterwards. It is so sweet to be subjected to punishment at your lovely hands.'

Flavia needed no prompting. Her right hand was rapidly exploring under Darline's mini-skirt and it went right up the luscious thigh to the close-fitting panties. She abruptly withdrew her hand as Patrick entered. They both sat up straight as he bowed.

Darline turned to her lover. 'Darling, are you ready for something to eat. I usually have only sandwiches at midday and I've had some special ones sent in to tempt you. We must also have some champagne to celebrate your return.'

'You are so kind, my love,' Flavia responded.

Darline looked up at her boy-maid. 'Patrick, you may serve the sandwiches now; and also bring a bottle of champagne well chilled.'

Patrick bowed and went out. The two lovers kissed again and this time Darline slid her hand under Flavia's blouse and gently massaged her back.

'I so love your dear back,' she murmured. 'I love your back in particular.' She could feel Flavia's hand under her skirt, her fingers getting very close to the heart of her arousal.

Just then Patrick entered with the sandwiches and champagne and they withdrew a little from one another. The boy placed a small table before his mistress and her friend and arranged the plates of sandwiches on it. Then he took the bottle of champagne from the bucket and wiped it, uncorked it and poured the pale gold liquid into two tulip-shaped glasses. He bowed and withdrew.

'Here's to you, my love, and to the prosperity of our union.'

'And to you, my darling,' Flavia responded. They linked arms and sipped the champagne. 'That boy seems very docile,' Flavia remarked. 'What was his family and school background like? He seems an utter neuter, but quite young and pretty.'

'He is from a working-class family. I gather that his parents were feckless and uncaring about him and used to spend a lot of time at the pub and playing bingo. I think because of this he developed a tendency to fantasise about being brought up very strictly. He was teased and bullied at school, but academically wasn't too bad at English, art and drama, although apparently he was a duffer at maths. It was only through the influence of his art teacher that he managed to get to art school.'

'Has he any friends?'

'He's very attached to a fellow fashion student, a girl called Pina who shares his taste for flagellation.'

'How about some coffee?' Flavia suggested. 'I am up at about ten thousand metres and I need something to bring me down to earth a little.'

Darline rang and Patrick appeared. She told him to now serve coffee. He entered moments later with a tray and bowed. Then he knelt before them in the manner of a geisha and started to pour. As he did so a small amount of coffee splashed on the hem of Flavia's long Californian skirt.

'Oh, my darling, your lovely dress. Patrick, how could you be so careless! Really, you deserve chastisement. But I'll be merciful with you this time. I'll content myself with giving you a spanking.'

'Darling, would you consider letting him off? Perhaps he was nervous at having a new arrival to serve; I'm sure he's doing his best.' Flavia smiled at the confused boy. She knew perfectly well that he was not averse to the suggestion that he should be spanked, but it seemed only befitting to put in a word for him.

'Darling, you are very kind. But I think it only right that he should be corrected. I shall administer a spanking here and now.'

Flavia smiled at the boy. 'And what do you think, Patrick?'

'You are very kind, madam. But if my mistress considers I should be spanked I am willing to submit.'

Darline rose from the settee and moved to the centre of the room and seated herself on a large pouffe.

'Come here, boy.' Darline's voice was stern.

Patrick went over to his mistress.

'Take down your trousers. Now your knickers. Now bend over my thighs. Right down.' The boy obeyed her. Darline raised his shirt.

'Good heavens! Hasn't he a lovely skin. I'm sure you'll want to paint him soon,' Flavia said.

'Yes, it's good that the whipping the other day was light and didn't mark him much. But a spanking won't do him any harm. I'll spank you for a minute by my watch,' she said, looking in Patrick's direction.

Darline pulled Patrick over her knees and started to spank him. Her mini-skirt, which covered very little of her thighs, had ridden up, and she could feel Patrick's semi-stiff phallus on them. As she spanked him she realised how much she was longing to be spanked by her lover.

'There, you may get up and adjust your clothes.'

There was a strange, almost ecstatic look on Patrick's face as he pulled up his knickers and trousers. He buckled his belt and bowed as if to go.

'No, I have not given you leave to withdraw. Go to the wall and stand facing it until you are told you may move.'

Flavia could not help noticing a look of pleasure on Patrick's face as he moved to the wall and stood facing it.

Darline went to the settee and lay down with her head on Flavia's lap. She kissed Flavia's thigh, lingering over the smooth skin with her lips. Then she felt her lover's hand on her own thigh, moving up to the delta of sensation.

Darline whispered huskily, 'Undress and let me feel you, darling.' She feverishly removed her own clothes, leaving on only the suspender belt and stockings, then she helped her lover undress. She took off Flavia's long, Californian skirt and top. 'Darling, what lovely underwear,' she exclaimed as she saw Flavia's silver lamé harnessings.

They lay naked together at last and could feel their bodies close, skin to skin. Their hands were exploring one another, moving over breasts and bellies and thighs; always moving closer to the main source of their pleasure. They were breathing deeply as each felt her lover's hand explore her vulva and deftly find the clitoris. They worked on one another with expert fingers and then they simultaneously climaxed, crying out together, as they felt the orgasmic pulsings.

3

Whipping Girls

Darline looked severely at Patrick. 'Tomorrow I shall ride with you and I shall punish you suitably in the spinney. You will run bare to the waist. You must not fail to take your swim.'

Patrick bowed and went out.

Patrick was ready on the forecourt in hot pants and running shoes as Lucan led Lightning Flash round from the stable yard; there was a cool morning breeze and he shivered slightly as he felt it on his skin.

Darline made a striking figure as she came down the steps in black jodhpurs and yellow shirt and black hard hat, crop in hand.

'Good morning, Lucan. Good morning, Patrick.'

'Good morning, madam.'

'And how are you this morning, Patrick?'

'Very well, thank you, madam.'

'Are you feeling in better shape as a result of your running?'

'Yes, madam, I think I am.'

'I am glad to hear it. Very well, let us move off.'

Darline placed a foot in the stirrup and swung up onto Lightning Flash. She dug her heels in and moved off with Patrick beside her.

There was a row of cars driving slowly along the road as they left her driveway. A van in front stopped and gestured for the rider to cross. Darline saluted with her crop and crossed the road with Patrick trotting beside her.

She put Lightning Flash into a slow trot on the gravel path. There was no sign of the grass-cutting men. She thought: I won't encourage him too much with the crop. I love doing it and he is not in the least averse to it but, after all, those women did notice it and say something on his behalf.

Three teenage boys were loitering by a chestnut tree. They had a rope and were attempting to throw it up around a high branch.

Darline reined in her mount. 'What are you doing with that rope?' she asked.

One of the boys said, 'There's a tawny owl's nest in a hole high up; we want to get up to see it.'

'What do you intend to do?'

'We were going to borrow one of the eggs.'

'Are you aware that the tawny owl is a protected species?'

'No.'

'You had better desist. Quite apart from your action being illegal, a photographer once lost an eye as a result of an encounter with a tawny owl. It is the practice now for people to wear goggles when approaching an owl's nest; I'm sure none of you would want to lose an eye.'

'No, thank you for telling us, miss.'

Darline dug her heels in and they went on.

There was a lack of discipline in these times. It began at home. If the young were disciplined better the country and the whole world would be better places. Punishment was certainly having its effect on Patrick. She quite loved him and it was good to discipline him. She gave him a light swish on his attractive back. She loved the back; it was such a subtle form. She enjoyed painting back views of nudes as much as frontal views. But much as she loved him she would give him his punishment. He had not taken his swim on the previous morning and, since he had been afraid to state any further falsehoods, she knew about it. She would give him twelve strokes across the log in the spinney but not lay them on savagely. A whipping was thoroughly enjoyable when whipper and recipient were attuned in their sado-masochism.

They were nearing the spinney and Darline brought Lightning Flash onto the sandy path leading to the pond. Patrick was now coming behind on the narrow track.

Darline dismounted and let Lightning Flash champ at the grass bordering the path.

She looked at her boy. 'Here we are, Patrick. I trust you have worked up a good sweat and are now ready for your swim.'

'Yes, madam.'

It never ceased to intrigue her; the boy was just completely submissive and happy with it.

'Strip off, then, and in you go. Fancy my saying that, you have very little to strip off. Oh my goodness, you really mustn't wear torn knickers. Have you no others?'

'I have only two other pairs, madam, and they are in the wash.'

'I'll take you out and buy you a dozen or so tomorrow.'

'Thank you, madam.'

Patrick draped his tiny garments on a branch and waded into the water. He swam gracefully across to the other side. As he was swimming back Darline remarked, 'Your breast stroke is improving.' He waded out before her, glistening wet.

'Have you no towel, you silly boy? Well, you'll have to take your punishment just the same, wet skin or no. I don't want my lovely crop to suffer but I think you have probably rubbed it well enough with saddle oil to make it water resistant. Lie along the log.'

The boy laid his wet body along the log and Darline had just raised the crop to deliver the first stroke when a voice sounded behind her.

'Please don't whip him wet.' It was Melissa, accompanied by Kirstie, Sarah and Gala.

Darline glared at Melissa. 'I should be glad if you would kindly not interfere.'

'Why is he being punished?' Kirstie asked.

'Not that it is any concern of yours, but he failed to take his swim yesterday.'

'But it's cruel to whip someone on their wet skin,' Kirstie remonstrated gently.

'It's his own fault for failing to bring a towel; he mus take his twelve strokes.'

Sarah spoke. 'May we confess something? It's really ou fault. We persuaded him not to take his swim yesterday because we had delayed him again and he might have earned another whipping.'

'I know. We'll take his punishment for him.' Melissa looked quizzingly at the other girls.

'Yes,' the three girls chorused. Then Melissa added, 'We can take three strokes each.'

'You appreciate it will have to be on your skin.' Darline's lips were tight pressed, and then they twitched a little.

'We don't mind,' Melissa said. 'It's only fair we should take it on our skin if Patrick has to.'

'Our skins are dry,' Sarah said.

'You're Darline Pomeroy, aren't you?' Kirstie said. 'We know of you because we're art students.'

Darline smiled and said, 'I am.'

'We saw a show of your work recently in Cork Street, Gala said.

'Your paintings of nudes with horses are fabulous,' said Melissa.

'We sketched some of your drawings,' Kirstie admitted, and added, 'It was lovely to see the nude in conjunction with horses.'

'How enchanting that you found my drawings worth sketching,' Darline cooed, regarding the four girls. 'Basking in your kind remarks I can scarcely see my way to continue with whipping you.'

'Oh, please do,' Melissa pleaded. 'If you don't we'll be afraid you might think we used flattery to get out of it.'

'Yes, please do whip us,' Sarah added.

Gala put in, 'If you don't whip us, will Patrick still have to be whipped?'

'I'm afraid so,' Darline said.

'Then you must whip us.' Gala was almost begging for it.

'Who is to be first?' Darline looked at them with tight lips.

42

'I'll be first,' Melissa said. She looked at Patrick, still shivering wet on the log. She took off her sheepskin waistcoat and tossed it to Sarah saying, 'Dry poor shivering Patrick whilst I'm being whipped.'

Patrick got up from the log and Sarah started to dry him.

Melissa looked at Darline. 'I take it you want my bare buttocks?'

'I'm afraid so.'

Melissa moved to the log. She unzipped her jeans and lowered them to reveal tiny sepia knickers which she slipped down to her knees. She manoeuvred herself onto the log and lay there as if waiting for a massage, with her face supported on her hands.

Darline stood over Melissa. The girl's skin was a healthy yellow colour, naturally tanned without sunbathing. Her buttocks were beautifully shaped, like plump fruit, reminding her of Rodin's drawing, *The Peach*. In one way it was a shame to mark them but discipline had to be maintained. In the arts there had to be obedience and self-discipline; and these girls would have to learn this fact of life. She was now their mistress.

Darline raised the riding crop and brought it down on the shapely buttocks. She saw Melissa flinch. A magpie cackled from high in a yew tree. She raised the crop and brought it down once more and again Melissa flinched and drew in breath audibly. For a third time the crop was raised and brought down and again Melissa flinched.

'That's it. You may rise.'

Melissa drew up her knickers and jeans.

'No hard feelings?' Darline was solicitous and caring.

'No hard feelings,' Melissa said.

Sarah was next over the log. She drew up her mini-skirt and lowered her white knickers.

Darline noticed that the girl's skin was very pale; as an artist she was forever registering colours and forms. The buttocks of the girl were quite beautiful. They put Darline in mind of apples modelled in delicate porcelain. But enough of that! What business had they in delaying her boy and encouraging him not to take his cold swim? This would teach them a lesson, all four of them.

Darline raised the riding crop and brought it down quite hard. Sarah's body jerked and she squeaked like a small animal. In the distance a police-car siren sounded, oddly incongruous as a background to whipping in a peaceful glade by a sheet of water. Again the riding crop was raised. Darline was now feeling a swelling pride as she whipped the girl. She would have liked to inflict more than three strokes. She brought the crop down and Sarah jerked but made no sound. A yellowhammer's song rattled and wheezed in some brambles nearby. Again Darline raised the crop and as she brought it down the girl made a slight whimper.

Sarah got up and drew up her knickers and smoothed her mini-skirt.

'Are you all right, you didn't mind it too much?'

Sarah smiled a little wryly. 'No, I suppose we deserve it.'

Patrick was now dry and dressed again in his hot pants. He was watching the scene as he sat on the stump of a tree.

Next it was Gala's turn and Darline saw that the girl was eager for it; there was a look of lustful excitement on her face. She raised her ankle-length skirt to reveal a slinky black G-string which divided her buttocks and defined her narrow hips below her small waist. She slipped the ridiculously tiny garment down to her calves. Her skin was of that very sexy grey-white that envelops the bodies of many German women. Her buttocks were like smooth grey pebbles.

Darline raised the crop and brought it down. A beatific smile appeared on Gala's face as she took the stroke. Darline raised the crop again and as she brought it down the smile on her victim's face grew rapturous. She raised the crop for a third time and, as it cut Gala's buttocks, the girl looked supremely happy. She continued to lie along the log.

'You may get up,' Darline said.

'Please. I have to say it. Please whip me more. I want to serve you and be punished by you; please flog me again.'

44

'Get up now, you've had your share,' Darline said sternly.

Gala slowly got up from the log, replaced her G-string and rearranged her skirt.

'I'm sorry about that. I just got carried away.' She looked shamefacedly at the company.

'That's all right,' Darline said, very kindly. 'We all have these desires. They are nothing to be ashamed of.'

Kirstie approached the log for her turn. She unbuckled her belt and slipped down her glistening PVC trousers to reveal tiny frilly red knickers which she slipped down as she lowered herself onto the log.

Darline was now glowing with sexual excitement which she kept tightly reined in. Gala's masochistic pleading for more had certainly aroused her.

As Kirstie spread-eagled herself on the log, her top had ridden up to reveal the most lovely tanned back. I'd like to have this girl in my studio and paint her beautiful back, Darline thought. The girl's rear view was truly beautiful and Darline wanted to love and honour it with the creativity of her painting.

Darline murmured unthinkingly, 'What a lovely back and bottom you have and tanned such a lovely brown, a wondrous raw-sienna shade.'

'It's going to have a different kind of tanning now and will probably be raw in a different way too,' Kirstie said, expectantly.

'It *is* rather a shame to mark you,' Darline said.

'Well, I have to take my share,' Kirstie said. 'If you leave me out I'll feel deprived. Please go on with it,' she urged.

Darline raised the crop and was just about to bring it down when a voice sounded behind her.

'What an extraordinary scene! Why is this girl being punished?'

Darline looked round and saw an elderly lady with a King Charles spaniel on a leash.

Darline said in surprise, 'Oh, Lady Dunbar. Good morning.'

'Good morning, Ms Pomeroy,' Lady Dunbar said. 'Why is this girl being punished?'

'It is because she and her friends delayed my boy-maid, Patrick, when he was on his run round the green yesterday. He was to have had twelve strokes of my riding crop and these girls, who were responsible for the delay, volunteered to take his punishment collectively, instead of him taking it all himself.'

'Yes, ma'am, we did,' Melissa spoke up.

'Yes,' Sarah and Gala put in together.

'We three have taken our three strokes,' Melissa said.

Lady Dunbar looked approvingly at Darline. 'I think you are doing something very sound to punish them, and it is noble on their part to take the boy's strokes between them. The young need discipline; my brothers had many a swishing at Eton. Well, I think you had better proceed with the strokes.'

Darline raised the crop and brought it down fairly hard. Kirstie flinched. There was an entranced look on Lady Dunbar's face and, as Darline raised the crop again and brought it down, she saw an unmistakable twitching of the Dunbar lips. As she brought it down again there was a look of exultation on Lady Dunbar's face.

Kirstie remained on the log for a few moments.

Lady Dunbar said, 'What a lovely brown body this girl has.'

'It seemed almost a shame to mark it,' Darline said. 'You may get up, now,' she added.

Kirstie got up from the log and rearranged the frilly red knickers and pulled up the PVC trousers.

'I must be on my way,' Lady Dunbar said. 'A lovely day to you all.'

Patrick bowed as Lady Dunbar and the spaniel continued on their way.

'No hard feelings?' Darline said, addressing the four girls.

'No hard feelings,' they chorused.

Melissa said, 'It was lovely to meet you.'

'Really quite an honour for us to meet such a distinguished painter,' Gala said.

'I take it you are all fine-art students?' Darline said.

'Yes,' Melissa replied for them all.

'Since you are obviously interested in my work I wonder it you'd all like to come to tea one afternoon. You could see my studio and some current work.'

'That would be fabulous,' Melissa said. Sarah, Gala and Kirstie agreed.

'Let me see, I usually keep Wednesday afternoon free for receiving people. Good heavens, it's Wednesday tomorrow. Would you like to come to tea tomorrow?'

'Thank you, that would be lovely,' Melissa said.

'It won't interfere with your school work?'

'No, not at all,' said Gala. 'We're in our third year and they let us off to visit artists' studios and things like that.'

'So I'll see you tomorrow, make it around three,' said Darline.

The girls thanked their chastiser and Darline swung herself up on Lightning Flash and she and Patrick continued on their way.

'Your boy is an interesting case,' Flavia remarked thoughtfully.

'He is,' Darline said. 'I've never known someone as totally submissive. There was a charming scene yesterday when I took him out for his swim. The poor ninny forgot to bring a towel, and I was going to whip him wet after his dip when four girls he has become acquainted with came on the scene. They offered to take his twelve strokes between them because they had delayed him. They were perfectly charming about it. It seems they are admirers of my work so I've invited them to tea tomorrow.'

'Hmm, interesting, darling. In the paper I'm preparing, it would be good to draw some comparisons with English masochists to point up what I've been able to say about Californians. In fact I've reached a stage now where I feel I shall have to expand the paper into a book. I shall publish a paper first and then work on a book.'

'I tell you what, my love, I have to go to Paris for a week soon for a show of my work. I could lend Patrick to you so that you could experiment with him continuously. You could do just what you like with him, day and night. What do you say?'

'What a splendid idea! You know, it might be an idea to make him serve naked. It would strip away even more of his persona, that mask we all wear.' Flavia grinned at her lover. 'And he would be all ready for chastisement should he merit it.'

'Sounds interesting. I might well emulate you. Darling,' Darline's voice was now hesitant, almost pleading, 'I have to confess something. I am an utter masochist myself as well as a sadist. I should love to be flogged by you. I know you've spanked me a few times, but I long for more.' Her voice became bolder. 'I have to say it, I am a masochist in relation to you. I'd like to be put over a flogging block and birched; I'd like to be strung up in the stable yard and lashed all down my body; I'd like to kneel before you as your footstool.'

They came together on the settee and kissed hungrily on the lips. Darline could feel Flavia's tongue enter her mouth and explore her tongue and her palate and her throat like a stiff phallus.

'The young ladies from the art school, madam. They are in the hall.'

'Thank you, Patrick. I'll come down and receive them and take them to the studio.'

Patrick bowed and went out. Darline rose from her chair. She had been sketching a vase of pink roses. She always had a sketchbook near at hand so that she could sketch all manner of things as inspirational pieces for use in her paintings.

As she entered the hall the four girls rose from an oak settle and all four smiled rather diffidently. Melissa held a bouquet of lilies. Darline could see that they were a little embarrassed, even a little overawed, at meeting her again in her impressive house and with the prospect of seeing some of her work *in situ*.

'Hello, darlings. And how are you all after your experience the other day?'

'Very well, thank you,' murmured all four.

Darline moved to each and they exchanged chaste kisses of welcome.

'We brought you these,' Melissa said, shyly proffering the bouquet of lilies.

'Oh, how charming of you all; you really shouldn't. But they are truly lovely.' She kissed Melissa again. 'Now let me take you along to my studio to see some recent paintings as promised. We have to go up some stairs. I made an upstairs room the studio because it overlooks the stable yard and the garden and beyond them the paddock where the horses are put out. The light is very good up there.'

The four girls followed Darline up the stairs to the studio, along a passage hung with drawings.

As they went in, the eyes of all four girls were drawn to a large picture on a big studio easel. It was of a naked girl with a bridled horse on a lunging rein. The girl held a long whip and the horse was caught in action as it made circuits at the end of the rein.

For a few moments no words were spoken and then Kirstie said, 'It's fabulous.'

Melissa said, 'You've caught the action of the horse as it makes the circuits.'

'And the naked girl at the centre,' Gala said. 'You feel as if she's the centre of her world, like a goddess.'

'And the horse is one of the planets turning around her,' Melissa said.

'It's truly fabulous,' Kirstie repeated. 'And you've created a feeling that the girl is in charge; the queen in control of her pawns in the game of life.'

'That's very poetically put,' Darline said.

Sarah spoke next. 'There is such contained energy in the horse. It reminds me of Watts's huge bronze of *Physical Energy* in Kensington Gardens.'

'Yes, we went to draw it once on an outdoor assignment. I remember a shower of rain came down all of a sudden and we sheltered under a tree and drew it with the rain drops streaming down it,' Melissa recalled.

49

'And I was drawing in ink, and raindrops streamed down the paper and created streaks and I left it as an unpremeditated effect,' Gala reminisced.

'Like Picasso when the doves shit down his paintings,' Sarah said.

'How very brave of you all,' Darline said. 'You weren't going to be put off by the vagaries of the weather. You were quite right. It was the lovely Matisse who said that an artist should be able to work under any conditions.'

'There really is such energy in the horse,' Kirstie said, focusing their attention back on the painting before them.

'You create such wonderful work,' Gala said. 'It almost makes me feel that I'd like to be the horse at the end of the lunging rein.'

'And feeling a touch of the whip?' Kirstie suggested, with a teasing look at Gala.

'Yes, you know you have a taste for that, Gala,' Melissa said.

'Yes, we'll never forget your performance at the party at the end of last term,' Sarah said.

Gala looked rather embarrassed and Darline said, 'We all have these desires, my dear. We are all of us part sadist and part masochist. Shall we move on to another painting?'

Against one wall was propped a painting of a naked girl astride a horse. They moved as a group and stood before it.

'This is a painting in which I wanted to express the synergism of the human body with an animal body. I don't know if you've ever ridden a horse bareback and naked yourself but it is quite an experience. Under your buttocks and thighs, under the smooth-haired hide of the horse, there is a tremendous feeling of animal energy stemming from universal energy. And as the horse moves you can feel the muscles move under the hide and you receive the sensation via your skin. I once had my groom clip a horse's back very closely so that I could the more feel the sensation.'

'So you've ridden a horse naked yourself?' Gala said wonderingly, and with a touch of admiration in her voice.

'Of course,' Darline said with a smile. 'I very much subscribe to the view that an artist must experience her subject matter as much as she can. When drawing or painting the nude it is good, sometimes, to put yourself in the pose of the model. Fortunately the paddock is not overlooked and I sometimes ride naked there before I pose the model on the horse. My horses are well schooled and are kind to an inexperienced rider although I've found that a good horse knows intuitively who is on board.'

'Yes, we sometimes get ourselves into the position before the models pose for us in the life-room,' Melissa said.

'Although we don't take off all our clothes for it,' Gala said with a tinge of regret.

'Although I'm sure you'd like to,' Kirstie said.

'Of course I would,' Gala responded, emboldened now to express what she really felt. 'A female model told me she'd always much rather pose in the nude.'

'I sometimes envy models in a studio with all their clothes off,' Darline said, adding, 'I suppose one could paint in the nude and I do sometimes. But it wouldn't be allowed in an art school.'

'Talking about having contact with the horse, I once saw a photograph in a magazine of a naked girl in a pose with a huge python.' Gala regarded the company lasciviously.

Melissa responded with a grin. 'I saw that too. It was very sensuous.'

Gala said, 'The great thick trunk of the snake was between her legs and you could imagine it crawling sinuously along, the muscles moving under the skin.'

'Ugh!' Sarah exclaimed. 'How disgusting!'

Kirstie came in, 'Yet I suppose it's no more disgusting than the closeness of any other animal to a human being.'

'I know what you mean,' Darline said. 'The evil may well be in the eye of the beholder.'

'Anyway,' Melissa said, 'I much prefer a human being in contact with a beautiful horse. Oh, that's a magnificent one.' The painting which had caught her eye was of a horse emerging from a pond with a naked girl on its back. The flanks of the horse were streaming.

51

'It's as if the horse is emerging from a great pool of water of life,' Sarah said, trying to arrange her confused thoughts.

'What you've said is very apt,' Darline said. 'Water is a symbol of the flow of the life force, of underlying energy.'

'I'd have liked to have been in that model's place,' Gala said.

'Who was the model for these paintings?' Kirstie asked.

'A girl called Carina. She has modelled for me for quite some time. She's a very good model; remains as still as a beautiful bronze.'

'It must be hard, being a model,' Sarah said. 'I mean having to remain absolutely still for long periods.'

Darline said, 'I think it's all right if you don't think of remaining still as a punishment.'

'But what a sweet punishment!' Gala said.

'I think she's heading for a punishment, the way she's going,' Melissa said. Gala grinned at the innuendo.

'Let's concentrate on the work,' Sarah said.

The group was feeling more relaxed now. To some extent the girls had overcome their initial awe in the presence of the internationally known Darline and her paintings.

Kirstie was looking at another painting. It was of the same naked girl lying on a towel on some grass, holding the reins of a horse which champed at the grasses. The effect was very serene.

'You paint animals and figures beautifully,' Melissa said. 'I wish I could be as good, one day.'

'But darling, you mustn't be overawed by my work or my style. Some day you may do even better. You have to find your own way. Never be intimidated by someone else's work. Learn from it, yes; but be overwhelmed, no.' Darline looked at her guests. 'How about some tea, now?'

'That would be lovely,' Melissa said.

'I think we'll have tea on the patio by the pool.'

Darline led them down the stairs and along a wide passage, this one also lined with drawings, then out through some open French windows to a paved area beside the swimming pool.

'Why don't you let Patrick have his swim here instead of in the pond?' asked Kirstie.

'I suppose I could, but I think it's so nice for him to break his run and have his swim halfway.'

'And it's a little more dangerous out there,' Gala said. 'There's a chance that someone could possibly come across you, like Lady Dunbar did yesterday.'

'But naked bathing is allowed there,' Melissa put in.

'I think I still find a thrill in things like that,' Gala said. 'It's just that you feel a bit naughty.'

'Somebody is going to get a spanking,' Kirstie said.

'Yes, please,' Gala said.

Melissa put on a mock severe expression. 'Now, that's enough of this line of talk.'

Darline rang a bell and a moment or two later Patrick emerged from the house. 'You may serve tea, now, Patrick.'

'How beautifully clear and light blue the water is,' Sarah remarked.

'It has those wavy lines from the reflections on the bottom, just like a Hockney painting,' Kirstie said.

Patrick reappeared in a few minutes with a silver tea tray and placed a teapot and cups together with a plate of cakes on a low table.

'Shall I pour, madam?'

'No, I'll do it, thank you, Patrick.'

Darline poured tea and passed around the cups and the cakes.

'You can have a swim after tea if you like,' Darline said.

'But we haven't any costumes,' Sarah said with a note of regret.

'You don't need them here, love,' Darline said with a smile. 'God gave you a lovely skin; the only swimsuit you need.'

The other three girls grinned.

'Could we – do you think we could see your horses before we go?' Melissa said.

'Of course,' Darline said. 'They're out in the paddock at present. They can move around freely there. But I tell you what, I'm sure you're dying to strip off and go in the water. Why don't you do that now and I'll make a few sketches of you?'

The four girls got to their feet. 'May we undress here?' Melissa asked.

'Of course,' Darline said.

The four girls stripped off their brief garments and stood there.

'What a handsome quartet you make! You all have different-coloured skins. I know, I must make a few sketches of you as you play and swim like water nixies in and around the pool.'

'Would you like us to pose now before we go in?' Melissa asked.

'Feel quite free to do anything you like. I know, we'll be like Rodin and his models; they were required to move around and strike attitudes and then he would say, "Stop, darlings", and they would freeze in motion and he would do those lightning line drawings to which he would sometimes add a touch of wash.'

The four girls moved and posed. Kirstie raised her arms and clasped her hands behind her neck, her expression pertly proud. Sarah slipped an arm around Kirstie's waist. Melissa assumed a majestic stance with hands on hips, like a queen regarding her subjects. Gala knelt before Melissa and took her hand and kissed it.

Darline's voice was animated. 'Hold those poses. They are perfect.' She stripped off her dress and she saw the girls eye her slinky black underwear. Her pencil hand was moving on the sketchbook page, dancing over the paper, creating a fresh beauty inspired by the splendid naked bodies of the girls. 'I'm not tiring you, am I, darlings? I know that posing can be hard, especially for inexperienced models.'

'No, we're all right.' Melissa spoke for the four of them.

'Tell me if you're getting cramped.'

'Even if we were it would be good to suffer a little for you and in the cause of art.' Gala spoke and then looked a little embarrassed, almost as if she wished she hadn't.

'You're at it again, Gala,' Kirstie teased.

'Let's not natter,' Melissa said. 'It may distract Darline.'

The practised hand was dancing over the paper, going in and out to create the volumes and rhythms of the figures and bringing them to life on the flat plane. She concentrated on the beautiful breasts and bellies and buttocks, synthesising them with the lissome structures of their young bodies.

'There, now; I'll release you from your immobility. You may enter the water. Thank you.'

Melissa dived in, closely followed by Sarah, Gala and Kirstie. Melissa and Kirstie struck out for the other end in fast and practised crawl strokes. Sarah moved into a slow breast-stroke and Gala swam a backstroke.

Darline turned the page and continued sketching, setting down impressions of the varied movements in the water.

'The four of you make such a picture in the water. I could draw you and draw you.'

The four nymphs swam back and emerged from the pool. As they walked up the steps, the water streamed from their bodies.

'You would look lovely as a quartet of Undines emerging from the water. Put your arms around one another and I'll sketch you like that. The girls stood; a frieze of lithe figures and Darline's hand moved the pencil over the paper.

'You look so lovely dripping wet and it makes your skin colours glisten beautifully. I'm getting all this down. It's wonderful to have such willing models and draw spontaneously. I must let you dry yourselves now. Oh, of course you haven't any towels. I'll get Patrick to bring some.'

She rang and in a few moments Patrick appeared. 'Patrick, bring four nice big bath towels.

He went and shortly reappeared with towels which he handed to the four girls who started to dry themselves.

'Let me help you with your backs.' Darline moved first to Gala and patted her back with the absorbent towel.

'That's lovely,' Gala murmured. 'It's a privilege to have your lovely hands dry my back.'

Darline moved to the other girls in turn and patted their

backs dry. 'I'd really love to paint you all one day,' suggested Darline.

'We could model for you again if you wish,' Melissa spoke up.

'Yes, it would be lovely to come again,' Gala said yearningly.

'Well, of course, that can be arranged,' the distinguished painter said graciously.

Gala said with longing, 'Would you towel me again; it was so lovely to feel your hands on me. I feel as if some wonderful electromagnetic charge will come from you to me as you touch me.'

'If it will make you happy,' Darline said, giving the girl a look filled with tenderness. She took the towel and worked on Gala with it. She could not help but touch the girl's body as she towelled, then she tossed the towel aside and took the girl in her arms and kissed her on her temple and then on her lips and then on her naked back.

'You have such a lovely back,' Darline mused. 'I love the bare back and yours is quite divine.'

Gala moved and kissed Darline passionately, with longing, on the older woman's breasts and throat and lips. Then she sank to her knees and kissed Darline's belly and then went right down before her and kissed her feet.

'I adore you,' she moaned. 'You are so wonderful. I want to serve you, to be your slave. Even if you are cruel to me I will still adore you. I can't help it. Please beat me, thrash me, whip me and let me serve you. I'd like to kneel down as your footstool. You are so wonderful and so beautiful. I so wanted to be whipped more by you yesterday.'

Darline thought that this was too good an opportunity to miss. A whipping would do the girl good.

'Don't be a nuisance to Ms Pomeroy, Gala. She has been so kind to have us here,' said Melissa.

Darline ignored Melissa's obvious embarrassment. 'I think you do deserve some punishment, Gala.'

'Oh, please punish me,' Gala begged.

'Very well, you shall be punished, Gala. You shall be

punished for so persistently pleading for it. I shall have Patrick bring my riding crop.'

'Yes, yes, mistress,' the girl yearned.

Darline rang and in seconds Patrick appeared.

'Bring me my riding crop,' Darline commanded. Her mouth was set cruelly.

Patrick bowed and disappeared and a few moments later came out with the riding crop on a salver. He proffered it with a bow.

Darline took the crop from Patrick. There was a haughty expression on her face. Her whole body was electrified in its nakedness. Then, on an impulse, she slipped her dress back on. Gala stood before Darline, looking down a little, compliant and adoring, then she dared to raise her eyes to her goddess.

'How many strokes do you think you merit?'

'As many as it pleases you to give me, noble lady.'

'You do not answer my question. How many strokes?'

'Er – well – fifty I should think, ma'am.'

'Indeed! When you have felt five on your backside you will be pleading for mercy because I intend to punish you severely.'

'Let it be whatever you decide, ma'am; I will accept your authority. Please show your love for me by whipping me. I feel I deserve it. I have been a nuisance to you.'

'Very well, I shall give you twelve strokes to teach you not to be importunate and greedy.'

'I will accept them from your gracious hand, ma'am.'

Darline moved over to a marble seat, every movement radiating feline grace. Her compliant victim followed.

'Stretch yourself over the marble slab,' she commanded.

Gala lay along the slab, her naked grey-white body in contrast with the white of the Carrara marble.

Darline raised the crop and then as an idea struck her she lowered it.

'Now, as you receive each stroke I want you to say, "Thank you, noble lady; I deserve it". Is that understood? Say it before I commence with the flogging.'

Gala murmured, 'Thank you, noble lady; I deserve it.'

Darline raised the lithe crop and brought the lash down on Gala's buttocks. The girl jerked and then murmured her litany. A radiant expression adorned her face.

Out of the corner of her eye Darline could see Melissa, Sarah and Kirstie watching, entranced. A horse whinnied from the stable yard.

Darline raised the crop and brought it down again and Gala murmured her line. The atmosphere in the secluded patio beside the pool was electric. All eyes were focused on the scene before them.

The ritual went on and Darline and Gala were now united in the love that accepts and inflicts pain and transports flogger and flogged into a region that comes near to nirvana.

Darline lowered the crop for the last time. She felt electrified and breathless. Her nipples were as stiff as bronze studs. She put aside the crop and approached the slab and bent and took the girl's shoulders in her hands and kissed her back. Then she took the girl's naked body in her arms and raised her and sat beside her. They kissed empathetically with open lips, each finding correspondent feeling and love and passion in the other. Melissa, Sarah and Kirstie watched the scene with faces radiating tenderness.

'I love you, mistress,' Gala murmured. 'I so took pleasure in the pain you bestowed on me. I want to love you and serve you.'

'And I love you, Gala, or I should not have given you what you yearned for.' Darline rose from the marble seat and said, 'Now, if you'd like to get your clothes on, I'll take you to see the horses.'

Gala got up slowly from the slab and moved to where her clothes lay over a chair. A calm and happy look shone from her face as she slowly dressed, giving the impression that she was reluctant to relinquish her nakedness. Melissa, Sarah and Kirstie also put on their clothes.

'It has been such a wonderful day,' Melissa said.

'It really has,' Kirstie added, 'it's a pity it has to come to an end.'

Darline smiled and said, 'There will be other times. Now let me take you along to the stables. Lucan may have turned the horses loose in the paddock.'

Darline led them through a doorway into the stable yard where Lucan was sweeping the cobbles.

'Have you turned them out already, Lucan?'

'Yes, madam.'

'We'll take them something to eat to encourage them to approach us and be friendly.'

'Shall I get it for you, madam?' The old groom started to put down his broom.

'No, you can continue with what you're doing.' She went into the feed room and emerged with a sieve of oats and led the party to the field gate, unlatched it and led them through and again latched the gate.

'I suppose it is safe for us to come in with them?' Sarah asked. 'Only they don't know us.'

'Yes, they are very well-schooled horses; two geldings and two mares. A stallion would be more temperamental.'

'What's a gelding?' Kirstie asked.

'It's a castrated stallion. You're not familiar with horses, then?'

'I'm afraid not.'

'What a shame. You'll have a chance to make good that failing now.'

Darline emitted a low whistle and the four horses came trotting up. She fed them each a handful of oats and they whinnied their appreciation. 'Now let me introduce these lovely animals. This glossy black one is Tempered Steel. He's a splendid creature. This chestnut is Lightning Flash. He's a lovely chap but still a little nervous with traffic. Then this white mare is Pandora. She's a lovely creature. She is an Arab and was a present from a Saudi prince. And this lovely skewbald is Halcyon. She is so beautifully patterned in raw sienna and white. I have drawn and painted her many times, simply because of her beautifully contrasting hide.'

'Aren't they lovely animals,' Melissa said. 'No wonder they inspire you so much.'

'What a wonderfully creative life you have!' Sarah said.

'I must say it is good to live a creative life and do what one feels a powerful inner desire to do. I consider myself very fortunate. So, now you have seen my small estate – we'll go through the garden on the way back – you must come again.'

'We'd love to,' Kirstie said. 'It has been most inspiring to see your paintings.'

'I'm so glad you found them of interest.'

Darline led them back into the stable yard and through a doorway leading into the garden.

'This is a very pleasant walk beside the great bank of flowers at this time of year. And the thick yew hedge gives such privacy for the swimming pool. I sometimes have swimming-pool parties here and I occasionally draw my guests as they swim or recline beside the pool. Just look at the array of colours in this herbaceous border. We have day lilies, campion and coral flowers; at the back goat's rue, campanula, delphiniums and lupins. They thrive very well here, thanks, to a great extent, to Lucan's devoted care.'

They were nearing the door leading to the forecourt and Darline opened it and let the girls through. 'I'll go as far as the gate with you.'

'It has been such a wonderful afternoon,' Kirstie said wistfully.

'It has,' Gala said, equally wistfully.

'You said we might come again some time,' Melissa said. 'We'd certainly love to.'

'I'd like to have you again. Before very long I have to attend a show of my work in Paris and I'm going to be fearfully busy with the arrangements, but I'll get in touch afterwards. Have you a number on which I can contact you?'

'I'll write mine down for you,' Melissa said. She wrote on a slip of paper and handed it to Darline.

The four girls kissed their distinguished painter host and prepared to leave.

Gala took Darline's hand and kissed it as if reluctant to let go. 'Thank you for what you did to me.'

'You are very welcome, darling. I received as much pleasure as I gave.'

Darline closed the gate behind the girls and, as they crossed the road, they looked back and waved.

4

Apprehensions

'Rest, please, Trisha.'

Darline put the brushes down as Patrick entered with a tray of coffee on which some letters also lay.

Patrick bowed and asked, 'Shall I pour, madam?'

'No, er, no,' Darline said absently. 'You may get on with whatever you were doing.'

Her mind was on her work and there was a problem in getting the right effect of scumble over an area of sunlit chrome yellow. She looked at the letters. One was from an agent in Berlin and the others looked like bills. But one caught her eye. The envelope carried a coat of arms which she recognised as the Dunbars'; she opened it and read the contents:

> *Dear Ms Pomeroy,*
> *It was good to meet you on the village green the other day and observe the activity you were engaged in with the young people. I would like to discuss a certain matter with you and should be glad if you would come to tea at Dunbar Hall on Wednesday next around three. My husband and I would so like to see you. Do please let me know if you can come.*
> *Sincerely,*
> *Agrippina Dunbar*

'Shall I pour coffee?' Trisha said.

'Mmm, yes. Please do.'

What might the Dunbars want to see her for with this missive out of the blue? There must be a connection with the happening on the village green when the four girls had taken Patrick's punishment for him.

The butler showed her into the Dunbars' drawing room and then withdrew.

Lord Dunbar got to his feet and said, 'What a charming visitation, the lovely Ms Pomeroy.' He took her proffered hand and kissed it.

Lady Dunbar got to her feet and they embraced and kissed. The butler re-entered with a tray of tea things and placed it on a low table beside Lady Dunbar.

'Thank you, Wilkins, I'll pour myself.' She looked at Darline and said, 'I recall from a previous occasion, you take your tea with lemon.' She tonged a slice of lemon into the cup and passed it to Darline.

'I see from your kind invitation that there is something you wish to discuss,' said Darline.

'There is, indeed, my dear,' Lady Dunbar replied.

'Is it by any chance connected with what you saw on the village green last Tuesday?'

'There is a connection with that incident.' Lady Dunbar sipped her tea thoughtfully. 'Are you aware, my dear, that you were committing offences in what you were doing?'

Darline saw Lord Dunbar looking straight ahead, with an air of wishing to dissociate himself from the immediate conversation.

'Well, no, I didn't think I did anything wrong.'

'Indeed, flogging four innocent girls in a public place; and you see nothing wrong in it?'

'Well, they volunteered to take Patrick's punishment. They offered because his skin was wet. They only had three strokes each.'

'And you would have flogged the boy on his wet skin?'

'Well, he forgot to bring his towel. They birch you on your wet skin in a sauna and I didn't think there was anything wrong with it. Perhaps I didn't think all that much.'

'Perhaps you should have thought a little more. As you are aware, I am the magistrate for this district. I have to tell you that I take exception to what you did in both my private and my public capacities. I propose to have you charged with an act of gross indecency in a public place, with assault on four female persons and with actual bodily harm.'

'Good heavens! Is there nothing that can be done? Is there no other way?'

'There is a possible way which, out of my kindness, I shall extend you. I might be prepared to punish you in a more personal way than taking you through the courts.'

'What would it involve?'

'It would involve accepting chastisement on your skin here at Dunbar Hall and perhaps other punishments and humiliations. There is a well-equipped chamber suitably appointed.'

'When you say on my skin, what would you do to me?'

Lady Dunbar's face creased into a cruel smile. 'We have an extensive inventory of instruments with which to sting skin and we have ways of restraining the recipient. Our equipment is varied and I think it suitable for you and us to be regaled variously.'

'But, I don't see why I deserve this. I've never been really cruel to Patrick. He likes to be disciplined a little and, when I had him whipped in the stable yard, I told my groom to lay them on lightly.'

Darline could see Lady Dunbar's eyes on her, steely and hard, vicious under the high-swept platinum-dyed hair.

'But why do you want to do this to me? I don't understand?'

'Shall we say, my dear, I believe in the personal touch in discipline. I could sentence you in court but I shall show a little mercy and bring a hands-on touch to the matter. What do you say?'

'No, no, I'm afraid I really cannot accept. This is really too much. I'm afraid you'll have to charge me.'

'I should think very carefully about this as you did not before. Can you visualise the reaction of the media – the internationally known artist caught flogging young girl art students with her riding crop on the village green – what a

64

luscious story for them! Just visualise the front page of the *Sun*. And I have it on good authority that you whipped that boy on his bare back as you rode beside him. A village woman who happens to be my cleaner saw you.' There was silence for a few moments before Agrippina Dunbar went on, and Darline felt herself close to tears. 'Perhaps I should acquaint you with another matter. I have had, recently, a most tempting offer for your paddocks from a property developer.'

'Oh no, please don't do that to me. I need those paddocks for my horses. I love the place and my father loved it before me, before he was obliged to sell it to you.'

'The decision is yours, my dear.'

'You say you want to sting my skin. I suppose – I suppose I could endure it once. Would you flog me severely?'

'It would not be once; it would be, shall we say, once a month. Your skin would have time to recover before the next beating; and it would go on as long as I see fit. As to severity, you are in no position to bargain. You shall leave that to my discretion.' Agrippina grinned and her lips twitched.

'Well, then, I suppose we should get the first one over as soon as possible,' suggested Darline efficiently.

'No, I think not. It will be good to let you have a little time to anticipate it. You can ponder upon it before you sleep at night and when you awaken. Think of your naked body strapped in position, so soft and luscious, awaiting the cruel strokes.' Agrippina rose haughtily. 'It has been so pleasant to have you. I'll see you to your car.'

5

Naked for Research

'Have you packed your things, Patrick? Are you ready to leave with Doctor Quayle?'

'Yes, madam.'

'Take your bag to the hall, then. Doctor Quayle is taking you in her car.'

'Yes, madam.' Patrick bowed and went out.

'The boy is so compliant,' Flavia remarked.

'He really is,' Darline agreed.

'I thought, also, he looked a little sad. Perhaps he's sad at leaving you and having a different mentor for a while.'

'I must say I feel flattered.' Darline smiled satirically.

'It shows your regime must have benefited him. We'll see how he reacts to my instruction, which will be orientated by scientific medical reasoning.'

They made their way to the hall where they found Patrick waiting with his bag. They saw at once that he was on the point of tears.

'There you are, Patrick, all ready to go with Doctor Quayle. I won't be seeing you for a short time so you must be good and unquestioningly obedient. You must do your best to help Doctor Quayle with her research.'

Patrick began to cry and, much as he tried to check it, the tears welled and streamed.

'Now don't be silly, Patrick. I'm sure Doctor Quayle will be kind but firm with you. You will have many pleasant experiences in the course of your talks with her.'

'Of course you will, and any chastisement will be for your own good.' Flavia looked at him rather like a puma at a hare.

'And reflect that in your small way you will be making a contribution to psychiatric science,' Darline said, looking almost tenderly at her slave.

Patrick got down on his knees and kissed Darline's feet, which were clad in leather peep-toe sandals of chestnut and silver, with bronze studs.

'I'm sorry to leave you, mistress,' he said, choking the words through his tears.

'And I shall be a little sorry not to have my slave at my beck and call. But it is not for very long and I shall soon be commanding and you serving me once again. Get to your feet now and behave like a responsible person. I don't like to say man because naturally they are inferior to women.'

The boy got to his feet. The two women embraced and kissed on their lips.

'Take care, darling. I love you more than life,' Darline whispered, with all the passion she felt for her friend. 'My sweetest lover; come back to me soon. I shall miss your lovely body.'

Flavia unlocked the doors of the Saab and Patrick got in beside her. She waved as they drove along the drive, then Lucan opened the gates and raised his cap, and they were away.

The gates opened automatically and Flavia drove in and parked by the front door. They got out. It was a strange-looking house; a tower of three storeys, set in a walled garden. The front door opened and a tall and very well-built young woman came down the steps. She and Flavia kissed briefly.

'This is Patrick Lovelace, Sally. This is Doctor Sally Dekker, Patrick.'

Patrick bowed and Doctor Dekker said, 'How do you do, Patrick.'

Patrick rose from his bow and said, 'How do you do, ma'am.'

'Bring your bag in, Patrick,' Flavia said. He took it from the back seat and followed the two women up the steps.

'We'll show you your room. It is next to Doctor Dekker's.'

They entered a small room. The walls were hung with several framed photographs of men and women clad in extremely kinky garments of what appeared to be black leather and PVC. Flavia noticed that Patrick's attention was at once arrested by a picture in front of him; it showed a woman whose breasts were encased in conical cups through which her nipples peeped. Below this she wore a tiny black skirt about six inches deep. On her ankles and her wrists were silver-studded black bracelets. From her ears hung long earrings shaped like wriggling snakes in green, with black outlining the scales. Another picture showed a pretty young man dressed in a skirt made of black PVC strips, kneeling before an extremely beautiful woman. The expression on her face was vicious as she looked down at him, whilst his entire demeanour and facial expression spoke entreaty. His arms were raised in supplication. The woman wore a silver-studded half-cup black bra which showed most of her beautiful swelling breasts, the pale-skinned flesh actually seeming to pour out of the cups.

Flavia saw Patrick glancing round the room and she said, 'You will have plenty of time to study the pictures, Patrick. We thought they might help you feel at home. Now, get your things unpacked and then come and see me in my study.'

The two women withdrew. As they went downstairs Sally said, 'He seems a nice young man.'

'He is,' said Flavia. 'He is a very interesting case of total submission. I need to have a few sessions with him to draw him out and see what he has to say about his earlier life and up to the present. What I would like you to do, Sally, is to take charge of his physical welfare. I think it would be good for him to do some physical exercises every day and you'd be the ideal person to put him through his paces.' Flavia smiled. 'I mean as an Oxford oarswoman and a famed runner. Also, as you are heterosexual, it will be interesting to see what sort of relationship develops between you.'

'Mmm, sounds intriguing. Do you think it could be developed as far as a physical relationship?'

'I think it quite likely that it might. I would like you to feel you have a free hand. If you feel you want to take it as far as having sex with him you are free to do so, but I would particularly like you to put him through some physical exertion.

'Like all of us he wears a persona and I think that at present he is wearing the mask of a slave. I think he feels safe as a slave, but we need to find out why and who he really is. I think that a good way to begin to strip away some of his fears would be to make him go naked.'

They were now in Flavia's study and Flavia seated herself at her desk and Sally on a chair nearby.

'Yes, I think twenty-four-hour nakedness would be a good experience for him. Perhaps stripping away his daily attire will reveal even deeper degrees of his masochism.'

'He is a long time coming. I wonder if he's all right,' said Sally.

'Perhaps he's having difficulty in finding the study.'

'I'll find him and bring him along.' Sally went out into the passage and found Patrick, cautiously looking into one of the rooms.

'Oh, there you are, Patrick. Let me take you along to Doctor Quayle's study. She's waiting for you there.'

Patrick followed her to the study and Sally looked in and said, 'Here's your young man. I'll leave you both together.'

Flavia looked up at him as Patrick entered the room. Her expression was kind. 'Have you unpacked everything, Patrick?'

'Yes, Doctor Quayle. I mean yes, madam.'

'There's no need to be too formal, Patrick. Don't be afraid, I want you to feel quite relaxed with me. Wouldn't you like that?'

'I suppose so, if it pleases you.'

'It is all right for you to please yourself as well, Patrick.'

'All right. Thank you.'

'Do you like your room?'

'Yes, thank you.'

'Do you like the pictures?'

Patrick smiled. 'Yes, I find them rather exciting.'

'We thought they might make you feel at home, coming as you do from a household where you were well disciplined.'

'It's very kind of you. I appreciate it.'

'Do sit down and relax, Patrick.' The boy seated himself on the edge of an armchair beside the desk.

'Now, tell me something about yourself. Do you like your life with Ms Pomeroy?'

'Yes, I was very grateful to find a place with her.'

'I understand she is very strict with you. She even gave you a spanking in my presence. Tell me about any other punishments you have had.'

'She has whipped me with her riding crop.'

'And what was the offence that earned this?'

'I spoilt an item of her lingerie.'

'What did you feel about this?'

'Well, I felt desperately sorry for having ruined the negligée.'

'Why did you feel so desperately sorry? Accidents will happen.'

'I felt sorry because I so love beautiful things, especially flimsy and soft things. I envy women the clothes they wear because the fabrics are so soft and they are made in so many beautiful colours.'

'Would you like to wear such things yourself?'

'I would, yes.'

Flavia could see that Patrick was relaxing now. He was gaining a little confidence in her.

'At art school, in the school of fashion, I designed underwear for ladies and for men.'

'I wonder why you particularly like to design underwear?'

Patrick blushed slightly. Flavia, with her acute attentiveness, did not fail to notice that he was drumming on the arm of the chair with stiff fingers.

'I'm fascinated by knickers because they are so brief, or at least you can make them very brief. And for ladies you

70

can design them with frills and flounces, although I also like them to be very sleek.' Patrick was silent for a few moments.

'Go on. Tell me exactly what you feel.'

'They are such an intimate garment. I asked a girl once what she thought the reason might be that I was so fascinated by knickers and she said, "That's easy, Patrick, it's because of the part of us they cover". She meant the genitalia, of course. Her name is Frederica. She used to model knickers and bras for me and tell me what she thought. She was a lovely girl. I used to design knickers for her in different colours, particularly red and various shades of tan and brown. But I particularly liked to make black ones for her. I used to make black ones for her in synthetic materials, usually nylon. You can get black nylon in very slinky textures, sleek and satiny. She used to look lovely modelling my knickers and bras. I used to want to kneel and kiss her feet.'

'Was there anything hurtful in your relationship with Frederica?'

Patrick licked his lips. 'There was one incident. I asked her to go out with me once. There was a play I thought she might like, but she didn't want to go with me. Next day I discovered she had gone to a sado-masochistic club with a sculpture student, a guy called Max.'

'That's very interesting. Did you design other things?'

'Yes, I designed skirts for men.'

'I see. What triggered this in you?'

'It began when a girl came round quizzing people for an article in the university magazine. One of the questions she asked was what you thought of men's clothes. Well, I replied that they were terribly dull because whatever a designer of men's clothes did they never got away from the basic concepts of jacket and trousers. I said that there should be gowns or robes for men to wear like there used to be. And it would not be anything new. The Greeks and the Romans wore tunics and robes. I love the way they exploited the draping qualities of materials in garments such as the chiton and the toga. And I love the garments the Greek ladies used to wear. Today a lot of men wear skirts, around the world. Not just the kilt. The Arabs wear robes, in the Pacific islands they wear sarongs. In Fiji the policemen wear skirts. At the end of her quizzing the girl asked if I would be prepared to wear a skirt and I said I would.'

'Going back to underwear, do knickers have any other associations for you?'

'Any other associations?'

'Yes, for example anything one might do with knickers.'

'Well – er – I suppose a thing one does as well as putting them on is to take them off.'

'Mmm, have you any particular associations with regard to taking them off?'

'Well, I like taking clothes off. I like taking them off for any reason, but also on some occasions you just take them down.'

'Go on.'

'I used always to fantasise about taking them down for a punishment sometimes but, on the few occasions when Pina whipped me, I stripped naked. It's lovely to be spanked or caned or whipped by a woman.'

'I wonder why you feel that, that it's so pleasurable to be beaten, to be made to feel pain, at the hands of a woman?'

'Well, I've never been beaten by a man and I wouldn't want to be. I don't want to be beaten by a bony, angular old man, a schoolmaster or my father. I like to be spanked or caned or whipped by a lovely woman dressed in soft and colourful clothes and with the scents of her cosmetics and perfumes in your nostrils.

'Ms Pomeroy had me whipped by her groom once when her right hand was sprained, but it was all right because I felt it came from her. She told him not to lay them on viciously and she was close by to watch.'

Patrick was silent for a few moments. Flavia said, 'You are talking about yourself quite freely.' She smiled gently at the callow boy. 'That's what I want you to do. Are there any other items of dress that fascinate you?'

'I love sandals, especially women's sandals. They come in so many beautiful designs and are made of such lovely materials. When I see a handsome woman wearing sandals I have flutterings in my belly and I feel I would like to go down and kiss her feet. I like them to be very strappy, often with thin straps and I particularly like the ones with a loop for the big toe, or with straps between the big toe and the next. When I first saw you this morning I wanted to kneel before you and kiss your feet. Your feet are really quite beautiful and your sandals set them off perfectly. Oh, I'm sorry; have I said too much?'

'No, that's quite all right. You may say whatever you like in your sessions with me. Do sandals or feet have any other associations for you?'

'Well, there is one thing. Ms Pomeroy sometimes makes me paint her toenails and I love doing that. She is seated and rests her feet on a footstool. I kneel before her and proffer the box of varnishes and she chooses one and then I carefully varnish her toenails.'

Patrick was silent for a few moments. The psychiatrist in Flavia saw that he was pondering whether to reveal something else.

'Is there something else you want to say? Feel quite free to tell me anything.' She smiled kindly.

'There is one thing. Or I should say two things. I'd like to be naked when I paint Ms Pomeroy's toenails and, when I've finished the painting, I'd like to take the place of the footstool. While the varnish is drying I'd like her to rest her feet on my naked back as I crouch before her. I find it a bit embarrassing to tell you but I'd just love to be her footstool. I want to be the footstool of a goddess.'

'So you feel that Ms Pomeroy is a goddess?'

'Yes. I absolutely adore her.'

'Lovely. Your masochism is a beautiful manifestation and I can see that it suits you. I'm glad you talked freely; you only needed a little prompting once or twice. We'll leave it there for this time. Before you go I will tell you something. You say you like to take all your clothes off; perhaps you like sunbathing.' Flavia smiled knowingly at her neophyte. 'Well, I'm pleased to say that I intend to have you go naked at all times during your stay with me. You had better wear sandals to protect the soles of your feet and set off your nakedness. And to titillate your flesh we'll have your ears and one of your nostrils pierced and fit you with some nice earrings and nose ring. It is good for the flesh to be pierced by metals because metal represents the valuable and enduring components of the psyche.'

'Thank you, doctor. You are very kind. If I may say so you look very attractive with your lovely jewelled stud and your long pendant earrings. Should I not say that?'

'That's quite all right. This afternoon Doctor Dekker will take you to have your nose and your ears pierced. If you have to answer the door you can slip on a housecoat which Doctor Dekker will give you. She will also take care of your physical well-being and will put you through exercises in the garden and will take you out jogging. Off you go now and remove your clothes.'

Patrick got to his feet, bowed low and said, 'Thank you for being so kind.'

'Good morning, Patrick.'

'Good morning, Doctor Dekker.'

'Now, let's put you through some exercises in the garden and then go jogging round the park. You can remain naked for the exercises. Have you something to wear for jogging?'

'Yes, ma'am, I've got some hot pants Ms Pomeroy gave me.'

Patrick could hardly take his eyes from Sally and she could see this. She had such a stunning figure which was barely masked by the brief shorts she wore, which were cut low to show some of her taut belly and tummy button and cut high to show a little of her curvaceous buttocks. She wore a bra from which the smooth mounds of flesh curved teasingly. He felt he wanted to kneel before her and kiss her feet. She was two or three inches taller than him and was extremely well built. A beautiful figure with a look of contained power. He had an impulse to kiss the lovely smooth curves of her shoulders but he scarcely dared entertain the thought, much less the action.

Sally could see that he was fascinated by her body in its near-nakedness. She thought how she would enjoy tantalising him. I'll now put him through some healthy exercises to take his mind off my body or perhaps concentrate him even more on it.

'Right, Patrick my boy, to the garden we shall go. Follow me.'

Sally led her naked charge through a conservatory and into the garden where there was a paved area.

'Now then, Patrick, stand before me and let me look at you. What a nice figure you have; such a tiny waist. You are almost too slim. Perhaps we'll build you a little more muscle. Now I'll demonstrate what I want you to do and then watch as you do it. Stretch your arms right up. Up high, as far as you can get them. Feel as if you are pushing up the sky. Now swing your whole body round in a circle with your arms still raised. There, I can feel my whole body stretching itself; all the muscles of my back stringing themselves.'

Sally could see Patrick doing his best. He certainly had a very slight figure. The tiny waist was very like a girl's and his small breasts were like those of a teenage girl. He could use a little more muscle but then he wouldn't look so girlish, which was very appealing in its way.

Patrick stretched up his arms for the next exercise. 'That's right; stretch right up. You can feel yourself stretching for the sky. Now, breathing out and holding your belly in, bend forwards slowly and smoothly. Carry on going until your forehead comes close to your knees. Yes, you can feel yourself going down, right down, and now place the palms of your hands on the ground. There, now can't you feel your muscles stretch? Hold yourself in that posture for four deep breaths. Now bring yourself up again.'

Sally thought: I'll make him do this ten times and then move on to something else. She watched as he repeated the deep obeisance.

'Now we'll try something else, the snake.'

Sally tossed Patrick an exercise mat and spread another on the patio slabs.

Sally could see Patrick watching her closely as she lowered herself to the mat. She could feel that her extremely short shorts had ridden up on her buttocks. She liked having this boy in her power and being able to tease him without it being too obvious. Her breasts seemed about to spill from their triangular bridles which only covered about half of them.

'Now I raise the front of my body by stretching with my arms until they are straight. My head goes right up and back like the head of a rearing snake and I look towards the sky.

Sally went through the snake posture ten times, feeling the muscles of her body moving on their framework. She could see that Patrick had an erection and felt deliciously and perversely pleased and indignant both at the same time. She would teach him if he stepped out of line!

'Now, let me see you do the snake posture. Up high with your arms and right over and take your weight on your hands and your toes, and now lower yourself right down, right down on your belly, and now you feel just like a snake on its belly.'

Seeing him like that with his slim body and tiny waist she felt that she'd like to whip him, really thrash him. She knew he needed and desired it. She could use one of the canes that Flavia had used occasionally on her. She knew that Flavia was a lesbian and was in love with Darline Pomeroy but she liked to express her Platonic love for Sally by caning her and Sally expressed hers by accepting it.

As Patrick exercised, Sally felt love for him and at the same time she wanted to beat him; how lovely it was to be perverse!

'There you are,' said Sally, breaking out of her reverie. 'Now I'll take you for a run in the park. Up you get and roll up your exercise mat. Get your knickers on.' The boy drew on his knickers and shorts.

76

'We'll go out through the garden door,' she said, unlocking the door. They went through.

Sally was aware of her whole body like a beautiful living sculpture. As her breasts bounced in their brief top, she could see that her pupil's eyes were on her, moving from her breasts to her buttocks and back.

They ran a few yards along the road and in at the park gates. She thought she should show him a little mercy as he wasn't as fit as her so she ran beside him, checking herself to his pace like a reined-in horse.

Two youths were lounging by a fountain and one of them whistled as they passed. Sally was oblivious to the action. She could hear the boy puffing just behind her and thought: he must be having a lovely view of her sinewy back and the cheeks of her arse peeping from the shorts. They passed a group of gnarled oaks that looked like strange twisted sculptures and Sally wondered if Patrick would like to draw things like that. Perhaps he would like to draw her. She paused, running on the spot.

'We'll go back now.'

As they ran back it was downhill and a little easier. She sensed that Patrick was relieved.

'We'll take a shower now. You can have a shower with me.'

They had reached the large bathroom at the top of the landing, stripped off their brief garments and got under the shower.

'I usually have it warmish at first and finish off with cold. We can soap one another's back.'

Sally took a tablet of soap and worked up a lather on Patrick's back.

'You have lovely skin, just like a woman's,' she said. Her hands circled over the soft skin of his back and she felt and lingered over his shoulder blades and the vertebrae of his spine. 'There! I've given you a good soaping. Now I'll use a loofah on you a little.'

Sally took a large loofah and began to scrub the boy's back in a circular motion.

'You have such a sensitive skin that I'm making you rather red. I dread to think what a whipping would do – make you scarlet! You really do have a skin like a girl's. There you are, that's you done. Now you can do my back.'

He took the soap from her and started to soap her back.

'You can press quite hard,' she said, and felt him increase the pressure. 'Now give me a jolly good scrubbing with the loofah to open the pores.' She felt him working on her with the loofah. 'That's it, scrub nice and hard.' She had not had a shower with a male for some time. But showering with this boy hardly felt any different from showering with a woman. He was so gentle and so compliant and he obeyed instantly. In company with him she felt like an Amazon.

'That's enough,' she said. He put down the loofah and they each soaped their own bodies, working over breasts, bellies, buttocks and pubes. She noticed that the boy's phallus was a little stiff and proud but by no means thrown out in a full erection. He needed a good whipping to bring him on!

'Now, shall we let the cold rain on us to rinse away the lather and perk us up?'

Sally turned the dial to cold and felt the disciplinary iciness attack her skin. She stood there taking it and watched the boy's penis slacken under the attack. After a minute or two she switched the water off.

'There's nothing like that to invigorate one's whole body and mind. Here, I'll pat your back dry and then you can do mine.'

She took the boy's towel and patted his back gently. 'There, now you can do my back.' Patrick took her towel and dried her back. She felt his hands once or twice and they seemed to linger on her skin. 'Thank you, that's enough.'

'I think a little talc is required now,' she said, as she took the talcum powder and sprinkled some on her underarms and crotch. 'Now I'll do you. Raise your arms.' The boy raised his arms and she sprinkled talc on his underarms. Then, on an impulse she sprinkled some on her hand and worked it into his genitals, rubbing it into the mat of hair and around his penis and scrotum. She felt him flinch like a startled deer as she did so and then felt his dangling pod stiffen slightly.

She was about to sit down when suddenly the boy took her shoulders in his hands and planted a kiss between her breasts.

She drew herself away. 'How dare you! How dare you be familiar with me! Get down on your knees and beg my pardon!'

The boy was shattered. He sunk to his knees and said, 'I beg your pardon.'

'I beg your pardon, what?'

'I beg your pardon, ma'am.'

'Say, "I humbly beg your pardon, ma'am".'

'I humbly beg your pardon, ma'am.'

'I consider that you deserve to be punished for this.'

'I am willing to be punished, ma'am.'

'I shall punish you after breakfast. Go and prepare it. You know that you are not to wear clothes in the house?'

'Yes, ma'am.'

The boy slipped his feet into sandals, bowed and went out.

Sally slipped on a transparent black peignoir and looked at herself in a full-length mirror. The splendour of her body was made mysterious by the dark filtration of the flesh under the filmy material.

She made her way to Flavia's study and knocked and went in. Flavia was studying some papers on her desk.

'Good morning, Flavia.'

'Good morning, darling. I like your negligée.'

'I'm afraid I have to ask for one of your canes. Patrick has been extremely impertinent. He actually had the temerity to kiss me.'

'Good grief! Where did he kiss you, darling?'

'Right between my breasts. I gave him some exercises in the garden and took him for a run in the park as you wished. Then – after we had showered – we towelled one another and put on some talc and he dared to take hold of my shoulders and kissed me between my breasts.'

'Good heavens! What did you do?'

'I made him go down on his knees and beg my pardon.'

'I should think so. Do take a cane and thrash him as you think fit. I know you won't flog him too hard, but I should make it fairly severe. A smarting impression on the body makes a lasting impression on the mind.'

'What do you think, say, six strokes?'

'I should think that would be fine. Perhaps this is a blessing in disguise. I had intended to be lenient with him during his stay, mainly because I wanted him to have confidence in me during our sessions, but this gives me the opportunity to impose a more disciplinary regime. I think it highly likely that he already admires you, in fact adores you as a goddess. But this morning's event is an aberration. He did not keep his place as worshipper but essayed familiarity. Yes, six strokes should do it. Although the pain of that will soon be over, so I should give him a further punishment, something other than flagellation, something that will last for a while.' Flavia smiled ironically. 'Take a cane from the cabinet. Take one and beat your boy but don't forget to think of a further humiliation for him; perhaps make him perform some menial task. Let me know how he takes his punishment.'

Sally went over to the cabinet and selected a long cane. She and Flavia smiled mischievously at one another as she went out. She swished it a few times as she went downstairs, remembering how Flavia had caned her.

In the breakfast room she found Patrick placing tea things on the table. She saw his eyes widen at the sight of the cane. When he had put down the tea things he bowed to her. He looked crushed, she thought, and she felt a little sorry for him, but she steeled herself.

'I'll bring the croissants and the muesli, ma'am.' He bowed and went out and came back with a tray and placed a box of muesli and a plate of croissants on the table. He looked at her questioningly, as if awaiting direction.

'I shall punish you after breakfast.' Her tones were icy.

She hung the cane on the back of her chair and they seated themselves.

There was silence during the meal and Sally knew that Patrick was anticipating the event soon to come. It was so lovely, the waiting, the meting out and the acceptance of punishment. There was a strange quality of love in it.

When they had finished eating Sally said, 'I shall punish you now.' She rose from the table and her expectant minion rose too.

'Mmm, now, we need a firm base on which to stretch you. Yes, I know, we'll put you over the kitchen table. Into the kitchen with you.'

Patrick said timidly, 'After you, ma'am.'

She smiled grimly and went into the kitchen. He followed her.

'Now stretch over the table.'

Patrick obeyed, prostrating himself on his front on the smooth Formica top.

'Now, Patrick, I am going to cane you for being familiar with me. After each stroke I want you to say, "I humbly beg your pardon, ma'am." Is that understood?'

'Yes, ma'am.'

Now that she saw his slim body with the peach-like buttocks, she felt a little compunction. But she felt cruel and angry and she raised the cane and brought it down. She heard him gasp slightly before murmuring, 'I humbly beg your pardon, ma'am,' then she raised the rod again. In her head was an image that she was a high priestess punishing an erring acolyte. I'll bring it down and cut him, she thought; and she brought it down as hard as she could and saw the boy flinch before he murmured his response. How dare he kiss me! That's what one gets for being kind! Be familiar with me? Indeed! She raised the rod and felt what a hard and cruel thing it was; like a long stiff phallus that was used to induce pleasure and pain. She brought the rod down, quite savagely now, and the boy gasped before murmuring his response. She felt like Venus whipping Adonis. She would 'rein his proud head to the saddle bow', as Shakespeare said.

The wretch did not seem very proud; he was so feminine. In fact he was a perfect girl. If he wears anything he should

81

wear girl's clothes, she thought. I'd like to fit him out with everything from knickers and suspender belts to flowered frocks. She brought the cane down again and empathetically imagined the pain she inflicted as she transmitted it through the rod. He moaned faintly with the sting of the cut and then repeated his litany in a voice that was broken. She was breaking him to nothing. She was his high priestess, his princess, his Amazon. Why, the creature could not even run very far without being distressed! She raised the rod for the fifth time, raised it high and brought it down with extra momentum. Her toy-boy squeaked like an animal and then begged her pardon in the prescribed phrase. What could there be more glorious than to punish the male, to keep him in check, to put a bridle on him. It would be good to make him wear a collar, a slave collar like the Romans put on their slaves. She brought it down for the final cut and made this the 'unkindest cut of all'. The boy gasped for the final time and murmured his line.

'There, you've felt the final stroke for this time,' she said to the boy who remained lying on the table. 'You may get up.' He rose and she said, 'Now you may kiss me; you may go down on your knees and kiss my foot.'

The boy bent his body and she felt his lips on her instep and on her toes. She could feel that his mouth was moving sensuously.

'You may get up now. And now, as a useful task, you may come to my room and paint my toenails.'

She went out and the boy followed her. She would enjoy this. Only a few times had admirers painted her toenails. It was a wonderful expression of love and desire.

She swept into the bedroom, tossed the cane on the bed, and seated herself in an armchair.

'On my dressing table you will find a box of nail varnishes. Bring them here.'

The boy went over to the dressing table and timidly approached her with the box. She looked at it and said, 'Mmm, I think we'll have the terre-verte today.'

The boy took the bottle of varnish and carefully unscrewed the cap.

'We had better have something on which I can place my feet. Bring over that camel saddle.'

Patrick brought the camel saddle and placed it before her. She raised her right foot. Patrick charged the brush and started painting her nails, commencing with the big toe.

She contemplated her foot as he knelt compliantly before her. The skin of it was tanned to the shade of a hazelnut. She loved a tanned body; loved her own. She loved Flavia, although her love for her was only physical in the sense of masochistic.

The boy was varnishing the toe next to the small one. It was a delicious, evil, green colour. She liked other colours for her nails, reds, yellows and blues; but this shade was truly of the earth, and it complemented beautifully the nut brown of her skin.

A wave of desire overcame her and her mind ranged over things to do with the boy. Perhaps she would make him sunbathe in the garden with her, make him oil her back. If he dared, perhaps she would actually initiate him in sex. She could ride him and drain him of what fluid he had and make him even more compliant, if that were possible.

He was now carefully working on her left foot. He appeared to enjoy the task and was charging the brush and laying on the varnish so delicately, taking great care not to overflow onto the skin. He painted the nail of the small toe with care. She could sense that he was sorry that his task was finished. He looked up timidly and dropped his glance to her feet again.

'Now put away the varnishes. On my bedside table you will see a book entitled *The Bronze Goddess*. Bring it to me.'

The boy got up and went over to the dressing table and carefully placed the box of varnishes on it. Then he went to the bedside table and brought the book over and offered it on the palms of his hands.

She took it from him. She wondered if she should make him go down as a footstool while the paint was drying, but thought it a bit extreme. There was no real pretext for it. The thoughts running through her made her clitoris stiffen. She felt she wanted to flog him again, harder, but she disciplined herself not to without reason. Then she had an idea; she would make him stand facing the wall while the paint dried.

'Now go and face the wall until I tell you you may move.'

Patrick bowed low and went obediently to the opposite wall and stood facing it. She looked at him standing there. He made a piquant sight with his attractive back and tiny waist and the long blond hair falling to his shoulders.

She turned the pages of the illustrated book. It was a first-hand account by a lady anthropologist, of her life amongst a Brazilian tribe on the upper reaches of the Amazon. There were many photographs of her naked, in company with members of the tribe. Sally put the book aside; her mind was too full of images and excitement. She would wait until the varnish dried and then make him clean her boots and shoes.

'Patrick, we are all alone, just the two of us on this lovely afternoon. When you have done the washing up you may come and sunbathe with me in the garden.'

Sally went out into the walled garden. She was wearing a transparent, short kimono which reached just below her pubic hair. Beneath the kimono she was naked and her athletic bronzed body showed smokily through the black net. She stood there, taking in the sounds of the garden. In the alders bordering the river, she could hear the exquisite descending descant chant of a willow warbler. She turned and regarded herself in the conservatory glass. The image of her bronzed body was made dusky by the filter of dark gauze.

She strolled down a path to a place which was a perfect suntrap, shielded on two sides by high yew hedges and on a third by the garden wall. She stood looking at a spotted flycatcher which flew out repeatedly from the garden wall to catch insects and then back. She loved birds; their varied forms and the coloured patterns of their plumage.

Patrick came into view. She removed her covering and

draped it over a garden chair, then reclined on one of the air mattresses over which was spread a huge towel. Patrick approached and bowed.

'You may recline beside me,' she said, grinning up at the boy. She turned over on her front and said, 'Oil my back for me. I don't really need oil with my tan but I like the feeling of oily hands on one's skin.'

The boy took the bottle of oil and poured some into his palm. He began with her back and shoulders.

Sally could feel the boy's hands sliding over her skin; the only thing better than this was a professional massage.

'Do it all over, on my thighs and buttocks as well.'

She felt her boy's hands move down to her firm buttocks and then over her thighs. From her prone position, with her face resting on her hands she could see that he had a partial erection.

'I think that will do nicely. Now I will do your back. Roll onto your front.'

Her boy lay down and she rubbed oil over his slim back and shoulders, moving down to his buttocks and thighs. It had been so titillating when she had caned him and now she was caressing his body with oil. She began to have an urge to possess him further; perhaps to ride astride him. It would be good experience for him, part of his education. She put down the bottle of oil and said, 'That's you done.'

She resumed her previous position with her face on her hands.

'Patrick, bring me a tall glass of lime juice with ice and have one yourself.'

The boy bowed and went towards the house. She watched his glistening back as he went.

She liked to be strict, even harsh, with him. It was pleasant and stimulating to have a slave at one's beck and call. She wanted to cane him again, but wouldn't without a pretext. Patrick scarcely knew whether he was coming or going and was so afraid to step out of line, yet yearned for a beating. He was returning with a tray with two glasses of lime juice. He approached his goddess and bowed as he proffered the tray.

'Thank you, Patrick.' She took one of the frosty glasses and indicated that he might recline on a mattress beside her. He stretched himself out. They propped themselves, Roman fashion, on elbows, and sipped the cool yellow liquid.

'Are you enjoying your stay here, Patrick?'

'Yes, thank you, ma'am.'

'But I suppose you'll be pleased to see Ms Pomeroy again.'

'Yes, I will, ma'am.'

'I trust I have not been too strict with you.'

'Not at all, ma'am. I'm sure I deserved it when you caned me. I never mind being caned by a lovely woman.'

'Do you miss anything here?'

'I miss Pina.'

'Who is Pina?'

'She's my girlfriend. She whipped me a couple of times, just for our mutual pleasure.'

'Go on, tell me.'

'She did it at my parents' house and at her friend Zenia's house. Oh, ma'am, excuse me – I feel so aroused.'

Sally felt suddenly moist between her thighs.

'You know,' she said levelly. 'You should have other sexual experiences; would you not like to?'

'I would, really, much as I like being whipped.'

'Come to me,' Sally said urgently, in a voice filled with intent.

Her boy came to her and she pulled him down beside her. She ran her fingertips over his belly and saw his reaction to the tickling of the muscles. Her hand strayed to his genitals and as she touched his phallus it began to lengthen. She gently teased it, touching the flange of its helmet.

'I'll tell you what; I'll give you real sex. You have nothing to fear because I'll play the dominant role. But first, be a darling, go to my room and bring the box of condoms from the top left drawer of my dressing table.'

The boy got up and made his way towards the French windows. His oily shoulders and buttocks gleamed in the sun and excited her as he went. He soon returned with the condoms.

As he neared her she saw that his erection had subsided a little.

'You naughty boy! You are relaxing. Bring me a switch from the silver birch over there and I'll soon stiffen you.'

Patrick eagerly went over to the silver birch and came back with a twiggy switch.

Sally rose and took the switch from him. Then she placed her left foot on a garden seat and bent the slim body over her knee, slipping her left arm over the appealing back and shoulders.

'I sometimes whip men to arousal,' she remarked nonchalantly. She started to swipe him at the point where his buttocks met his thighs, deftly swishing the twigs into the crevices. Then she swished him lightly between his legs, on the soft skin on the insides of his thighs. She was gratified to see his phallus lengthening and thickening.

'That's better,' she said, tossing the switch aside. Like the masterful goddess she was, she took him and laid him down on a mattress.

She took the box of condoms and extracted one of the foil covers and tore it, drew out the viscid oily condom and rolled it deftly down over the erect penis. On a whim, she took some oil from the bottle and rubbed some over his belly.

'Does it tickle?' she asked, looking down into his eyes.

'It does, ma'am,' he said.

She put down the bottle of oil and took up a position astride the lithe body with its stiff rod upstanding. Her eyes gazed into his and her expression was determined. Slowly she lowered herself onto the erect member, feeling it enter her innermost regions. Her clitoris, proud and stiff, was rubbing against his groin, and she raised and lowered herself, feeling exquisite sensation as she kept her body in contact with his. One could do anything with men; one was a goddess in relation to them.

She continued her up and down movement as she rode him, then, as she felt his mounting excitement, she increased the speed by degrees, thinking, idly, that it was like the rising and falling in the saddle on a trotting horse. Then she began to move her hips in a circular motion, feeling all the time his muscled phallus in her as though she were scrubbing her insides with it, feeling that she wanted him deeper and deeper. His penis was a corkscrew going round and round and up and down, and she was riding him, and rubbing herself against him, using him to excite herself. And then she felt him coming and she drew him deeper and met his thrusts with her corkscrewing. As he reached the climax of orgasm he moaned with sensation and his seed spouted. She could feel it within the end of the condom and she screwed and screwed his member more until he was utterly finished.

She felt now that she could do anything with him. She would spank and thrash and whip and flog him. She would make him crouch down as her footstool. She would not have him for much longer but she would make the time full of sensation. She whipped the condom from him and tossed it aside and grasped the sensitised member and squeezed and oscillated on the flange of the glans and he moaned with pleasure.

'Now you are going to work on me,' she said decisively. She lay back on the mattress and opened her legs. 'Kneel between my legs and go to work on my clitoris with your tongue. It is the ancient art of cunnilingus. Do you see the clitoris at the front of the vulva? I'm holding the lips open to expose it. Stiffen your tongue and lick me. That's it, press as hard as you can with your tongue; go on, go on.'

She could feel the most exquisite build-up of sensations as he worked deftly with his tongue, keeping it as stiff as the head of a snake. Then she felt herself exploding on a wave of ecstasy, and she was beyond the point of no return. She cried out in delight as her body and belly writhed and heaved in a current of release.

6

Nakedly Vulnerable

'So I take it you enjoyed your stay with Doctor Quayle, Patrick?'

'Yes, madam.'

'It must have been quite an experience to go about naked all the time.'

'It was. I felt so free, madam.'

'Well, you'll be able to feel free at home now, you may still leave your clothes off.'

Patrick entered the kitchen with a tray containing the remains of Darline's afternoon tea.

'Here he is again, doesn't he look sweet.'

Lilian smirked lasciviously at the naked boy who put the tray down on the draining board and said nothing.

'Nothing to say for yourself, cat got your tongue this afternoon?'

The hefty woman snatched playfully at Patrick's genitalia and he drew himself aside, like a fencer.

'There, what does it feel like, no clothes on? Strewth, in my younger days they did some things but they never made them go naked.' She pinched his bottom as she spoke and he flinched.

'Please let me get on with my work. I can't if you keep teasing me.'

'Ah, there, what a good boy. He wants to get on with his work.' With a sudden movement she pinched him below his ribs.

'Please – please leave me alone. I've got to clean the mistress's shoes.'

'And he's so polite and he talks so good – although he comes from the working class just like me.'

'Why do you torment me like this? Please let me get on with what I'm doing.'

'There – and he's got no guts – can't even get a hard on.'

Patrick was polishing one of Darline's riding boots.

'And be sure you polish her whips as well – her lovely riding crops. I've heard about what goes on when she makes you run beside the horse; when she lashes your naked back. You enjoy it, do you? I'm told you don' object.'

All that afternoon the hefty woman tormented the naked boy. In her eyes he was not a man. He was sensitive so he had to be bullied to elicit a rough reaction that would coarsen him like her. She mercilessly pinched and poked him until he was spotted with brown bruises like a leopard and she jeered as she physically tormented him. She couldn't understand how someone would take it without retaliation.

As the morning went on she started to feel more crude and more cruel. She wanted to spank him; yes, she would give him a spanking like the ladies did, like the upper classes used to do to their children. Took their knickers down and spanked them, her mother, who had been in service, had told her. Oh yes, there was many an exciting story about spanking as practised by the gentry.

Patrick came in with some of Darline's lingerie which he proceeded to arrange on an airer.

When he had finished Lilian approached him and said with a grin, 'Now, my boy, or is it my girl? I'm going to toughen you. I'm going to make a man of you if it's the last thing I do. I'm going to put you across my knee and spank you.'

Patrick moved as if to run away but Lilian grabbed him. She sat herself down, then drew him on to her lap. He struggled, but she grasped his wrists in her left hand and

90

held them tight behind his back, then began to spank him hard, with stinging slaps on his buttocks, and she continued spanking until her arm was tired.

Patrick entered with Darline's morning tea and placed it on her bedside table. He bowed low.

Looking at him Darline saw that his body was spotted all over with brown and purple bruises.

'Good grief! How did you get those bruises, Patrick?'

'I'd rather not say, madam.'

'Now, don't be silly, tell me how you got those bruises.'

'Lilian did it, madam. When I was working in the kitchen yesterday she teased me a lot and kept pinching me. I have a very sensitive skin and bruise easily. She finished by spanking me until her arm was tired.'

'Why on earth should she torment you like that?'

'I don't know. She just said she wanted to make a man of me.'

'As soon as she arrives this afternoon, tell her she is to come and see me.'

'Yes, madam.'

'I will not have you treated like this.'

Patrick bowed and, as he was going out, Darline called after him, 'Don't forget, you have a driving lesson at eleven.'

There was a knock at the studio door and Lilian entered.

Darline turned from the canvas she was working on. The highly dramatic painting showed a rearing horse with a naked girl on its back, holding the reins tight as if to make the horse rear.

There was a severe look on Darline's face as she spoke.

'Lilian, Patrick has just served my afternoon tea and I was astonished to see that his body is a mass of bruises. I understand that you were the perpetrator of these injuries.'

'Oh well, madam, I thought you would have no objection to that. I was just teasing him because of seeing him starkers, and I just pinched him a few times. I really thought you'd have no objection. After all he gets a lot of spankings and whippings. I watched him being flogged by Lucan in the stable yard.'

'When you should have been getting on with your work. As to your first assertion I have every objection. I will not have my personal boy-maid subjected to ill-treatment by other servants. I intend to exact retribution for this. I shall punish you severely. You have the choice of accepting the punishment I deem proper or being dismissed instantly. Which is it to be?'

'Well, if you put it like that, madam, I don't want to lose my job here, so I'll accept your punishment.'

'In that case you will keep your post for now. Your punishment will be twelve lashes of a whip of my choosing. You will be strung up in the stable yard and flogged naked, which is appropriate since you teased Patrick when he was naked. I shall lay on the strokes myself. I take it you are still willing to accept.'

'I still accept, madam.'

'And you will apologise to the boy for molesting him.'

'Very well, madam.'

'Your punishment will be administered tomorrow afternoon. You may go.'

Lilian bowed and went out.

Darline did not like bullying. The woman had had the boy there in the kitchen, naked and completely vulnerable. For herself, physical discipline had to be ceremonious, a lovely enjoyable ritual involving mistress and slave or mistress and pupil. The recipient had always to be willing, she reflected.

Ingrid Riding was at the gates with the Fiesta at eleven. Patrick was waiting for her and got into the driver's seat beside her. As he got in she saw that he had noticed the long and whippy-looking cane lying on the rear seat. She had taken it from its wrapping as a psychological ploy.

'And how are you, Patrick?' Ingrid asked cheerfully. 'I saw you glance at the back seat. Don't be alarmed, it's a cane I occasionally use on my husband. Being a policeman he appreciates the value of discipline.'

Patrick concentrated hard on putting the Fiesta into gear and started moving fairly well and without any jerks.

'That was a reasonably good take-off. We'll see later how you can manage a hill start. I understand you've been away for a week while Ms Pomeroy was in Paris.'

'Yes, I stayed with a friend of Ms Pomeroy's, Doctor Flavia Quayle.'

'And did you have a pleasant time?'

'Yes, it was quite enjoyable. Sally Dekker, Doctor Quayle's assistant, put me through yoga exercises and took me out jogging every morning.'

'I must say you look fit and well. Take the next turning on the left and we'll try you with a three-point turn and see how you manage it.'

As Patrick took the left turn competently Ingrid thought that she could not recall ever having had a more nervous or uncertain pupil. One part of her wanted to cane him again, as she had previously, with him bent over the bonnet in Oxshott Woods, but another side of her felt a little sorry for him. He was very feminine for a boy of his age. She would be gentle with the boy for a while.

'Now slow down and stop just beside that lamp-post and we'll try a three-point turn. That's it. Now put the car into gear and we'll take off slowly. What should you have done first?'

'I should have looked in the mirror.'

'Then why didn't you do it?'

'I'm sorry.'

Flustered by now Patrick made a poor three-point turn. 'No, Patrick, that was not good,' said his teacher. 'However, don't despair; we'll try again.'

They went through the three-point turn again and Patrick made an even worse job of it.

'All right, let's try a hill start,' Ingrid suggested. She was feeling she wanted to beat him again. She had scarcely ever had such unpromising material, but she made herself be kind.

'Now for the hill start, you bring up the clutch and feel the pressure on the footbrake. Nicely off with the handbrake. Slowly and smoothly up with the clutch and we're away.'

The car started to roll back and Ingrid put her foot on the brake to correct her pupil's poor performance.

'Let's try again until you improve a little.'

They tried a second and a third and a fourth time and Patrick's performance worsened with each attempt.

'All right, Patrick, I'm afraid I have no choice but to punish you again as Ms Pomeroy wished. Change seats and I'll drive us to Oxshott Woods. I take it you are willing to be punished?'

'Yes, ma'am.'

Ingrid drove effortlessly, with mastery, to Oxshott Woods. She felt an excitement in herself in anticipation of what was to come and she felt a little sorry for him. But the exasperating thing was that she was trying her very best and however patient she was with him, he did not improve. Perhaps there was something in the medieval idea that knowledge could only be flogged into people.

As she was driving along the track towards the clearing it started to rain, long lances of rain that impinged on the windscreen and trickled down. She switched on the wipers. A wild idea came to her, to whip him in the rain, lay on the strokes while the rain streamed down his buttocks. It would be a bit extreme though to cane him in the rain and it would be bound to sting more. Besides, she was wearing only a short skirt and a flimsy blouse and she didn't want to go back to the office soaking wet.

'I'm afraid the weather is against us. I'll just have to cane you in my office.'

She turned the car round and drove them back to her office through the downpour. She was feeling a sort of sexual superiority. The poor ninny deserved to be flogged. She parked the Fiesta in front of the office. Taking the cane from the rear seat she replaced it in its wrapping and they ran into the dry building.

They exchanged greetings with the receptionist and went into her office where she locked the door after them.

She looked at him with tight lips. 'I'll cane you across

94

my desk. Take your trousers down.' The boy undid his belt and unzipped. His trousers dropped. 'Now your knickers.' He took down his tiny black knickers. She felt arrogant and cruel when she saw him with his briefs around his ankles. The boy was so sensitive; he so much desired to be dominated. She compared him with her husband who was tougher, yet still liked to be flogged unmercifully.

'Take those papers from the top of the desk and put them on the filing cabinet.'

The boy did as he was bid. She could see that he was trembling with excitement.

'Now lie across the desk,' she ordered.

Patrick eased himself up on the desk and lay across it. Ingrid pulled his shirt well up.

'I shall give you nine strokes this time. Do you think that is fair?'

'Yes, ma'am, whatever pleases you.'

'I want you to count the strokes to give you something useful to do. Your driving by the way, is quite useless.'

'Yes, ma'am.'

Ingrid raised the cane. She brought it down quite hard so that it cut across the skin sharply. She reflected that her husband liked the strokes to be laid on hard. The boy jerked slightly on the desk and murmured, 'One.'

She raised the cane again. A police car screamed in the street. She brought it down hard and the boy jerked and mouthed the count, 'Two.'

A pigeon cooed on the window sill. She raised the cane again. She was feeling high and mighty now, quite the goddess. It was such an opportunity to exert mastery over the male.

'Three.' She raised the cane. She brought it down very hard, aiming at the point where buttocks met thighs. The boy wriggled slightly and mouthed, 'Four.' Ingrid was now glorying in her role of dominatrix. The wonderful opportunities life offers! This boy had been delivered into her hands. She raised the cane and brought it down. 'Five.' Floggings unlimited! She would be like the medieval masters and flog skill into the boy as they had flogged in

Latin. My God! She should have flogged him in the woods
with the rain streaming down his buttocks. But there might
be a further opportunity for that! Down she struck with
her rod and the boy jerked and squirmed a little and
murmured, 'Six.' Men were just there to be dominated and
she would dominate. She would take him back to her place
next time. She brought down her instrument of pain and
love and her subject squirmed. 'Seven.' There was a tap at
the door. She laid down the cane on the boy's buttocks and
unlocked the door and opened it slightly. It was her
secretary.

'Some letters for you to sign.'

'Thank you, Helga, I'll sign them presently. Don't
disturb me again, please, I'm giving a pupil some
individual tuition.'

She relocked the door. Now I'll lay on the final two as
hard as I can, she thought. He deserves it and it will do
him good. She brought up the cane and struck down and
stroked him with it. It was a little like tenderly stroking a
loved one; but going to the other extreme of inflicting pain.
'Eight,' he murmured and squirmed. Another police car
screamed in the street and faded out. The cane was coming
up and then she delivered him his pain and he murmured,
'Nine.' Ingrid was by now in a state of near-ecstasy, feeling
herself the mistress of this body and psyche before her.

She put the cane down. 'You may get up now.'

The boy eased himself up off the desk and drew up his
knickers and trousers.

'No hard feelings?' Ingrid was looking at him almost
tenderly; he had afforded her such exquisite pleasure.

'No hard feelings.' The boy looked entranced, uplifted
by his abasement, serene and calm.

'I'll sign these letters and then I'll take you home. And
remind me to give you your letter for Ms Pomeroy.'

Darline was working again at her painting, when there was
a knock at the studio door and Patrick entered with a tray
of tea things. He put it down on a painting table and
bowed.

He looked sweet in his nakedness, Darline felt, yet she could not forbear to chide. 'The report from Mrs Riding yesterday was not very good, Patrick.'

'No, I'm sorry, madam. I do try my best.'

'So she punished you again?'

'Yes, madam.'

'Again in Oxshott Woods?'

'No, it was raining, madam, so she took me back to her office and caned me there. She put me across her desk for it.'

'Well, I hope it does you some good. I hope she doesn't have to wear out canes on you. Perhaps she should use a whip instead.'

'I will accept whatever she decides, madam.'

'On to another question of flagellation, is Lilian here?'

'Yes, madam.'

'Tell her to be ready for her whipping in fifteen minutes. Take the long whip which you'll find on the desk in my study, take it to the stable yard and wait there for me. Get a lunging rein from the harness room and have it to hand. Lilian is to be stripped off ready.'

'Yes, madam.' Patrick bowed and went out.

The prospect of whipping Lilian was not as exciting to her as when Patrick was the recipient; but it had to be done because the slattern deserved it. Pinching the boy until he was bruised all over! She would teach the great fat bitch. If her cooking had not been so good she would have sacked her.

She sipped her tea and stood back from the painting and studied it. It was coming along; the naked girl mastering the great stallion as he reared with mane flailing. She finished the tea and made her way down to the stable yard. Patrick was waiting there with the whip and the lunging rein but there was no sign of Lilian. She looked round and saw the fat woman through the kitchen window. She was obviously reluctant to undress and come out naked. Darline took the whip from Patrick and went into the kitchen.

'How dare you keep me waiting! My instructions were

that you were to be ready for your whipping. What is the meaning of this?'

'I'm embarrassed to take my clothes off, madam.'

'Then you must overcome it. You were happy to torment the naked boy when he had no choice but to be in your company. Take off all your clothes at once. I shall give you two minutes. Either that or you are dismissed!'

'All right, madam.'

Darline went back into the yard and stood by the tethering rings. She kept the time by her watch. In exactly two minutes Lilian walked out, naked but for her shoes. She had a gross white body which reminded Darline of a fat model they had once had in a life class, an immense lady on whom breasts and belly and thighs were huge and flabby hangings.

'Offer your wrists.'

Lilian, crestfallen, put out her wrists and Darline put the clip end of the lunging rein round them, slipped the rope into the clip and drew it tight. She felt a delicious sense of power as she put the free end of the rein through a high tethering ring and drew the woman up as far as she could.

'Hold her tight up while I secure the rein.' Patrick jumped to it and held the rope while Darline secured it to a lower ring. 'You may stay and watch,' she told him.

Darline stood back and to the left of the strung body. How gross the woman was! She would stroke her grossness with the whip.

She swung the whip back and then in a wide arc to crash on the fat naked back and shoulders. Yes, she would work on her like that, moving down with each stroke. She swung it again and brought it down a little lower and it curled around the fat body. One of the horses neighed from the paddock. How unrelated images will strike us when we are engaged on a different activity! Down she brought the whip, again a little lower. Lilian moaned quietly as it stroked her. Three welts were appearing like a developing photographic image on her skin. Darline swung the instrument of pain and pleasure back. A wood pigeon cooed from the stable roof and performed its courtship display, a deep, puffed-breasted bow with fanned tail, for its mate. Darline swung the whip once more, and brought it round to curl around Lilian's back.

She said to Patrick, 'That was four strokes. Keep count of the remaining eight.' She wanted to lose herself in her lashing and not be concerned with arithmetic.

'Yes, madam.'

Darline was now feeling all-powerful. She was to remember this afternoon. She was glorying in lashing this fat creature strung up before her. She wanted to be lashed herself; she would ask Flavia to whip her the next time they met. It was good; it took one right out of the greyness of life. She felt a slickness between her thighs. How would she get her lover to whip her? Perhaps kneeling and bending over a camel saddle. Perhaps stretched across a hard table. Should she ask Flavia to tie her hands behind her back? That would make her feel deliciously helpless. The sounds and smells of the warm afternoon went on around her; the whinnying of horses, the song of the yellowhammer and the cooing of the wood pigeon. A bee buzzed around Lilian's shoulders and then flew off as the lash crashed down. Darline felt herself empowered by punishing this creature for tormenting her boy. She would rule them in her domain, her word would be law!

'That is twelve strokes, madam.'

Darline was pondering whether she should let the woman hang there for a while, then decided against it. She still had to prepare the evening meal to which a dealer had been invited.

'All right, release her.'

Patrick untied the rope from the lower ring and loosened it from Lilian's wrists.

The fat woman had an odd expression on her face; as if she had discovered something strange and new. Darline thought: perhaps she even enjoyed it in a strange way!

Lilian bowed and turned to go.

'Haven't you forgotten something? I said you were to apologise to Patrick.'

Lilian turned to Patrick, looking down. 'I'm sorry for what I did.'

'Very well, you may go now.'

Lilian went towards the kitchen door, her skin aflame.

They were reclining naked on sun beds on Darline's patio. Patrick emerged from the kitchen with two tall and frosty glasses of pale green liquid. He bowed and placed them on the low table between the ladies.

Flavia looked after him as he retired towards the kitchen. 'That boy is quite pretty, you know. One could almost imagine him dressed as a girl.'

'The idea had breezed through my mind,' admitted Darline.

'Instead of having him go naked, you mean?'

'He would certainly make a very attractive girl.'

'Darling, one thing I've been pondering is that it might be good for him to have lessons in mathematics. He seems rather too dreamy and the discipline of mathematics would be good for him. In one of his sessions with me he admitted that maths is his weakest subject. And it would be good for him if he had to study one subject which he finds very difficult.'

'Do you know, darling, I'm rather taken by that idea. It might make him a bit more structured in his approach to design. He has designed nice knickers and bras for women and acceptable skirts for men. But art needs structure and a course in maths might instil some structure into his approach.'

'I introduced you to a mathematician of my acquaintance once, Julia Compton. She is a senior wrangler. She's a brilliant mathematician and has done special work on the relation of mathematics to psychology.'

'Sounds interesting.' Darline paused for a few moments and there was silence between them. Then she spoke: 'I must tell you something, you are closer to me than anyone else and I must tell you.' She paused again. 'The fact is – I am in a certain amount of trouble.'

'What is it, Darline?' asked her lover. 'You know you can confide in me.'

'Well, do you remember I told you about those four girls

Patrick met, who offered to take his punishment for him? Did I tell you that Agrippina Dunbar came on the scene and saw me swishing one of them?'

'She's the local magistrate, isn't she?'

'Yes, that's right. Well, at the time she took no exception to it, said the young needed discipline.'

'Then what's the problem?'

'A day or two later she invited me for tea. She intimated that she would have me charged on several counts – actual bodily harm, an indecent act in a public place – that sort of thing. She wants me to submit to whatever she likes, probably once a month. She said she has a special chamber.'

'And, even though you are a masochist, you feel aversion for this?'

'Of course I do. Flagellation should be concomitant with love; an experience between two willing people. Have you no sympathy, no feeling for me?'

'I do sympathise but, as a doctor and analyst, I have to be clinical.'

'My God! And I thought you loved me. Christ! I used to thrill to be spanked by you. I loved it when you took my knickers down. You just treat me like a specimen. The truth is I'm just part of your bloody research!'

Flavia looked coolly at Darline. 'I see nothing that I can do to help or intervene.'

7

Aromatherapy and Swedish Massage

They lay side by side on massage tables in the Aphrodite Health Centre.

Darline turned and addressed Flavia. 'It's lucky this massage has made me feel kinder towards you. I no longer resent what I thought was your cold and impersonal attitude the other day. I must accept it as a punishment from my mentor. It is my discipline to accept it.'

Romana smiled knowingly as she continued her kneading.

Flavia said, 'I do have your interests at heart and I feel that I must let you work out your own solution. Tell me more about what she said she would do to you.'

'She said they had an extensive collection of restraining and correcting instruments. I suppose I'll be hearing from her soon. My God! This massage is so heavenly that I can almost face the prospect.'

'I'm quite sure that the effect of massage on the body is also felt on the mind,' said Flavia dreamily.

'Well, you're the psychiatrist, you should know.'

'Well, even a psychiatrist is always learning. I must say, I've learnt quite a lot from my sessions with Patrick.'

'He must be quite an interesting case study for you.'

'He certainly is. He seems to be a total masochist.'

'I sometimes wonder if I'm not playing with Patrick,' mused Darline. 'I'm intrigued by the idea of dressing him in girl's clothes. I think the novelty of having him go naked all the time is beginning to wear off, for both of us. Besides, it slows him down when he always has to whip on a housecoat to open the door.'

'Yes, that must be a little inconvenient sometimes.'

'It's so exciting when it's a novelty to be naked, for specific things like swimming and sunbathing or for life drawing and painting. I didn't tell you, did I? I've found a beautiful new model, a girl called Trisha. She's a really excellent model, remains as still as a Rodin bronze, and she's quite beautiful.'

'Do you look for particular qualities in a model? Is beauty a particular qualification?' asked Flavia

'Well, of course, beauty is very much in the eye of the beholder. I've seen and used all sorts of models from the petite to the huge. When I used to teach, the schools used to engage all sorts of models. I remember one very gross lady at the Wimbledon school. My God! The creature was vast: huge breasts, belly and thighs, and folds of fat would hang down her back from her shoulder blades. Apparently she used to write poetry but I never read any of her work. But the answer to your question is that I need to draw all sorts of models. Working overmuch from one model leads to clichés.'

'Yes, I suppose that's true. Oh, this massage is superb,' she purred, changing the subject.

'Do you think we should have them give Patrick a massage?' asked Darline.

'He's still in the sauna, I suppose. Well, why not; it would be only fair to let him experience this kind of pleasure.'

Darline addressed Romana, who was working on her belly muscles. 'Do you think you could give my boy a massage when you have finished with us? He's a little dreamy and we'd like to perk him up a little.'

'You say he is in the sauna at the moment. The best thing would be to give him a Swedish massage when he comes out. We needn't interrupt your massage. I'll call Santha and she'll fetch him from the sauna and attend to him.' Romana ceased kneading Darline's belly, glanced through into an adjoining room and called to another masseuse to administer to Patrick.

'Oh, please don't stop working on my stomach. I love it when you take those folds of skin in your hands, just above my hips, and then release them.'

Patrick felt Santha's arm around his slender waist as she brought him into the massage room.

'Lay yourself down over the table,' she ordered.

Patrick stepped up to the table and laid himself over it. The towel fell away as he did so.

Santha said, 'Your employer said she wanted you enlivened, but it doesn't seem fair to give you a Swedish massage only. I'll pummel you first and swish you with birch twigs and then give you a soothing massage with some special aromatherapy oil. You've had your cold plunge so the pummelling and birch twigs should refresh you and the oil will relax you again.'

Patrick lay there and felt Santha's energetic and deft fingertips pummel his flesh. She plucked handfuls of skin and then released it, then plucked again all over his back and shoulders, belly and thighs.

'Oh, my God! What an experience!' he moaned ecstatically.

'Now I'll swish you with birch twigs,' she told him.

She took a light birch rod and he felt the delicate, stimulating sting as she swished his skin, working deftly and easily from his shoulders down to his buttocks and thighs and up again.

'It doesn't sting too much, I hope.'

'No, its absolutely heavenly,' he replied truthfully.

'Have you had a Swedish massage before? Felt the birch twigs on your skin?' Santha asked in a teasing voice.

'No, never. Although I've often yearned for it. I've read about boys being birched in public schools, but this is quite different.'

'Mmm, I've always thought that's rather cruel!' said Santha.

'I don't think I'd like to be birched by a man,' he said, 'but it's lovely to be swished by a lady.'

104

'I'm glad you enjoyed it. Now, I think that's enough swishing, for now. I'll leave the birch twigs and use some lavender oil now.'

Santha poured some of the sweet-smelling oil into her hands and rubbed them together, then worked it over Patrick's back and shoulders.

'That's really lovely. I should have had this before,' he moaned. 'And you have such soft hands.' Patrick spoke as if he were experiencing something very special.

'That's because I'm a masseuse. We work such a lot with fragrant oils on soft skins like yours. You really do have a lovely body.'

She began to make great sweeping movements right up on either side of the spine and then down on the other side. He sighed deeply.

'Now, I'll move down and do the backs of your thighs.'

She began to press at points between his thighs and buttocks.

He gasped. 'Oh, I like that effect.'

'It's a crucial point in massage.'

'It sends sensations right up my body.'

Santha finished his treatment with long swirling movements at either side of his spine – from coccyx to neck – and then he felt the delightful dance of her fingertips all over his back.

'There! That's you done. I'll return you to your mistress; stimulated, swished and soothed, all in one session.'

'Thank you, I'm most grateful to you. I'd like to kneel before you and adore you.'

Santha laughed lightly and teasingly. 'I don't think you need go that far.'

When they got back to Pomeroy House, Darline had Patrick serve them tea. She wondered if her friend would like to have Patrick paint her toenails? She checked herself and said nothing. She herself was feeling quite masochistic. She acknowledged that one side of her envied Patrick. Life for him was so simple; he simply had to do what he was told and serve his mistress. No, she would like to paint her friend's toenails herself. And maybe she would plead to be allowed to do so. Maybe she would kneel before her mistress and offer her back. She would ask her lover when the boy had left. She would ask to be whipped first. Yes, it would be better to be whipped first and then paint her toenails.

Patrick placed the tea things neatly on the low table before the settee.

'Shall I pour, madam?'

'Er, yes,' Darline said absently. Her mind was full of more erotic images. The flesh; it was the flesh. She loved flesh and skin. She loved to create from flesh and skin. A whipping would be a stimulus for her creative work. The big brush would sexually touch the canvas. She recalled reading something about a writer writing with a stiff penis; perhaps a woman could write or paint with a stiff clitoris. Creation was positive. It was glorious. Whipping was glorious too. Perhaps even a Lady Dunbar stinging would be a stimulus! All sex was glorious because in it one cast away all pretence and lovers did what they wanted to do; what the flames in their bodies insisted upon.

Patrick finished pouring the tea and straightened up.

'Thank you, Patrick. You may go.' The boy bowed and went out.

Darline's mind was on things other than tea, but she picked up her cup and sipped.

'You seem miles away,' Flavia remarked.

'Flavia,' Darline sighed. 'Half of me still resents your coolness, but I am on fire for you, right now. I bloody-near feel I can face the prospect of a Dunbar stinging at the moment. You make me want to be dominated. May I talk with utter honesty? I'd like to be whipped by you. Please whip me. Do what you like with me. Please, treat me as your slave, your thing, your footstool.'

Flavia turned and kissed her lover on the lips and Darline responded passionately. As the stiffened pairs of lips touched and brushed, Darline felt her lover's flesh stirring her insides. She wanted to lie down before her mistress and lover and feel the strokes on her buttocks. She needed to be punished.

'Please whip me, darling. Stroke and mark my backside with your whip. Let's cast off all caution – whatever the hell is going to happen will happen – let's play games while we have one another. Like I whip my minions so I want to be whipped, lashed at your hands. I want to kneel and bend over; be your footstool.'

'All right,' murmured Flavia. 'I understand your desire to play the masochist. Perhaps you are finding your true self. Bring me a whip and I shall flog you.'

'I love it when you say that. Please say it again,' moaned Darline.

'I shall flog you.'

'Why are you going to flog me?'

'Because you are naughty. You have not fully accepted what life offers – even if your skin *is* to be stung by someone you don't like, you must learn to accept it and use it. Perhaps even put it into your art. Also you must not resent my sometimes objective attitude. Don't forget I am a doctor as well as your friend. I feel you should cast off any remaining trace of inhibition and let your art become even more explicit. Yes, I want to see sadism and masochism right there in your paintings. Bring me a whip at once and get yourself stripped off.'

Darline's body was a mass of flaming desire as she got up. She no longer cared if Agrippina Dunbar wanted to sting her skin. She bowed humbly before Flavia and hurried to her room.

She undressed, tingling with passion. Should she leave her knickers on? She liked to feel them froth around her ankles. No. She would strip naked and put on a teasing peignoir so that Flavia could see her body through it. She selected a slinky black garment. She slipped it on and looked at her reflection. She looked marvellous. There was a smoky quality to the gauze and she could see her outline through it; shadowy and mysterious. She felt fully alive, as if she could have done anything. She was trembling with anticipation because she was about to surrender to her mistress and lover. She slipped her narrow feet into some strappy sandals, pushing her big toes through the loops and strapping the single thin jewelled leather over the insteps. She took up her riding crop and made her way back to the drawing room.

She went in and stood poised in the doorway. She could see Flavia taking in the sight of her body through the sheer fabric.

'My God! What a sight you make!' Flavia was visibly electrified and her eyes darted over the luscious body she was to lash and sting.

'I have come for my punishment.' Darline bowed and, as she straightened up, offered the crop.

Flavia took the leather-handled stick and rose from the sofa.

'Now, I am going to punish you severely. Do you know what you are to be punished for?'

'Yes.'

'Yes, what?' she asked patronisingly.

'Yes, mistress. I am to be punished for resenting your professional interest at the prospect of my correction by Lady Agrippina Dunbar, and for not being sufficiently sado-masochistic in my art.'

'Those are the reasons. You must not resent my coolness as a doctor and you must learn to cast off inhibition and use your talent to its utter fullness. I trust that the strokes, the pain, you are about to experience, will liberate your creativity more fully. We shall go on working on you to this end. Remove your garment.'

Darline slipped off the peignoir and stood naked before her handsome lover. She could see the gleam in the eyes of the dominatrix.

'Stretch yourself over the pouffe.'

It was a large, circular pouffe, almost like a padded altar. Darline went to it and laid herself on it. She was feeling liberated, now, yet at the same time she was nervous in anticipation of the strokes. From the corner of her eye she saw Flavia approach and stand over her with the crop. It was a vicious-looking instrument, the one she had used on Patrick.

'Now, Darline, I am going to give you six strokes. I shall deliver them slowly and each time I cut you and you feel the sting I want you to say, "I love you, darling, I will have no resentment". Is that understood?'

'Yes, darling.'

'Say it now.'

'I love you, darling, I will have no resentment.'

'I want you to understand that I whip you with love. Do you understand that?'

'Yes, darling.'

Flavia raised the whip. Darline was feeling deliciously abandoned. She knew well that the more aroused you are, the more you enjoy the pain of the whip.

She heard the swish and felt the cut on her smooth buttocks.

'I love you, darling, I will have no resentment.'

Swish down and cut! And then the sting as the whip was raised.

'I love you, darling, I will have no resentment,' she repeated.

Darline writhed delectably on the pouffe under her body. She felt that this was the whole meaning of being: to stretch out and be flogged by the one you admired. She felt a spiritual heightening in this lovely discipline.

The remaining cuts were delivered and it was over much, much too soon. She lay there on the padded leather, her buttocks burning. This was even better than a spanking over Flavia's thighs. It was delicious to be treated like this by her lover. She found such pleasure in suffering pain for passion's sake.

'You may get up now.'

'Please go on – I love you, I will have no resentment.'

'I said you may get up.'

Darline got up slowly from the pouffe. She felt such unabandoned desire in her flesh and her belly. There was an oozing between her thighs and her tiny bud was stiff and proud in its hood. Then she sank to her knees and kissed Flavia's feet. She felt her lips on the slopes of the insteps and savoured the taste and smell of bathed and perfumed skin; the loved skin of an adored body.

'I worship you, darling. I would do anything for you. You have given me such pleasure, such pure joy, by

109

whipping me, that I would like to do something in return. My backside is burning. I'm on fire. Let me kiss you between your thighs. Lie down on the altar of love and let me kiss you. Lie down and part your legs.'

Darline felt as if they were both moving in slow motion. It was like an erotic dream, a slow ballet of love. They embraced and kissed, their lips meeting and stiffening and then parting and meeting again. She pushed her nakedness against her lover's thin clothes and then she was helping her to undress. She unbuttoned her dress at the back, then removed it completely. She unhitched the bra, allowing the harnessed fruits to bounce free, then slipped down the petticoat and brief knickers. She took her time in removing the silky sheath from her lover's exotic area, and breathed in the scent. She was on her knees when Flavia stepped out of the knickers and Flavia raised Darline up to her level where they kissed, their fleshy lips opening as their tongues entwined.

Darline's body tensed and shivered with pleasure.

'Darling, I love you, adore you. Thank you for beating me. But let me kneel before you. I want to explore between your legs with my tongue. I want to taste you.'

Flavia lowered herself onto the circular altar and opened her legs. Darline knelt between her luscious thighs and licked slowly. She loved the sweet salt taste of the clitoral flesh and felt the clitoris stiffen as she worked on it, massaging it with her tongue muscles. She could feel Flavia responding and sensed the effect on the adored bitch body. The belly was heaving, the breasts bouncing as tension built, within the loved flesh.

Flavia groaned with the stirring of her insides. 'Tear it! Bite it!' she commanded. 'Pull it to bits!'

Darline started to nibble on Flavia's clitoris with her teeth, feeling the tough purple flesh between her incisors, biting almost to the point of breaking the skin. Then she worked on the nub with the tip of her nose, going at it like the end of a penis or a dildo.

Then there was a surging of Flavia's belly, spreading to her whole body and she shuddered to a thundering climax.

As she was heaving, Darline moved slightly to rest with her lover across the altar and rubbed gently between her legs with her hand, massaging softly to bring her back down. They lay there for a while, at peace. A starling whistled outside and it mimicked the mew of a gull and the 'ya ya ya' of a green woodpecker and Darline smiled. She had her own madrigal within her.

'Oh, that was beautiful.' Flavia's voice was a gentle sigh, going out of her and draining her as if all the tensions within her were dissolved.

'I'm so glad. I'm honoured to serve and thrill you because you have given me such pleasure emanating from pain. Let me perform a service for you now, let me paint your toenails. Or perhaps you would prefer to paint them yourself and use my back as your footstool? Yes, please do that, darling, rest your feet on my back. I'll bring you some varnishes so that you can choose.'

Darline slipped on her peignoir and danced out of the room. She returned to find Flavia seated regally. She bowed and then knelt before her goddess and proffered the box of varnishes.

Flavia selected a bottle of bright red and took up a brush. Darline turned and offered her back and Flavia placed a foot on it and started to paint.

Darline knelt on her hands and knees with her lover's foot on her back and was high and happy.

Patrick felt Julia Compton's eyes on him, stern yet with a certain inner kindness.

'Really, Patrick, I have never known anyone have such difficulty with Pythagoras's theorem. You should be able to grasp how the square of the hypotenuse equals the sum of the squares of the other two sides of a right-angled triangle. Perhaps this is too far advanced at first. After coffee we shall go back to the study of fractions. Good grief! It's nearly time for coffee. Take a break from Pythagoras now. Would you like to go and get us some coffee?'

The boy looked deliciously vulnerable as he got up from his desk, clad only in sandals, earrings and nose ring. She had observed that he was a titillating sight, with his very tiny waist and his long blond hair falling to his shoulders. She had noticed him thrill when she had said that his skin was just like a woman's! She had gathered there was the prospect of his being dressed in girl's clothes and that might be more exciting than being always bare.

There had been talk of whether he should have lessons at Pomeroy Place or at her own flat. It might be nice for him to have lessons at her place where she would be able to do what she liked with him, although, of course, she was able to do what she liked with him here. Darline had given her authority to cane him if he did not make progress and she was thrilled at the prospect. She had not caned a pupil before. She had never caned anyone; she usually taught university students and with them caning was not customary. She had often thought however that it might have done some of them good!

When he returned with the tray of coffee she was still seated at her desk and was glancing through a copy of *Elle*. He carefully placed a cup of coffee on a table mat on the desk.

'Thank you, Patrick. Do relax, now, and enjoy your coffee.'

She looked at him as he sat at the pupil's desk. She felt that perhaps he was a bit too compliant, even a bit feminine. They had told her that his mental make-up needed structuring a bit more rigorously. Mathematics, they had said, would be good for that. She began to feel that she wanted to cane him, felt the impulse in her taut belly and between her thighs. She continued to coolly regard her pupil. It was a bit much for them to make him go naked all the time.

Flavia had thought that it would strip him of some of his persona! But then what would you get down to? Maybe a feminine inside, a feminine unconscious!

'I understand you like being with Ms Pomeroy, Patrick.'

'Yes, ma'am, I like it here. I think I was very lucky.'

'But I understand you are treated rather strictly.'

'I don't mind that.' Suddenly he blurted out: 'I used to

fantasise about being treated strictly. I like it here. I don't mind when a lady whips me.'

'I wonder why that is?'

'Well, ladies are so beautiful. And when a lady lays on the strokes you can just somehow accept it. I love women. I love everything about them. When I was at art school I used to design ladies' and men's underwear, bras and knickers mostly; and I used to design skirts for men.'

Julia felt quite aroused by the mention of designing knickers for both sexes and skirts for men! Flagellation fantasies too! She was aware of a familiar throbbing between her thighs. It was extraordinary how just the idea stimulated her. She knew that she wanted to cane him. She acknowledged that she had always wanted to cane men and boys.

In the university art-school library she had been looking at books on erotic art which had illustrations of women being whipped by other women, tied up in certain attitudes or just lying there demurely. She had noticed a new book there, which showed women and men in all sorts of kinky black plastic and rubber wear; tiny black straps between the thighs, the breasts harnessed in black straps. Straps – the very word was evocative, suggested things. Strappings, kinky practices. Someone had once told her that she was austerely beautiful. The austere senior wrangler in an austere discipline who was austerely beautiful herself! She had been given authority to cane him if necessary and she accepted that she wanted to do so. She would like to be like some of those women in the book, in the lovely shiny black harnesses. She could picture herself wearing a black high-rise one-piece, which would reveal nearly all of her buttocks, with a little strap coming between her thighs, just hiding her depilated vulva and then dividing to leave her belly bare. And cone shaped bra cups with open ends through which her nipples would peep. The boy was still there in front of her. Dammit! She would cane him! He deserved it for being so compliant and so feminine; and his work was not good.

A great rush of power flooded through her; she would

113

cane him on the slightest pretext. She would set him some difficult mathematical problems. They would be child's play for any reasonable student but they would be difficult for him. She would mark his work and then – she would mark him with the cane!

'The BODMAS rule tells us the order in which we must carry out the operations of addition, subtraction, multiplication and division,' she lectured.

Julia looked at her pupil and felt herself very beautiful and powerful. She felt a little sorry for the boy – he must feel very vulnerable dressed in just his skin and the weather! Yet another side of her wanted to cane him hard. And she had such opportunity! He was absolutely in her power. She was a high-priestess and he her acolyte.

'Now, are you with me so far, Patrick?'

'Yes, I think so, ma'am.'

'You think so. Well, I hope we can make you know so, Patrick. What does BODMAS stand for?'

Patrick stumbled over his explanation, and she chastised him firmly. She explained the mathematical rule again but knew there was no chance of him understanding it.

'Now, I'll set you some problems and leave you to work on them for a while.'

Julia got down from her desk and placed a sheet of paper before Patrick, on which she had set the problems. 'There, I'll leave you with them,' she said sharply.

She was feeling splendid in herself, now. She was the bitchy dominatrix. She wandered out to sit for a while on the patio by the swimming pool. Her nipples felt proud and stiff and she felt she would like to strip off her clothes and dive into the pool; it would cool the sexual heat within her. She was very excited and she was aware of the fire underlying her austere beauty.

An art book lying on the table caught her eye. It was called *The World of Darline Pomeroy*. She picked up the book and opened it, turning the pages. There were colour reproductions of many striking and highly erotic paintings, many of them nudes. They were mostly female and took a variety of sensual poses: embracing and kissing, sunbathing and swimming and emerging wet from the water. Then there was a series showing a girl gardening in the nude. Julia read a little of the text. There was a sentence that ran: *Darline Pomeroy, a declared lesbian, has derived a great deal of her inspiration from the contemplation of female bodies and through her friendships with other women*. Julia thought the paintings beautiful and the title of the book very appropriate. The book really did reveal the world of Darline Pomeroy.

Julia felt a sexual arrogance rising and contemplation of the paintings merely added fuel to her sexual fire. She had decided that she would cane him if he had not solved all the problems correctly, give him no let off for getting some of them right and, however pleasant it was sitting there turning over the pages of painted eroticism, there was even greater pleasure to come.

She rose and went back towards the schoolroom. Her nipples stiffened until they felt like marble, as she anticipated his failure.

As she walked in, Patrick was still bent over his books.

'You haven't finished yet,' she declared angrily.

'No, I'm afraid not, ma'am.'

'Let me see what you've done.' She picked up his exercise book and scanned it. His work was terrible. He simply had not remembered anything she had taught him.

'This is not good, Patrick. You have not memorised or applied what you've learnt. You know that I'm authorised to cane you if your work isn't satisfactory?'

'Yes, ma'am.'

'There is no choice but to cane you. Are you willing to accept a caning?'

'Yes, ma'am.'

'I consider that six strokes would be appropriate this time, one for each letter in BODMAS. Do you agree?'

'Yes, ma'am.'

'Then bring me a cane.'

The boy got up, bowed and went out. Julia was glowing now that his caning was imminent. Should she make him bend over or make him lie over a desk?

He came back in with a long cane, bowed and handed it to her. It was a formidable-looking instrument with a curved handle. Julia took it from him. She had better take the lead.

'Come here, and lie across your desk.'

Patrick eased himself up on the hard desk and lay over it. As she contemplated his nakedness she was inspired as to how to punish him. As each stroke was delivered she would make him recite the six parts of the rule. She would let him read from the book in front of him, as he would never remember otherwise.

'As I cane you I want you to recite each part of the rule as you receive the stroke. Is that understood?'

'Yes, ma'am.'

'I want you to say what each letter of BODMAS stands for.'

'Yes, ma'am.'

Julia raised the cane. She felt magnificent now, a patrician goddess with a minion in her power. She brought the cane down and it cut his buttocks. She saw him flinch.

'Go on, dullard; what does B stand for?'

'B stands for brackets, ma'am.'

'Which priority is it?'

'First priority.'

She raised the cane, her breasts firm and large under her upstretched arm. Then she brought it down, angry with the stupid boy. She brought it down hard, and he gasped as he received the cut.

'Go on, stupid! Do you forever need prompting?'

'O stands for of, which means multiplication.'

'Which priority?'

'Second.'

She raised the cane, suffused with an almighty feeling of power; then she brought it down and saw him writhe as it stung.

'Don't keep me waiting.'

'I'm sorry, miss. D means division.'

'And its priority?'

'Second.'

She raised the rod again. She could feel her clitoris stiff and proud between her moist thighs and felt she was whipping him with it, via the tough unyielding rod in her hand. When she brought it down she saw his body jerk. She noticed the welts appearing.

'M means multiplication. Second priority.'

She said, grimly, 'You improve slightly. Let's see if we can make you improve further.'

The cane was raised and brought down again viciously. The boy flinched as it cut him and writhed at the after-sting.

'A means addition and it is third priority.'

Julia felt herself gone now. She was in a state of something like nirvana. There was the realisation that she could do anything with this slave boy. She raised the rod and brought it down and this time she saw an expression approaching ecstasy beginning to suffuse his face.

'S means subtraction and it has third priority.'

She stood there over him. She felt such a sense of power. She felt supremely beautiful! She had never done anything as exciting as this before, and she wanted more.

The boy lay there over his desk, gazing at the open book. There was a beatific smile on his face.

Patrick served coffee for Darline and Trisha, the new model, in the studio. As he went in he saw the naked Trisha, perched on a high stool, her legs crossed. He placed the coffee on a painting table.

'You may break the pose now, Trisha,' Darline said.

Trisha came down from the stool and rubbed her thighs.

'Did you find it a hard pose?' Darline asked.

'No, not really, it was just that I was sitting on a hard surface. The edge of the stool cut into my thighs a bit, that's all.'

'Oh dear! How thoughtless of me! I should have given you a cushion.'

'That's all right.'

'Let's have some coffee and then we'll do some short poses for a change.' She looked at Patrick as he bowed and was about to go. 'Stay a moment, Patrick.' He stood there, awaiting her word.

'I think we'll try you in some poses with Trisha. We'll put some duality into it.' She looked at Trisha. 'I take it you have no objection to posing with a male?'

'No, not in the least. I've frequently posed with other models, female and male.'

'Good,' Darline said. She finished her coffee and put the cup down. 'Now, I'd like you to take up some poses with Patrick and I'll draw you very quickly. I'd like you to take the lead and arrange yourself and Patrick in any pose you like. I'll tell you when to change. I want you, Trisha, to be the dominant one. You can do anything you like; feel utterly free to invent.'

Patrick felt his belly flutter with excitement as Trisha approached him. He found her stunning, with her dangling earrings and the jewel in her tummy button.

She addressed him solicitously, 'I take it you don't mind if I touch you?'

'No, not at all.'

She stood behind him and slipped her arms around his waist and joined her hands over his taut belly. How gentle it felt after the harshness of the caning during the recent maths lesson!

'Good, that's it, hold it there.' Darline had sketchbook and pencil in hand and was drawing swiftly, the point of the graphite dancing over the cartridge paper. Patrick was reminded of his own nude sketchings. His art school days seemed far distant. He had sometimes drawn Pina in the nude and it would be good to see her naked again. It was a never-ending mystery how one could capture on a flat surface something of the essence of the beauty of the naked body.

'Change the pose,' Darline commanded.

Trisha moved to Patrick's front and gazed into his eyes. He felt her gently take his face in her hands and heard her soft and sexy voice saying, 'I'm gazing upon the face of my lover.'

'Good,' Darline said. 'You're an imaginative model and you seem to pair well with Patrick.'

Her hand moved over the paper and he saw her eyes scanning quickly over their bodies to sketch the entire pose. Then she worked on a detailed drawing of his face in Trisha's hands as the model gazed lovingly, strangely, into his features.

'The two of you are working well. I feel I'd like to reward you in some way.' She laughed. 'Perhaps with a spanking. There's a compelling expression in your two faces, the one captive and the other exploring actively. Change the pose.'

There was an elusive atmosphere, that comes about in a life studio when things are beginning to go well, when artist and model are beginning to feel some dynamism between them.

Trisha moved to Patrick's side and slipped an arm around his waist, then turned herself so that her eyes were on his profile. Her pouting lips planted a kiss on the corner of his mouth. She rested her left hand on his hip. He thought how lovely it was, sometimes, to be treated with tenderness.

'That's perfect,' their employer said. 'It's as if you feel overwhelming love for him.' Her hand was darting furiously over the paper. She said, musingly, 'I like sometimes to draw very swiftly. It's almost as if the ego is suspended. I can feel and see very acutely and your pose has become profoundly meaningful. I know – we'll have you more and more intimate as you go on, as the series of drawings progresses.'

After a few minutes she ceased drawing. 'Come out of the pose now. This is good. I think I've just created a new series. You may or may not know that my work is largely inspired by sado-masochism. In sado-masochistic acts all inhibition must be cast aside – there is no place for it in art or in love. I want you now to be totally uninhibited. Trisha, you can take the lead. I want you to lead Patrick into the simulation of all sorts of daring sexual acts. Is that all right with you, darling?'

'Yes, that's all right with me. Is it all right with you, Patrick?'

'Yes, it's all right with me. Whatever you say.'

Trisha's voice became soft and seductive as she began to lead Patrick. 'Now, let's lie down together. This is a better position for love and dalliance and spankings.'

She tossed a light mattress to the centre of the floor and spread a large sheet of black satin material over it. She lay down, her superb pale body contrasting strikingly with the black satin. She drew him down with her and he felt her soft flesh against his own. 'Let's pretend we're mutually masturbating. You can thrill me between my legs and I'll thrill you just in front of yours.' She took his right hand and guided it down between her thighs, pressing on her vulva so that his middle fingers were on her clitoris. With her left hand she grasped his penis and it twitched and lengthened as she did so. Her fingers searched for the helmet of the glans which now stood out proudly.

'This is the pose,' she said, addressing Darline. 'Is it all right?'

'It's excellent,' Darline said. They could see her hand moving swiftly over the sketchbook page. She added, 'Can you hold this for ten minutes?'

'Of course,' Trisha said.

The woman and the boy lay there, splendidly revealed in the studio light, in the intimate attitude of giving themselves each to the other.

Trisha whispered softly, 'Oh that we could go on, but in the line of duty we must hold it here with me holding you and your hand on me.'

'Darlings, that was fantastic,' said Darline when the ten minutes had gone by. 'How about some real sado-masochism, now, to counterpoint the mutual masturbation and get you both fired up again.' She looked around the various props in the studio and seeing a beautiful whip she took it up. 'Here we are. Let's have a tableau in which you whip Patrick in a humiliating position. I must say you look the part, Trisha. A goddess.' She tossed the whip to Trisha who seized it and swished and cracked it in the air. Then she enacted whipping Patrick as he stood before her.

'Now,' Trisha said decisively, 'what is the most

humiliating position I can put you in? I know, we'll have a mirror image so that we can see ourselves. Is that all right with you?' she asked, addressing Darline.

'Of course.' Darline grinned lasciviously.

Trisha wheeled over a large portable mirror and adjusted it. 'Now,' she said, and Patrick felt himself thrill. 'We'll put you in the most humiliating position possible, which is kneeling and bowed over so that your forehead touches the ground. There you are.' She guided his body into position and bent his head to the floor. Then he felt her foot on the nape of his neck and, as he glanced up and looked in the mirror, he saw her standing proudly over him, holding the whip.

Darline started drawing. 'I'm on fire now. I feel I'd almost like to change places with one or the other of you.'

Patrick could see from the corner of his eye that she was drawing hard and fast. Then she exclaimed ecstatically, 'I'm etching out the figure of this proud young woman as she stands over the abject boy crouching before her. I wonder if Trisha's nipples are as hard as mine. You certainly have lovely firm breasts, Trisha, and pert nipples which stand out well. I'd almost like to take you in my arms and feel your lovely flesh.'

Then she was silent for some minutes as she drew hard and with concentrated effort. She mused aloud again, 'I almost wish we had decided to make this a painting.' Then, she said decisively, 'I think that will do for this pose, darlings. Would you like to move on to something else?'

Trisha came out of the pose, stretched languidly, and put down the whip. She said, softly to Patrick, 'I think we'll simulate fellatio and cunnilingus now. Let's lie down.' She lay on the black satin and drew Patrick down beside her. 'We'll lie head to toes. There you are. I'll take the upper position. If I open my legs it will give you access to my clitoris. There we are. Your prick is nice and hard like my nipples and my clitoris. Now with my ruby lips I simulate the act of being just about to suck you. Mmmm! Your cock is standing out nicely. There, we need not actually make contact or we might just make each other come. Is this all right?' she said, addressing Darline.

'Darling, it could not possibly be better.' It was apparent that Darline was all-absorbed by the pose.

Patrick could see Trisha's startlingly beautiful lips scarlet painted and pouted just about to enclose themselves around his glans. He reflected how they were like a lovely vulva, open to receive the attentions of a lover. He and his model partner were both very aroused now, burning with sexual excitement. He could hear the sound of the graphite moving over the paper as if of its own accord. It was almost as if Darline had become a channel through which the sexual energy flowed.

'Oh your bodies are so beautiful!' Darline declared heady with joy. 'The two of you paired are just what I needed to launch myself into a new series. I shall take you both to the private show when they are exhibited in Cork Street. Darlings, wonderful as it is, that is our ten minutes.'

Trisha got up from her prone position over Patrick and he could almost see the thoughts moving through her head. What was coming now?

Trisha looked around and spotted a gilt armchair with crimson upholstery. She moved to it and seated herself regally and addressed Patrick. 'I think we will now play the queen having her valet paint her toenails.'

'You ought to have the correct props, then. Patrick, run and get my box of varnishes,' exclaimed Darline.

Patrick obeyed and when he returned Darline was already drawing Trisha as she sat like a queen on the crimson and gilt chair. He took a rush-topped stool, placed Trisha's right foot on it, knelt before her and took a brush and simulated the act of painting her toenails.

'I know,' Trisha said in a soft and sexy voice. 'We'll have you painting my toenails and then you have to turn your back to be a human footstool.'

'Lovely!' Darline declared. You've found yourself a new occupation, Patrick. How truly beautiful and significant it is to see the male abased, kneeling before his superior and attending to her lovely feet. Trisha, you play the perfect aristocrat with your minion kneeling before you. It's a shame the poses are so short but then we can always se

122

hem up for long painting sessions. I think you can change
now, darlings.'

Trisha bent forward and looked significantly into
Patrick's eyes. 'Now the moment has come. You can put
down the brush and turn and be a footstool of flesh.'

He put down the box of varnishes and turned and knelt
before Trisha and offered his back.

Trisha placed her feet on him and, as he felt them on his
back, he felt a rush of ecstasy.

8

The Chastisement Chamber

Wilkins, the butler, opened the door and regarded her with what could only be considered an aloof smirk. He bowed slightly and said, 'Her ladyship is expecting you, madam.'

He showed her into the drawing room where she found Agrippina seated with Lord Dunbar, who rose and bowed.

'We have been so looking forward to this occasion. Doubtless you have also been anticipating it, one hopes.'

There were butterflies in her stomach and she hoped she was not visibly shaking.

'There is no need to be too apprehensive, my dear – perhaps you, too, will enjoy what we are shortly to indulge in.' Lady Dunbar turned to the butler and said, 'I think you may serve tea, Wilkins. I should think that some slim cucumber sandwiches would be in order.' She turned again to Darline. 'And how have you been spending your time?'

'I have been painting, of course. I hope to set up a new series with a new model and Patrick.'

'Oh, yes, your pretty, slim young man. I trust you have been taking care when you chastise him.'

'Yes, yes. I have been taking care.'

'These things are acceptable if they are done with discretion; our forthcoming session will naturally be conducted with discretion.'

Darline could see Lancelot Dunbar smile slightly. She wondered what on earth they were going to do to her. Perhaps she should try to bear it, brave it out – perhaps it wouldn't be as bad as she anticipated. She felt so confused; what with Flavia's cool, detached attitude and her own trepidation at what was to come. She might even take pleasure in what they were going to do to her; she just had to wait and see.

Wilkins came in with a tray, poured tea and offered the cucumber sandwiches.

She began to panic and she hoped she was not going to crack or break down and give them the pleasure of seeing her in tears. She felt half-inclined to drop her front and ask this sadistic woman to get on with whatever it was she wanted to do. She sipped her tea.

'Art has become very strange these days,' said Agrippina, trying to make conversation. 'Animals looking as if the slaughtermen had been at them. I can only say that I prefer your work. The nudes with horses are superb.'

'Thank you. I'm glad that you like them.'

'Now, my dear, if you've finished your tea I think we should move on. First, I think we will have you more suitably attired. My maid will take you and fit you out.' She rang and a few moments later a maid appeared, a tall woman with blonde braided hair.

'Erna, you have your instructions. Take this lady and help her into the outfit I chose for her, earlier.' —

Erna bowed to Darline and said, in a distinct German accent, 'If madam will come with me.'

Darline rose and followed Erna through several corridors and into a room lined with tall wardrobes.

'Now, if madam will undress. Should I help?' Erna unbuttoned the back of Darline's dress and helped her off with it and then helped her out of her slip.

'Madam has the most beautiful underwear, if I may say so.'

'Thank you. You seem quite used to this sort of thing, you're very efficient.'

'Madam is kind to remark so.'

Erna knelt and slipped down Darline's knickers and she stepped out of them. In spite of her trepidation she felt thrilled.

The blonde maid rose and unhooked her bra and Darline felt a hand brush across her breasts as they fell loose. And then Erna undid her pretty satin suspender belt and slipped down her stockings.

'So, madam is naked. What can we attire her lovely body in?' She moved to a cupboard and took out a black leather garment. 'Now this should fit nicely; if madam would step into it.'

It looked like an extremely high-rise swimsuit but was much more kinky. It left nearly all the buttocks bare and Darline grew excited as Erna drew it up on her body.

'There – a perfect fit; I'll draw in the little strap at the back through its buckle to make it nice and tight at madam's waist – so. If madam would like to look in the mirror.'

The outfit was extremely sexy and Darline's fear was mingled with, and almost overcome by, titillation as she regarded herself. The high rise of the leather sheath barely covered her pubis and an oval cut-out left her belly bare. She looked down and saw with alarm that fringes of hair were visible at either side of her pubic area.

'Madam has some reservation?'

'Er – well – I suppose not; I was looking at the visible pubic hair.'

'Easily dealt with.' Erna went over to a wash basin in one corner and returned with a damp sponge, a tube of cream and a razor. She knelt and moistened the fringes of hair, creamed them and deftly shaved the skin smooth. 'There, it is better. Now a little cologne to brace the skin.' Darline felt the sudden sting as Erna applied the cologne.

'Madam looks so attractive. She would like to see her back view?' Erna held a mirror and Darline saw how she looked from behind. A leather strap rose to cruelly divide her buttocks; the buckled strap drew in her waist and above it her back was bare. 'Now, I think a little black leather skirt is necessary, which can be removed as required at a later stage.'

Erna smiled as she brought out a tiny black skirt and, as Darline stepped into it, she drew it up and tightened its belt around her hips.

'Charming. So very brief. I can see that madam is

thrilled by her outfit. Now, some shoes to complete the ensemble.'

Erna brought out a pair of high-heeled black shoes. 'If madam would be seated.' Darline sat down and Erna knelt and slipped the shoes on and buckled them.

'There – superb. Madam looks the part for what is to come. I will leave you for a while and her ladyship will come to view your outfit.'

Darline sat there, feeling alternately nervous and excited. Her trepidation was almost overcome by the outrageous outfit the efficient German maid had dressed her in. Part of her felt no resentment, just elation. But what in heaven's name was to come next? Could it be that she was being left for a while to anticipate her vulnerability?

Lady Dunbar entered, her appearance altogether transformed. She had become regal and haughty and was now dressed in slinky black trousers which rode low on her hips. Her belly was left bare to display a miniature silver cat-o'-nine tails, the haft of which pierced her fleshy navel and above it a black bra, designed with open straps, which left her nipples pushing through. To Darline's excitement she noticed that tiny silver riding switches pierced them. Her hair was arranged high and surmounted by a coronet. The outfit was completed by high spiked heels. She carried a long and slender whip.

Darline got to her feet as her tormentor looked at her.

'A curtsy or a bow would be in order.' The aristocratic lips curled cruelly. 'I'll make you grovel yet, I'll have you beg for mercy and kiss my foot with gratitude when I lay down the lash – and that will not be soon. A swish of my whip should correct your omission. Do you agree?'

Darline managed a bow and said in a trembling voice, 'Yes, all right. You may do with me what you wish.' For now she thought it safer to play along with this sadistic woman.

'Bend over and raise your skirt.'

Darline bent and raised the tiny skirt, a delicious thrill coursing through her, even though she did not like Agrippina. She felt a single cut of the whip on her buttocks.

127

'There is much more to come,' Lady Dunbar said grimly. 'Now I think it appropriate that you should perform some menial task – follow me.'

Darline followed her along a corridor and into a large and luxurious bathroom equipped with an oval bath, toilet and bidet.

'Now, I want you to scrub the toilet pedestal and bidet until they are spotless. Furthermore, I want you to employ nothing more than the toothbrush and tooth powder you will find on the wash basin. I shall leave you and will return in a while to inspect your work.'

Darline took the toothbrush and tin of tooth powder, squeezed a little cleaner on the inside of the pedestal and started to scrub. It was ridiculous and humiliating to work like this – and all at the whim of that sadistic woman. Who did she think she was? She was close to tears but managed to hold them back. Then a surge of masochism swept through her. 'Perhaps I deserve it,' she murmured to herself. 'After all, I have made Patrick do many menial tasks at my whim. This is my come-uppance.' What would Flavia think if she could see her now? Would she maintain her cool reserve? She finished the toilet pedestal and moved to the bidet. After some minutes of scrubbing, Agrippina returned and in her hand was a birch.

'Stand up and bow when I enter. I shall now inspect your work.' Darline complied. 'Your work is not satisfactory. You deserve to be swished. Remove your skirt and bend over and touch your toes.'

Darline did as she was bid, imagining the picture she made, and felt the sting of the twigs as Agrippina applied strokes of the birch to her backside. What was happening to her? She was almost beginning to feel a strange admiration for this sadistic woman. Or was she – no – you can't love a creature like this.

'Get to work again. I shall stand over you this time,' barked Agrippina.

Darline knelt and began to scrub again with her inadequate tool. She felt her tears brimming, but managed to quench them. She scrubbed for long and tedious minutes.

'We shall see what a little stimulation will do.' Darline immediately felt the sting of the twigs on her back.

'Get to your work or have your skin stung.'

'I am doing my best with this ludicrous tool.'

'Don't speak unless given permission.'

Long minutes passed, broken every few seconds by the birch on her back and, with each stroke, Agrippina urged her on in the most contemptuous terms until finally she was told to cease.

'A swishing is obviously insufficient.' Agrippina went to the door and called to Erna who entered a moment later.

'Erna, take her to the chastisement chamber and arrange her suitably.'

'If madam will come with me,' said the maid.

Darline followed Erna along several corridors and down several flights of stairs until they finally came upon a massive studded door. She unlocked it and led the way in, then switched on some suffused lights. One wall was hung with instruments of correction – whips, canes, crops and birches of every description, together with straps and harnesses in black leather, rubber and shining plastics. The remaining walls were painted with scenes of punishment: slaves, submissives and masochists adopting every possible attitude to receive punishment. Some were bending, some kneeling, others strung to crosses, frames and whipping posts. Darline was particularly riveted by a series of three paintings in which a slender young man was being whipped by a sinewy woman attired in a garment similar to her own. In the first picture the naked man lay on his front, taking it on his backside. In the second he lay on his back, his small genitals narrowly missing the whip as he took lashes on his belly. In the third he was on his back with his genitals tucked between his thighs. His tormentor was grinning lasciviously as she whipped him.

'My God – what a place!' she exclaimed as she looked around the room.

'If madam would let me help her undress.'

She yielded as Erna undid the buckle and slipped down the wondrous garment.

'What are you going to do with me?'

'I am instructed to strap you for a flogging, madam.'

'Do with me as you will,' complied Darline, feeling a sudden rush of love for the blonde.

Erna led her over to a skeletal fabrication of black painted wood which rested against one wall.

'What in heaven's name is this?'

'It is a flogging frame, madam. I am going to strap you to it. Now, if madam would lie down over it on her front.'

Darline lay down on the frame which was strung with transverse straps to support her body.

Erna passed a strap over her upper back and buckled it tightly.

'So, now I will strap madam just above her buttocks.' Again a strap was tightened. 'Now we will secure madam's thighs.' She felt straps being secured around her thighs, high up against the buttocks. Next her ankles were secured. 'Now for madam's wrists.'

Finally, she passed a thin strap between Darline's thighs and up between the division of her buttocks. She pulled it around the waist strap and tightened and tied it.

'This is more to thrill the secured one than anything else.' Erna laughed lightly. 'At least I have found it so when I have been secured in this way. Madam is ready now for her chastisement. I will retire.'

Darline was left alone in the strangely appointed room. She was bound tightly and could not move. Her heart beat strongly in anticipation and she could feel the leather straps exciting her sex.

'Excellent, Erna is most efficient. She has prepared you well,' said Agrippina suddenly, as she entered the room. She pressed a bell on the wall and Erna reappeared.

'I am disinclined myself, Erna. I want you to lay on the strokes. I think you can employ the little knotted cat-o'-nine-tails. Work well from her shoulders down to her thighs but don't flog her within an inch of her skin.' Agrippina laughed, and sat down.

Erna took a cat-o'-nine-tails from the wall. Darline was relieved to see that it was not a particularly brutal type,

130

like those once used in the Royal Navy, yet it was knotted along each of its nine thongs.

'You had better remove your dress,' Agrippina said to Erna.

Erna put down the cat and slipped her dress off to reveal slinky black knickers and bra, with a suspender belt holding up net stockings.

'Now go to work on her; give her thirty lashes.'

As Erna began to lay on the lashes, Darline felt them sting her skin. She felt strangely relieved at being able to take it; the pain was not unbearable. And out of the corner of her eye she could see the tall German woman laying them on. Erna's skin was the same exciting white-grey as Gala's. Oh, how lovely it had been when she had acceded to Gala's pleading for punishment by the swimming pool.

'You have been laying them on lightly, Erna. Now let her feel the final ten sting her skin or I'll put you in her place.'

Erna laid them on hard and Darline writhed ineffectually in her straps. Yet even then it was not unbearable. The German girl stood to one side when she had finished, still holding the cat, and Darline felt a strange dark love for her.

'Now that you have been conditioned somewhat we will use you in an experiment in slave breeding. Erna, go and bring my husband. You may go as you are.'

Erna went out and in a minute or so returned with Lancelot who was naked but for a tiny snakeskin loincloth.

'Release her from the frame.'

Erna swiftly unbuckled the straps, as she was ordered.

'My husband here is a masochist and I treat him as a slave. Isn't he the perfect slave?' Agrippina lifted the front of the loincloth to show a tiny G-string over Lancelot's genitals. 'Slave breeding was practised sometimes by the Romans. I will have him serve you as a stallion is made to serve a mare or a bull a cow. Get down on all fours like the animal you are. A slave in Rome is not a person.'

Darline quickly got down on her hands and knees and Agrippina turned to Lancelot. 'Remove your G-string.'

There was a serene look on his face as he slipped off the snakeskin.

Agrippina turned to Erna. 'Treat his phallus suitably.'

Erna took a tube of cream and applied some to Lancelot's partly erect member and, as she did so, it increased in length and became proud under her hand. She took a condom and unrolled it onto the penis that reared like a mindless python.

'Now treat her thighs, and make sure you get it up into her vulva.'

Erna bent and applied cream as directed. Darline became instantly aroused as she felt the hand moving over the soft skin of her inner thighs and up to her clitoris.

'Now: serve her,' Agrippina ordered her slave boy. 'Lash him lightly to make him harder,' Agrippina commanded and, as Erna complied, Lancelot mounted Darline like a bull. Darline felt his hard manhood and clenched her thighs to hold him in. His hands were on her shoulders as he thrust and thrust with his cock deep inside her. And then she felt him spurt and he collapsed over her and then fell to one side and lay there.

'Mmm, you came rather soon – but there will be other occasions. That will be all for this time. Erna, help this lady get dressed.' Agrippina went out, leading her submissive man with her.

'So, it is over. Now madam, let me take you and help you dress. One moment, let me wipe between your legs. There is a little surplus cream.'

Having been swabbed dry Darline got to her feet and let herself be taken to the room where she had left her day clothes.

Erna was solicitous as she knelt and hooked on Darline's suspender belt, rolled up her stockings, securing them gently, then drew up her knickers. She then assisted with her bra and slip and buttoned the dress.

'I hope, madam, as you say in England, that there are no hard feelings – I mean because I lashed you?'

'No, you simply did your duty. And it wasn't excruciating, apart from the last ten strokes.'

'I am indeed glad about that. If you would come to the drawing room I think the mistress would like to offer you something.'

They went to the drawing room, Erna still only wearing her underwear.

'There you are, my dear.' Agrippina smiled brightly. 'You will take sherry with us, I trust?'

Erna poured out the sweet wine and offered it to the ladies and to Lancelot, who was now conventionally dressed.

'I am intrigued by your work,' said Agrippina conversationally. 'Do let me have a preview of your latest series with your boy and your new model. I take it she is female?'

'She is, actually.'

'And how have you been posing them together?'

'In quite exciting poses.'

'Sounds interesting. Perhaps you will be further inspired by your experiences this afternoon.'

Agrippina smiled knowingly as she sipped her sherry.

9

Solace in the Midi

'There is mystique in the Midi; there is magic. It's not surprising that Picasso could only paint his fauns and cacodemons here in this sacred landscape!' Darline said poetically.

'It's certainly a wonderful region,' Flavia agreed.

They were in Heliopolis, the sun city, adjacent to Cap d'Agde. They walked leisurely through the spectacular, circular city with Patrick behind them. They were all three naked except for jewellery and sandals. Patrick carried the bags.

The previous evening they had all three been to the naked cinema, where they had fallen into conversation with a Frenchman, François Loup.

'That Frenchman was extremely friendly, last night,' Darline remarked.

'Yes – as he said, he seemed delighted to have found people on whom he could practise his English,' Flavia replied.

'I wonder if he'll be there at Rocher d'Agde,' Darline said.

'We'll soon see.'

'Are you all right, Patrick?' Darline glanced behind at him.

'Yes, madam.'

'The bags not too heavy for you?'

'No, madam.'

As they neared Rocher d'Agde they saw François waiting, propped against a low wall.

He stood up, obviously delighted to see them. 'Bonjour mesdames. Bonjour monsieur.' He bowed and kissed the hands of the two ladies. 'What a pleasure to see you again! May I accompany you down to the beach? Monsieur, let me take one of your bags,' he said, addressing Patrick.

'Oh, how glorious to see the Mediterranean in the sun!' Darline's voice was joyful.

'Shall we settle down here for a while?' Flavia suggested.

'Yes, and then we can decide how to spend the day.' Darline was looking around.

Patrick spread a large padded waterproof sheet on the sand and they reclined on it.

'Give me my sketchbook, Patrick,' Darline said. 'I can't resist drawing, even though I'm on holiday.'

She deftly sketched the three figures in their various attitudes on the sheeting.

'So you are a painter, madame,' François said. 'Of course, how stupid of me; you are Darline Pomeroy. I saw some of your work at your last show in Paris. I very much like your paintings.'

'Thank you,' Darline said absently, as she sketched away swiftly.

'And monsieur Lovelace I understand trained in fashion design.' François glanced at Patrick.

'Yes, but I am now employed by Ms Pomeroy.'

'How charming. In what capacity?'

Patrick looked embarrassed and said nothing for a few moments.

'Go on, Patrick,' Flavia said. 'You may talk freely. You will not be punished for talking.'

'I am employed as a boy-maid at Ms Pomeroy's residence.'

'I see,' François said softly. He was obviously intrigued.

'Yes, I do all sorts of chores around the house and serve as Ms Pomeroy's valet,' volunteered Patrick.

'He does, and he is fairly satisfactory. Recently I have been using him as a model.'

'Really, madame. And what kind of poses have you been using monsieur in?'

135

Darline felt that this Frenchman was really a little too pushy but she would play along for a while. 'I have been posing him with a female model. As you may very well have divined for yourself when you saw my recent show in Paris, my work is largely inspired by sado-masochism. I find all that I need in my art by portraying figures in sado-masochistic situations. Even in my series of nudes with horses the magnificent beast is in bondage to his nude mistress.'

'It is an honour to converse with you. I read a book about you, published in French.'

'How charming, my fame has gone before me into France.'

'More than that, madame, you are internationally known.'

'You are very kind, monsieur. But I think you flatter me a little.' Darline turned and looked at Flavia. 'I think I know what I'd like to do today. I'd like to ride bareback along the beach and have you ride beside me. Then I'd like to draw you with your horse.' She turned back to François. 'Is there anywhere we can hire horses? I've seen postcards of naked girls riding horses.'

'Yes, madame, there is a stable quite close with magnificent white Camargue horses. Shall I bring you two?'

'How kind you are,' Darline said, giving him a five-hundred-franc note. François got up and walked away up the beach.

'That Frenchman is extremely helpful,' Flavia said.

'He is. I'm sorry, I should have asked you first. I take it you don't mind riding bareback with me?'

'You impetuous sweet creature. I'd love to ride bareback with you.'

She turned to Patrick. 'You're very quiet. You may join in the conversation, you know. I won't punish you for that.'

'Thank you, madam. You're very kind.'

'I want you to enjoy the holiday as much as anyone else.' She looked up the beach. 'Oh, what a splendid sight!'

François was coming down the beach leading two magnificent white horses, bridled but not saddled. Their manes and tails were blowing in the offshore breeze, their nostrils flaring.

Darline got to her feet and said dramatically, 'Let us ride wildly along the beach. Let us feel our horses under us.'

Darline took the reins of the nearest horse. François offered his cupped hands as a stirrup for her to mount and she swung up and gripped the horse's barrel girth with her legs. Patrick did the same for Flavia.

'Let's go. Let's ride together.' Darline dug in her heels and the horse went into a canter. She felt splendid and wild, riding with her companion along the great wide open beach with the sea to the right, and a sandy bluff to the left. She found the haired hide of the horse under her thighs very sensuous. She felt his heat and strength coursing through her as his hooves threw up spurts of sand.

She said wildly, 'Oh, this is the meaning of life for me, to ride a horse naked with my lover riding beside me.'

A mile along the beach Darline reined in her mount and he stood there snorting and pawing a little at the sand. He sniffed and blew through his nostrils.

Flavia reined in beside her and she leant over and put an arm around Flavia's waist and they kissed tenderly on their lips.

'Let's take them into the sea.' Darline's voice was now husky with desire. She urged her mount down the sand and he went willingly into the cooling sea where it splashed around them. Flavia followed as they went out deep, until the water washed around the chests of the horses.

Darline dismounted into the water, still holding the reins.

'Come in with me,' she said to Flavia, who obediently slipped down from her horse. They stood in the water and embraced, feeling the warmth of their bodies in the cool water.

With the reins trapped in a crooked elbow Darline held Flavia's body to hers. 'I can feel your blood coursing with

137

mine. I can feel your heart beating against mine; I love you in spite of your coolness.'

They kissed again, feeling the sea washing around them. Their lips met, the muscles stiff under the glossy lipstick. They moved their heads sideways so that their mouths engaged one in the other, their tongues were stiff and phallic. Darline felt Flavia's tongue snake into the depths of her throat. Then they both let their fingers explore the other's body. Hands glided over belly and buttocks, moving to explore between oily thighs. Flavia felt Darline's full breasts while Darline pushed her wet pussy against her lover, their vulvas now mingling their moisture with the great careless wetness of the sea. Each felt the clitoris of the other, proud and hot in the sea, and each massaged the stiffness, at first gently, and then with gathering momentum until it was a furious friction. With loud cries they both came orgasmically holding their bodies close together and feeling the warmth of one another in the cool water. The horses waited patiently and dipped their heads and blew and snorted at the shimmering surface.

At length Darline spoke. 'Loved bitch goddess, come and lie in the sand with me. I want to hold you and feel your wetness.'

They led the horses out of the sea and lay down on the warm sand. They kissed again with open mouths and held each other tightly.

'Darling,' Darline enthused, 'I feel so naughty now after we've made love. Do you know, I think François would also like to be a slave.'

'I think he probably would.'

'We must take him on as a temporary slave. Then we shall each have our personal boy-slave for the holiday.'

'It sounds intriguing,' Flavia said, her handsome face keen and her crimson lips twitching a little.

'It's perfect,' Darline said. 'Darling, you're sandy all over,' she laughed, as she embraced her lover. Flavia responded, as Darline ran her hands over her gritty body. It hurt a little as the sand ground into her soft breasts and thighs. Sand was biting into Flavia's buttocks but she didn't care. They kissed again on lips that were stiff and then soft and yielding.

Darline said softly, 'I feel like I'm in a whirl of creativity, after sex with you.'

'There is a correlation between the erotic and the creative,' the psychiatrist said.

'I think the erotic and the creative are one in me.' Darline said the words quietly, almost breathlessly. 'I want to have a session of drawing you while I'm this elated. Shall we go back?'

'We'd better wash the sand off first,' Flavia said.

Reluctantly they released one another and rose. As they led the horses back to the sea and waded in, they felt the cool sea wash away their encrustations of sand. Then they remounted. They cantered the horses back along the beach, their hair and their horses' manes streaming in the wind. As they reined in their mounts they found Patrick and François in conversation. The two men got up and took the horses' bridles.

'Oh, we have had a glorious time. It's too divine to ride wildly along the beach and take one's horse into the sea. What have you two been doing?' Darline was wildly dynamic and animated.

'Monsieur has been telling me about his life with you.'

'Indeed. What sort of things has he been telling you?'

'About the sort of work he does for you and a little about your strictness with him.'

'And what do you feel about my strictness with him?'

'Do you know, madame, I can only feel envy. I wish I could have such a life myself and serve a noble lady,' said the Frenchman.

Darline looked at Flavia. 'What a coincidence. We have just been saying how delightful it would be for us each to have a personal slave on this holiday. What do you think, darling? Shall we take François on as a temporary slave.'

'It's an intriguing idea,' Flavia said. 'But I hope monsieur understands that the regime would be very strict and that he would have to undertake all sorts of personal services.'

Darline looked at François. 'Yes, you would be at our beck and call. You would have to indulge our every whim. You would have to fetch and carry. You would have to give pedicures, paint our toenails, massage us.'

François looked overwhelmed with joy. The two lesbians did not fail to note that there was a certain stiffening of his phallus, by no means a full erection, but certainly a noticeable swelling.

'Oh, mesdames,' the Frenchman said. 'I should be delighted. I should deem it an honour to serve you. I can think of nothing more splendid.' He went down on his knees and kissed the feet of the two women, Darline first and then Flavia.

'It is done,' Darline said emphatically. 'You are now our slave.' She kissed her lover on the lips. 'Shall we assign him to one of us? Shall I take him for a while and you can have Patrick, since you do not have Patrick as much as I do?'

'That will suit very well,' declared Flavia, returning Darline's kiss.

'My sketchbook, Patrick,' Darline ordered. She took it from the boy and took a graphite stick. 'Doctor Quayle and I have been discussing the powerful forces that eroticism and bondage can be in art. I'm going to draw her with the horses. Which of you would like to be in the most humiliating pose?'

'I would, madame,' François said instantly.

'Very well, you can be a mounting block to assist a noble lady in mounting her horse. Patrick, you can hold the horses. François, I want you to crouch right down beside the horse; that's it, right down. And hold yourself to take the noble lady's weight. Now, Flavia, would you make as if to mount?'

Flavia moved and took the reins from Patrick then she placed her left foot on François' back.

'That's it, splendid, darlings. We'll make these ten-minute drawings. How I love to draw wildly on a beach with the sapphire sea in sight.'

Her hand was moving rapidly over the page. She felt herself possessed. Her nipples were as stiff as the graphite

140

stick she drew with, and her creative and sexual juices were flowing. She felt as if she could have drawn for ever.

'I love people and I love horses,' she cried out ecstatically. 'I love the lightning speed of the horse and I love his power and his energy and I love to see him tamed. We are coming to the end of this one, darlings. Another few seconds. There we are now – next in the sequence. Darling, would you now raise your right leg and put it over your mount's back, but not fully seated on the horse. That's it, lovely. We're doing very well. This is a lovely pose. You are now united with both horse and man. Your left foot is still on the back of your slave and you can feel your mount's hair under your right thigh.'

Flavia looked fantastically arrogant in this pose. 'I can't believe it,' she exclaimed. 'I'm aroused both by the horse's back on my leg and François' back on my foot.'

It was a glorious morning. Darline had almost cast off the memory of her recent experience with Agrippina. The wild ride along the beach and having sex in the cool of the sea had left her feeling sublime.

She began to imagine what they could do now that they each had a slave. They could whip François as well as Patrick, of course. They could have each slave give them simultaneous massage. They could make each slave lick them to orgasm; that was as far as they could allow the slaves to go in respect of sex with a lady. But her tortuous mind wanted to go further than that and then she had an inspiration. For their edification they would make the slaves wrestle on the beach. And the loser would have to submit to the victor in any way the victor desired. It would be an intriguing spectacle to see the slaves straining in combat. Slaves were not persons, of course, and had no choice but to obey. Then she saw how the wrestling would be a way of stripping even more of the persona from Patrick.

She came out of her reverie and said, 'That's it, Flavia, ten minutes. We'll change the pose. I know, now we'll have you lying along the horse, face down. Can we try that?

Maybe if you mount first so that you're sitting and then wriggle around and ease yourself into a prone position. You're all right, are you? I'm not being too demanding?'

'No, of course you're not.'

Darline thrilled at the sight of Flavia astride the horse: imagined the animal horse-power beneath her. She watched her lover ease herself into a prone position, the back of the horse in contact with her thighs, belly and breasts. The image of contact with the horse along the length of the haired body was beautifully sensuous, if anything better than having the thighs astride the horse.

'That's lovely, darling!' Darline exclaimed ecstatically. 'Your breasts are on either side of the horse's withers.' Flavia remained posed there, her arms on either side of the horse's neck, her hands holding tufts of mane.

Yes, that is what they would do; make the two slaves wrestle. Suppose they did not agree? The question would not arise. As slaves they had no choice but to accept the will of their mistresses. She wondered if Flavia would go along with it. She almost certainly would; they knew one another very well!

'All right, my love. Thank you very much. We'll take a break now.' Darline put down the sketchbook. 'Patrick and François, you can take the horses back now. You may as well both go.' The two slaves obeyed their orders.

The two women lay down and Darline said, 'Thank you. I enjoyed drawing you in those poses.'

'I had an idea while I was posing,' Flavia said, looking at her lover. 'And it might be a way of stripping a little more dignity from Patrick, seeing how far down we can bring him. Let's make the two of them wrestle when they get back. And the loser has to submit to the winner in any way he desires.'

'Do you know, I had exactly the same idea!' said Darline, her face lighting up.

The two slaves were coming back down the beach. 'Which of us should tell them?' Flavia asked.

'You can be first,' Darline said. 'Then maybe I'll join in as well.'

'Here you are, chaps,' Flavia said as they drew close. We have thought of another activity for you both. You are to wrestle on the beach for us and – wait for it – the loser must submit to the winner however the winner desires.'

'Is this an order, madame? Only, I have had no experience of wrestling.' François seemed at a loss.

'It is the wish of your mistress. And the wish of your mistress is the finest order I know,' replied Flavia.

'I've never wrestled either, ma'am,' Patrick said nervously.

'That makes two of you,' Flavia said with finality.

'You can simply wrestle as best you can,' Darline suggested. 'I shall be sketching you. I watched wrestling a long time ago and I think the aim is to get your opponent's shoulders down on the ground. If either of you should want to give in, simply beat on the sand with your hand.'

'Now, go to it,' Flavia ordered.

The two inexperienced wrestlers faced one another. Both had their hands outstretched. Then François suddenly lunged forward and grasped Patrick around his tiny waist. Patrick put his joined hands in front of François' throat and tried to force his head back. His hands slipped upwards under his opponent's jaw. François was trying to unbalance Patrick sideways, but Patrick had his legs braced on the sand.

The two instigators had their arms around one another as they watched. They were enjoying the spectacle of their handsome slaves trying to wrestle.

At last François managed to force Patrick over. The boy was down on the sand and François was on top of him. François was forcing the boy's shoulders down and he held them there. He sat astride the boy, holding him tight until Patrick slapped his hand on the sand.

'That's it,' Flavia cried. 'François is the winner.'

The slaves got up from the sand and stood before the noble ladies.

'You are the victor, François,' Flavia said. 'What is your pleasure?'

143

François looked slightly uncomfortable. 'Well, madame, if Patrick is agreeable, I would like to have sex with him.'

'Indeed?' Flavia said. 'I had thought you were heterosexual.'

'I'm afraid not, madame. I'm bisexual.'

'Really!'

'Yes, madame. So, if you ladies and monsieur Patrick are agreeable, I would like to make love to him.'

'Well, darling, we did say that the victor could have his pleasure with the loser,' Darline interrupted.

'That's right,' Flavia said. She looked at Patrick. 'What do you feel about it, Patrick?'

Patrick was looking down at the sand. 'I'm willing to obey you and submit to François, ma'am.'

'So be it,' Flavia said. 'It only remains for us to decide upon a suitable venue for this event.'

'Well, it's a little too public here on the beach,' Darline said. 'I think we should make it in our apartment. On that subject, since François is to be a slave for the duration of the holiday, had he not better move into the Minotaur with us?'

'I think that would be ideal,' Flavia said. She turned to François. 'We shall book you a single room at our hotel. Patrick also has a single room in our suite.'

'You had better go and bring a few things and meet us at the Minotaur later,' added Darline.

'I shall be honoured to move in with you, madame,' François said and bowed deeply.

'Darling,' Darline said. 'I think we should make it a very kinky evening. What can we do to make it very naughty?'

'Let me see,' Flavia pondered. 'We could buy them some sexy black plastic or rubber gear.'

'I tell you what. We could dress Patrick as a girl.'

'What a splendid idea.' Flavia was obviously becoming excited. 'Let's buy him a few special things.'

'Also it might be an idea to give them each a swishing before they have sex,' Darline said.

'No problem – we've got a whip.'

'But it would be nice to whip them simultaneously

144

taking one each. We'd better buy another whip. I saw a sex shop on the way down.'

'You are a clever bitch goddess,' Flavia said, smiling excitedly at her lover.

The two ladies made their way up the beach with their slaves following them, carrying the bags.

The shop had a sign proclaiming UNISEX D'AGDE. They went in and an extremely beautiful saleslady, naked but for jewels, came towards them.

'Bonjour, mesdames. And how can I be of assistance?'

Flavia spoke. 'We wish to fit monsieur out with ladies' underwear.'

'How charming,' the saleslady enthused. 'Yes, indeed, I see the point. Monsieur has a beautiful figure.'

'We would like him to have some very soft and slinky things,' Darline said.

'Knickers, bra and suspender belt,' Flavia put in.

'And probably net stockings and some provocative shoes.' Darline's voice was husky with excitement.

'Of course, mesdames. We have some very beautiful lingerie in his size.'

To enthusiastic cries and coos the sales assistant brought out a selection of knickers and bras, suspender belts and stockings. She waxed lyrical over them, praising the qualities of the sleek or lacy materials and the quality of the workmanship.

'We have every possible style of knickers. Most of them are very brief. Perhaps monsieur would like to go into the cubicle and try some on.'

The saleslady took Patrick into a fitting room to which she left the curtain undrawn. There followed a veritable orgy of trying on every possible combination of underwear. The saleslady and the two lesbian dominatrices exclaimed their delight. Finally they settled on some tiny black G-string knickers and a half-cup bra to match. The undie ensemble was completed by a ruched black suspender belt and several pairs of net stockings with a motif of a snake climbing up to the thighs.

145

'It's a fabulous outfit,' the saleslady cooed. 'It suits him very well. He has small breasts and they peep so beautifully above the bra cups.'

'Now we must fit him with shoes,' Darline said. They moved on through the store and Patrick tried on several styles.

'It would be nice to have him in high heels,' Flavia said with a daring twitch of her lips.

'Oh, yes. That is a must,' Darline put in.

'And they should show his toes. He must paint his toenails,' Flavia cried sexily.

'How about these?' the saleslady suggested. She showed them a pair of shoes with chunky high heels and minimal strapping over the insteps. Patrick slipped his feet into them.

'Come out and walk up and down,' Flavia said.

Patrick came out of the cubicle and promenaded up and down, very much in the manner of a model on the catwalk. He made an elegant and titillating figure. 'What a picture he makes!' Darline exclaimed.

'How feminine he looks,' Flavia said. 'We are not stripping him of his masculine persona, we are simply endowing him with a feminine one.'

'Shall we take this ensemble for him?' Darline said with excitement in her voice.

'Yes, we'll take the whole lot,' Flavia said with decision.

The saleswoman made out the bill and they paid. As they were about to go Darline whispered to Flavia, 'Of course we need another whip for this evening; shall we ask?'

Flavia said to the assistant, 'Do you have a department specialising in sex goods?'

'Of course, madame. It is downstairs.'

They went downstairs to the department which proclaimed itself ACCESSORIES. They went in and their eyes were assailed by an array of skimpy, fetishistic underwear and rubber and plastic wear. There were dildoes in various colours, and every possible lotion and cream and unguent. But they were drawn at once to a display labelled

CORRECTION and the two dominatrices gazed at the whips and switches with eager eyes.

Flavia fixed her eyes on Patrick as he stood there. 'Look at this wonderful display, Patrick; everything possible for titillating the skin. Wouldn't you love to be punished pleasantly with one of these instruments?'

'Yes, wouldn't you,' Darline purred. 'I wonder how we could have François do it? Perhaps bending over a chair with your knickers down, your lovely new black G-string panties. Or perhaps we could make you undress bit by bit so that he could lash you naked?'

'There is no need to look so perplexed, Patrick.' Flavia turned to her lover. 'Tell you what, darling. Shall we let him choose his own instrument?'

'Yes, let's,' Darline enthused.

'Can I be of any assistance, mesdames?' The voice came from behind them. The salesgirl had a face in which sado-masochism was written all over and deep within. She wore a décolletage from which the ripe fruits of her breasts looked as if they strove to escape.

Flavia looked round at the woman. On an impulse she forced herself to be explicit. 'We want a whip for this evening. We are going to make two boys whip one another.'

'Of course, madame. I understand. As you see, we have a great selection.'

Looking at Patrick, Flavia said, 'We have decided to let the young man make the choice. Which do you think, Patrick?'

Patrick blushed and then stammered, 'I think I would like to make it the cat-o'-nine-tails.'

'A charming choice, monsieur,' the saleslady gushed. 'Take one from the rack and I will wrap it for you.'

Patrick chose one of the whips, which were beautifully made, the nine tails plaited tightly and knotted at intervals along their lengths. The assistant took it and put it in a smart black carrier bag with gold lettering, and handed it back to Patrick, while Flavia settled the bill.

* * *

147

As they entered their suite of rooms Darline said, 'Shall we give him a bath to make him soft and sweet for his lover?'

'Darling, what a splendid idea!' Flavia's lips quivered with excitement.

They hustled the boy into the bathroom and ran a warm bath and got to work on him. As he sat in the warm water Flavia gave him a shampoo and Darline scrubbed his back.

'One thing, I think,' Flavia said, as they worked. 'We should shave his legs and underarms.'

'We'll have you as smooth as porcelain, Patrick,' Darline cooed.

They each took a ladies' razor. 'Raise your arms and legs,' Flavia ordered. The boy rested his heels on the end of the bath and raised his arms. Flavia shaved his legs and Darline his underarms.

'There you are,' Darline enthused. 'What a lovely soft body you have!'

They made him step from the bath and dried him with vast fluffy towels and talced his body. Then they led him into their bedroom and arrayed him in his black underwear, the G-string knickers, the half-cup bra and the ruched suspender belt. They each rolled one of the net stockings up on his legs so that the head of the crawling snake was high on his thighs. Finally they made him put on the shoes and parade up and down while they admired their handiwork.

The doorbell rang. Darline felt her excitement mount as she admitted François, who was dressed in black PVC trousers and a black silk vest. He took one look at Patrick and said in admiring amazement, 'How magnificent. You look wonderful, mademoiselle; I may call you mademoiselle, may I?'

Patrick said nothing and Darline prompted him. 'Give your admirer an answer, Patrick.'

'Yes, you may,' Patrick said.

'I think we could maybe call her Pat, now,' Flavia said.

'What a good idea,' Darline responded.

The two women were themselves magnificent sights.

148

They each wore a rubber garment like a very daring high-cut swimsuit which only barely concealed their depilated vulvas and left their buttocks bare. Each had a cut-out circle which revealed their bellies.

'Now, you can both quite literally get down to it,' Flavia said. 'On your knees, and you know what is expected of you.'

Patrick and François knelt before their dominatrices and kissed their feet, lingering long over the suntanned insteps.

The submissives got to their feet and Darline said, 'Patrick, parade up and down before your admirer.'

Patrick walked up and down, for all the world like a willowy model showing off underwear. François was rapt in admiration.

Flavia's voice was commanding. 'Enough of that. You are now to give one another a light swishing to bring you on and make you feel fiery and sexy. You can do it any way you like, knickers down or naked. Which do you prefer?'

'If we strip naked we'll be ready for the next stage,' François said bravely.

'Yes,' Patrick put in, as if he hardly dared speak.

'Would you like to be first, mademoiselle?' François said. 'Perhaps you could undress slowly to excite me.'

Patrick stripped as provocatively as he could. He unhooked the bra and removed it.

François gasped in admiration and said, 'You look so ravishing, would you whip me as you are? You're so beautiful I have no desire to whip you in return. I don't want to mark your soft skin.'

Flavia handed Patrick the cat-o'-nine-tails. François lowered his PVC trousers, took down his knickers and bent over a chair. Patrick started to lash François lightly on his buttocks and, as he did so, François' phallus began to lengthen.

After a minute or so of the whipping Flavia said impatiently, 'Enough of that. I want to see you touch each other.'

Patrick took down the G-string knickers and stepped out of them and stood there wearing only his black ruched suspender belt, net stockings and high-heeled shoes.

Darline could see that François was overcome with mingled admiration and sexual desire.

'Don't take off more than that, mademoiselle,' begged the Frenchman. 'You look so beautiful like that. I envy the snakes rearing upward.'

'You may go into action,' Flavia ordered. 'Pat, you lie face down on the bed.' The boy did as he was told. His buttocks pointing upwards, between the suspender belt and stockings.

'Now, you are not to enter his anus,' Darline commanded. 'You may rub yourself between his thighs as he holds them together.' She took a condom and unrolled it down the length of the Frenchman's phallus, then she took a bottle of massage oil and greased the insides of Patrick's smooth thighs.

François approached the body stretched prone for him. He eased himself onto the bed and kissed Patrick's back. Then he eased his phallus between the soft and oily thighs and began to slowly move his pelvis from side to side. In and almost out; backwards and forwards. The movement continued slowly for a while and then increased in tempo until it was like a fast and smoothly working piston. The two lesbians could see that there was now an ecstatic look on Patrick's face. Then, with a cry, the climax of the ride came and the Frenchman began to spurt his seed. As it was spurting he moved his member from side to side, obviously to increase the intense sensations he was experiencing. Then they saw that he was spent, entirely spent, and he lay himself beside the bare back, suspenders and stockings of his desired one and remained still.

The two lesbians began to kiss passionately. The homosexual act had aroused them beyond belief.

After a while Darline said, 'Shall we be wicked and make them give us cunnilingus?'

'Maybe, maybe later,' Flavia said, her hand straying between her lover's moist thighs.

'Maybe we shouldn't take it too far with them,' Darline said, her face clouding. 'I'm just thinking about what was done to me – and what I may yet have to endure.'

10

Cross-Dressing and Other Pleasures

There was a knock at the door and Patrick entered and bowed.

Darline looked at him. 'Patrick, my boy-maid, I have decided to dress you as a girl. This has been partly inspired by our recent French experiences, but also I've consulted with Doctor Quayle and she agrees that this will be a good experience for you. So, after your driving lesson, in the afternoon you will go to be professionally depilated at the Aphrodite Health and Beauty Centre.'

Patrick went out and got into the car beside Ingrid. She saw at once that he had noticed the whip and coil of rope, and the shiny black raincoat and hat, lying on the rear seat.

Ingrid made him drive to an area without much traffic. She put him through various manoeuvres and he was completely hopeless. Attempting a hill start he stalled the Fiesta several times. On the three-point turn he made two feeble attempts and on the third damaged the bumper by driving it into a low sign which he had not noticed projecting from the grass verge. The last straw came when he was about to head out at a T-junction into the path of a fast-approaching meat lorry. Ingrid put the handbrake on just in time.

'Jesus!' she exclaimed. '*We'd* have been so much mangled meat if I hadn't stopped you. Change seats.'

She drove in the direction of Oxshott Woods. She was

angry now, filled with a feminine-Amazon fury at the inferiority of the male of the species. They deserved to be crushed, ground under heel, flogged until they could take no more. As she headed the car into the woods it began to rain and she was glad she had brought the raincoat and hat. She knew what she was going to do. She brought the car to a halt in a clearing, at the edge of which reared an immense beech tree, its verdigris-greened bole like a great bronze phallus, patinated by the rain and wind. The downpour was now heavy and continuous.

'Get out,' she ordered. The boy stood before her and she looked with scorn into his eyes.

'I'm going to flog you. Take off all your clothes; every stitch. Put everything in the car.'

She watched the boy as he stripped naked. The rain began to wet his skin. 'Hold out your hands.'

She took the rope and tied his slender wrists tightly so that the hard nylon cord cut into the skin. She tossed the free end of the rope over a projecting branch and pulled him up. She could feel the power in herself – the green-skinned brutality of the beech bole in contrast with the soft flesh of the naked body. She hoisted him until he was on tiptoe, the rope taut as a bowstring, the body hanging. The warm rain was now streaming down his back and buttocks and his blond hair hung wetly to his shoulders. Protected by her black plastic raincoat and hat she felt a pang of pity for him. But his poor performance had raised the hackles between her thighs and at the points of her breasts. She put her face close to his, his features were streaming, his eyes half-blinded. She said, cruelly, 'Do you think I should punish you so?'

'Yes, ma'am.'

'I intend to give you eighteen lashes. I could have made it two dozen, but I have some pity for you. Do you agree that eighteen is just and fair?'

'Yes, ma'am.'

She stood back and swung the whip – which hissed in the wet air – before crashing on his back and shoulders. Then the cruelty rose in her as she swung the lash back and lashed with her tongue as well as the whip.

152

'I'll cut you.' The whip cracked.

'I'll teach you.' Again.

'You shall obey me.' With each crack of the whip she had a new sentence to recite.

'You will concentrate. You are a ninny. You are wet. I will make you kneel to me. You shall kiss my feet. You will learn if I have to skin you. You shall have it flogged into you. You will thank me for being a disciplinarian. I have tried with you. I have been kind. I have been patient. I have explained. I have encouraged. I now lash you and you have felt the last stroke this time.'

She stood there in the rain for a few moments, the drops pattering on her hat and streaming down the slinky black raincoat. From the boy's shoulders to the curves of his buttocks he was welted red. The whip had curled round him so that the red scars curved around his right side, his ribcage and his hip. She was panting from her exertions but also with excitement. Yes, she would let him dangle there for a while.

She got into the dry of the car and sat, feeling uplifted, as she gazed at the hanging body, being rained on until it could not have become more wet. She began to fantasise that she would like to degrade him more. Perhaps she would take him home and make him go down on her. Wouldn't that be nice to round off the morning with an orgasm! Two magpies flew down and perched on the branch from which the boy hung. They cackled raucously and it seemed as if they were laughing at his plight. Suddenly one sent a stream of shit down the naked back below; then the other followed suit.

Ingrid began to laugh as the surrealism of the situation hit her. She said, aloud, 'Oh no, it's too bad, too much. Whipped in the wet and shit on by magpies. Oh, no more, I'll take him down.'

She got out of the car and untied the rope to let the boy down. There was a strange look on his face, almost ecstatic, as she untied his wrists. She hustled him into the car, wiped the shit from his back, and started to dry him with a large towel. She looked at him kindly. 'You've had enough for today,' she said. She continued to dry him, comfortingly, with obvious concern. 'Now wriggle into your clothes.'

Patrick squirmed and dressed as best he could.

'I'll take you home and give you a hot drink,' she said, as she put the car into gear and drove them out of the woods with her accustomed mastery. She felt now that she wanted to talk.

'I wanted to do that. I was even delighted when the rain came; I was hoping it would. The forecast was rain for the late morning. It's funny, when I was whipping you I was thinking that it would be odd if someone came upon us in the woods like that, a naked boy tied to a tree being whipped in the wet by a raincoated woman. Just imagine a mounted policewoman or policeman coming upon us. I feel I want to discipline you and in another way I feel rather tender towards you. We'll soon be home. You haven't been to my place before, have you?'

Ingrid drove the car into the driveway and led Patrick inside. She couldn't decide whether to seduce him now and make him perform cunnilingus, or to wait for a more propitious time? No, she would just give him a note to give to Ms Pomeroy saying that he needed more lessons.

'Now, I'm afraid we can't be too long about it. Your mistress will want you and I have to get back to the office. How about a nice cup of coffee?'

'That would be lovely.'

Handing him a mug of coffee Ingrid said, 'I think it might be good for you to have some tuition on the Highway Code. I'll give you a note for Ms Pomeroy.' She took a pad and began to scribble a note.

The boy gratefully sipped the coffee.

'You don't feel too chilled after your exposure, do you?'

'No, ma'am, I feel all right.'

'Would you like to be coached on the Highway Code?'

'I think I would, ma'am. If you think it best.'

'I think it would be good for you to go through it with me. Sometimes words can remain dead on the page if we don't discuss the meaning with someone else.'

'I'm sure you're right, ma'am. We used to find that at art school. I mean that it was best to talk about it.'

'There you are,' Ingrid said kindly. 'So give this note to Ms Pomeroy. Now, if you've finished your coffee I'll take you home.'

A tall and beautiful young woman emerged from the treatment room and said, 'Mr Lovelace.'

'Yes.' Patrick got up and went towards the door of the treatment room.

'Hello, I'm Zena.'

'I'm Patrick.'

'So, I see Darline wants you to have complete body depilation.'

'Yes.'

'If you'd like to go behind the curtain and get undressed I'll prepare the wax.'

Zena put some waxy strips in the heater and switched it on. In a minute or so Patrick emerged from behind the curtain.

Zena regarded him reassuringly. 'Now, if you'd like to lie on the table on your back. It's quite comfortable, just the same as a massage table. There you are, we'll just push your lovely blond hair out of the way because I'll give you a little waxing on your breasts as well as the other area. So I understand you are employed by Darline?'

'Yes.'

Zena could see that the boy felt vulnerable lying naked on the table.

'What sort of work do you do?'

'I'm employed as a boy-maid. I serve in a general capacity, serve light meals, do housework; clean, dust, that sort of thing.'

'Lovely.'

Patrick was beginning to relax. 'I also do things like painting her toenails.'

'That's interesting. What made you take up this kind of work?'

'I trained in fashion design but found it difficult to get a job in that.'

'Yes, I see. Now I'll just put some wax strips on your breasts, you have a little coarse hair just under them. There we are. I should imagine it would be difficult to get a job in that sector. Raise your arms, that's right, and I'll wax your armpits.'

'It is; so I was very pleased to get a job with Ms Pomeroy.'

'I saw some marks on your back when you got undressed. How did you get them?'

'I was whipped this morning.'

'Whipped! Who whipped you?'

'My driving instructor, Mrs Riding.'

'Good grief! What did she whip you for?'

'For not doing well in the lesson. I fluffed a hill start several times and stalled the car. Then I did badly doing three-point turns and finally I damaged the car on a road sign.'

'Goodness gracious! But it's a bit extreme for driving instructors to give pupils corporal punishment, isn't it? They don't even do that in schools now.'

'The initiative was not Mrs Riding's. Ms Pomeroy authorised her to punish me if I didn't make progress. Mrs Riding has to write out a report on my performance after each lesson and if I'm unsatisfactory she's required to punish me.'

'Good heavens! Do you like driving?'

'No, I don't really.'

'Then why do it?'

'Ms Pomeroy insists that any servants employed by her should be able to drive.'

'Couldn't you find something else where driving isn't necessary?'

'Well, I don't really want to leave Ms Pomeroy.'

'I see. I'm now going to apply the wax on your pubic hair. In one way it seems a shame because you have lovely ginger hair in that region. People with blond hair often have ginger pubic hair.'

'I was a bit embarrassed when it first appeared but I'm used to it now.'

156

'Girls usually have that combination as well; I mean ginger pubic hair when they have blonde hair. I'll just get the wax strip nicely into your groin. There we are. So you are treated strictly?'

'Yes.'

He felt himself gaining confidence and began to talk quite freely to Zena.

'I'm sometimes caned by Ms Pomeroy, and once she had her groom whip me when her wrist was sprained.'

'Whipped by the groom? What on earth was your offence to merit such a severe punishment?'

'I'm afraid I told a lie.'

'What about?'

'Ms Pomeroy makes me take a run round the village green every morning and I'd been talking to four girls I got to know and I said I hadn't.'

'Gosh, that still seems a bit excessive. I don't say that I'm entirely against a bit of spanking; my boyfriend and I play spanking games but it's all in fun. It stimulates us sexually and we kiss and cuddle afterwards. Now I'll just move down on your thighs with the wax. There we are – it's going on beautifully.'

They chatted until the wax on his front had cooled and hardened. 'Now we'll get down to stripping off your hair.' Zena laughed slightly. 'Just relax, don't tense your body or it will be worse. Here we go, on your right breast. There, it's off. Now your left breast. A quick pull of the cotton strip – and it's off. Now we'll go down to your pubic hair. This is a sensitive area, so just relax. There! And it's nearly off. Just a bit left in the groin. There! And it's off. Now we go down to your thighs. You have lovely thighs. Very like a woman's. They'll be even more so when we make them velvet smooth. There! That's one. Now the other. And it's done. Now below the knees. You have lovely calves and ankles. There! That's the right one. And there! That's the left one. Now, don't you look and feel lovely. Just like velvet. Now turn over and I'll do the backs of your legs. Good grief! The marks on your back! They go from your shoulders all the way down to your buttocks. I'll just put

157

the wax on your thighs and calves. What did she use on you?'

'A long whip she'd brought in the car.'

'And how did she actually go about it?'

'She drove us to a secluded clearing in Oxshott Woods, then told me to strip naked. She tied my wrists with a nylon rope and strung me to the branch of a tree.'

'Were you whipped soaking wet?'

'Yes, it was pouring this morning.'

'And I suppose she had her clothes on, so she didn't get wet.'

'That's right.'

'And what happened afterwards?'

'She got into the car and left me hanging there.'

'Good God!'

'Then a peculiar thing happened. Two magpies came and perched just above me and sent streams of droppings down my back.'

'You poor darling.'

'But after that she came and took me down and took me into the car and dried me. Then she took me back to her place and gave me a hot drink.'

'You did have a morning of it. Now the wax is nice and hard. So a nice pull of the strip and it's off; and another. Now the calves. First this one; that's it. Now the other. There! What lovely smooth legs; just like a girl's. That's you done.'

'Thank you very much.'

'You're welcome.'

Patrick got up from the treatment table. He was now smooth all over.

Zena looked at him rather fondly. 'You look lovely with your skin all smooth and velvety. Is there any particular reason why Darline had you depilated?'

Patrick felt himself blush a little. 'Well, the reason is that Ms Pomeroy is going to make me dress as a girl.'

'What? All the time? My boyfriend sometimes dresses as a girl just for the fun of it. But all the time?'

'Yes, Ms Pomeroy's friend, Doctor Quayle, thinks it will help make me less inhibited.'

'Well, you certainly look more feminine. You can get dressed now.'

He felt extremely aroused in the cubicle and was sure that Zena felt the same. He felt lovely with his body all smooth. When he emerged Zena looked fondly at him and stroked his cheek.

'Thank you for treating me.'

'You are very welcome, Patrick.' She took his face in her hands and kissed him gently on his lips. 'Take care, doubtless I'll be seeing you again when you need rewaxing.'

There was a tap at the door and Patrick entered.

'Hello, Patrick,' Darline said.

Flavia looked kindly at the boy. 'How are you, Patrick?'

'Very well, thank you, doctor.'

'So you've been depilated?'

'Yes.'

'What do you feel about it?'

'Well, actually, doctor, I feel beautifully soft and smooth, just like velvet or silk.'

'Mmm, do you feel rather like a girl?'

'Yes, I suppose I do.'

'Do you feel, shall we say, undefended and exposed because you have been stripped of hair?'

'I suppose I do, really.'

Darline put in, 'Why don't you take your clothes off and let us have a look at you?'

'Yes,' Flavia said. 'The proof of the depilation will be on the skin.' She smiled at the boy as he began to undress.

'Oh, you are beautifully smooth,' Darline purred.

'Parade up and down a little, let us see your smooth body in action,' Flavia commanded.

He began to walk up and down like a fashion model on the catwalk. 'Oh!' she exclaimed. 'You are quite lovely. I begin to visualise further poses I can make you take with Trisha.'

'He's like a lithe young woman now,' Flavia said. 'When you have a girl's wardrobe the transformation will be complete.'

Darline said excitedly, 'The crowning touch will be to

159

take you to the hairdresser and have your hair shingled. I want to see your blond hair descending in sinuous waves.'

'That would be the final mistress stroke,' Flavia said.

'I've made an appointment for you and I'll be taking you along early this evening,' Darline said. 'Well, Patrick, we are pleased with you and I think you may get dressed and leave us now. I'll see you later.'

The boy put his clothes on, bowed and went out.

They entered the hairdresser's, Darline in tight snakeskin pants and a close-fitting backless top, Patrick in a pair of his mistress's shorts and a chocolate-coloured vest, also his mistress's.

'Madam, how pleasant to see you,' Hilda, the manageress, gushed as she came out to greet them.

'I've brought my boy to have his hair done,' said Darline brusquely.

'Of course, madam, and what style would it please you to have his hair dressed in? You can, of course, look through our book of styles.'

'I'm sure they would be charming and very creative but I have some sort of idea how I'd like it. I want it to cascade in shingled waves.'

'What a charming notion, madam. I'm sure the young man would look most attractive with hair dressed so. He has beautiful blond hair.'

'And I would like to have my own hair cropped short.'

'Oh, madam, it's almost a shame in a way, if I may say so, you have such lovely dark hair.'

'But I particularly want to have it short. I want to look like a boy. Well, I think you will understand what I mean. I want still to be feminine but I want to look boyish.'

'Of course, madam, I understand. Ladies can appear most charming with a short style. In fact I think I will cut your hair myself.' Hilda looked to the far end of the salon. 'Lucy, I have a client for you.'

The girl addressed came forward and Hilda said, 'This is Madame Darline Pomeroy. She wishes to have her young man's hair dressed in a shingled style.'

'Like descending waves,' Darline repeated.

'I understand, madam,' Lucy said.

Hilda turned to Darline: 'Now, madam, if you would like to take a seat, I will attend to your beautiful locks.'

Darline seated herself and, for a moment, felt a pang of regret at what was about to happen.

'So madam wishes to have it cut short, to look rather like a boy. If I may say so, you will make a very pretty boy.'

'Thank you.'

Hilda was snipping away with the scissors and already Darline felt her long dark hair falling to the floor.

'Was there any particular reason, madam, that you decided to have it cut?'

'I think the reason was just to feel a little different.'

'Of course, I understand.'

'And perhaps I just wanted to please my lover.'

'How charming. I'm sure he will be pleased by the boyish cut I'm giving you.'

Darline hesitated for a moment. She oddly found herself resenting the suggestion that she had a male lover. Then she decided to tell her; why should she be afraid to reveal what she really was? Well, the whole international art world knew she was a lesbian.

'My lover is actually another woman.'

'Oh, how lovely,' said Hilda. 'Well, I am sure she will like what I am doing to you.'

'I hope she will.' Darline felt a certain lightness around her head as the long locks of hair fell to the floor.

'Are you working at your painting still, madam?'

'Of course, I am always working at my painting.'

'I saw your exhibition of nudes with horses and I found it utterly thrilling. The girls are so beautifully painted, and the horses so muscular and powerful, and yet subjected to the female will.'

'That's a theme in much of my work. The masterful feminine goddess and the subjection of the male to her.'

'How exciting! What sort of paintings are you currently working on?'

161

'A series exploring sado-masochism practices involving women and men.' Darline now felt that she could be quite explicit and daring. Why the hell should she hold anything back?

'How lovely!' said the hairdresser. 'I find it charming. Sado-masochism can be such a liberating thing.'

'I find sado-masochism a very creative and dynamic force in my art,' said Darline, warming to her subject.

'I think I see how it could be so,' agreed Hilda. 'Well, madam, that's you finished.' Hilda held the mirror behind Darline's head and moved it from side to side.

'Oh, I think that's very nice. What a very creative cut.'

'I hoped madam would be pleased. You look just like a very pretty boy.'

Darline got up from the chair and turned her head to look at her new style. She certainly looked quite changed in appearance.

'Now, madam, Lucy is still at work on your young man. I'm afraid you will have a short wait. Would you like some coffee or a cool drink? Some lemon cordial, perhaps?'

'Some cordial would be very pleasant,' replied Darline. She picked up a fashion magazine and leafed through it.

Lucy was working deftly on his hair.

'I sometimes go swimming with my boyfriend. But where we go you have to wear something,' she was saying to Patrick.

'You feel much more free when you wear nothing,' he replied.

'I only wear a very tiny bikini. And my boyfriend wears a slip that's not much more than a G-string.'

'But you'd find it much better to wear nothing. The water envelops you entirely and there is nothing to impede your body as you glide through it,' he explained. He had been telling her of his experiences.

'You make it sound very attractive. We must try your pond in the spinney some time.'

'You really must.'

'We do sunbathe in the nude in his parents' garden,' she

added. 'It's a very private garden surrounded by high yew trees. His parents actually encourage us to sunbathe nude because they are naturists.'

'That's wonderful. Ms Pomeroy took me to the naturist city of Heliopolis recently. It's close to Cap d'Agde.'

'Oh, a girl friend told me something about it. She said you can go nude everywhere.'

'Yes, you can walk around the city completely naked. You go into shops and cafes nude; even go to the cinema nude.'

'Sounds delightful.'

'Ms Pomeroy and her friend, Doctor Quayle, even went riding in the nude along the beach.'

'Did you go too?'

'I didn't, actually, but I held the horses while Ms Pomeroy was drawing Doctor Quayle with them.'

'Oh, it sounds lovely. Well, that's you finished, Patrick. I'll just put you under the dryer.'

Lucy arranged the dryer over his hair and turned and went out.

'That's your young man finished, madam. In a few minutes we can take off the dryer and see the finished result,' said Lucy.

'I look forward to seeing it.'

'Patrick tells me you took him to Heliopolis. He said you had a wonderful time there.'

'Yes, it is quite a delight. Such a change from herds of the clothed.'

'And were you able to do some drawing there?'

'Yes, I found it inspiring to draw in the open air under the sky. Of course I had my partner, Doctor Quayle, as a model. And also Patrick and a Frenchman we met there.'

'I think Patrick should be ready now. I'll take him from under the dryer and we'll see the result.'

Lucy removed the dryer and Patrick got up from the chair. His blond hair fell free.

'There, is that how you wanted it? Just like the waves of the sea.' Lucy took him out and showed him to Darline. 'What do you think?'

'It really is quite lovely, just like a shimmering waterfall shining in the sun.'

'Thank you, madam, I'm pleased you like it. He looks gorgeous.'

'What do you feel, Patrick?'

He looked at his mistress. 'It feels very nice,' he said softly. 'I feel quite different.' He looked at himself in the mirror. 'I feel rather changed; as if I'm beginning to have a different personality.'

Darline smiled mischievously at him. 'This is just the beginning. Wait until we have fitted you out with a new, more feminine wardrobe.'

In the ladies' fashion store Patrick was fascinated by the choice of clothing available. He was taken first to the lingerie department where a magnificent array of underwear was brought out by the saleslady.

There were knickers of all shapes and sizes – from G-strings to French knickers – depending on how much you wanted to cover. He chose some of each to try. There were also bras of every conceivable sort. Some had lacy half-cups, and some had hardly any cup at all. There were strapless bras to wear with evening wear. There were suspender belts with wide elastic strips for the hips and there were suspender belts with ruched lace. Yet others were shiny and slinky satin. There were basques of the most exotic kind. His favourites were cut high on the thighs so that they bared the groin and buttocks to the hips and were cut so low at the front that they revealed most of the breasts. Patrick now felt as if he had small breasts like a slim girl, the flesh being forced up by the boned corsetry. The saleslady cooed over them and he felt himself tingle.

He tried half-slips and full-slips, loving the feel of the soft material against his skin. The saleslady would have Patrick slip on an ensemble, say knickers and bra, suspender belt and stockings, and then she would draw the curtain to show him to Darline.

When he was suitably attired they moved on to dresses and skirts and blouses and tops. He enjoyed being made to try on many items, particularly several mini-skirts in which he paraded up and down for his mistress and the sales assistant. Darline remarked that he looked quite delectable in the mini-skirts and dresses. They then moved to consider shoes and sandals in a unisex footwear section. He felt himself now beginning to look quite like a girl as he was fitted out with several pairs of extremely sexy sandals and shoes, some of which had very high heels.

When they had tried a wide variety of clothes to make up an extensive wardrobe, they paused. He was, for the moment, dressed in a shiny mini-skirt which exhibited his smooth thighs to good advantage and a top which displayed his bare shoulders and a good deal of his back. Darline exclaimed, 'I think that's enough for one day. You can leave your present outfit on and I'll take you home.'

'It's a charming and very eye-catching outfit,' the saleslady said, as she made out the bill.

Next they went to the cosmetics department and Darline bought him lipsticks, foundation, powder and rouge. She took great care over the selection of suitable mascara and eye shadow. She made him try the lipstick and he thrilled as he applied the red stick, stretching and stiffening his lips as a woman does. She wanted the red tint to beautifully complement his skin colour, she said, and the eye shadow was to enhance the shape of his eyes.

As they walked into the car park they were whistled at by a rabble of unemployed youths lounging at the entrance. Neither Patrick nor Darline cared whether or not the compliment was directed at the other. They both felt good.

As Darline drove them home Patrick was feeling extremely horny. He knew it gave her the most delicious thrill to dress him in this way. She glanced at his almost naked thighs, so smooth and silky, and she moved her free hand to stroke the nearest. He could not help but hope she would give him a spanking. He visualised her raising the tiny skirt and taking down his sleek knickers and then slapping his tiny bottom. He felt liberated, by his dress, to indulge in ever kinkier behaviour and fantasies.

* * *

As Darline drove the car up to the house, Lilian and Lucan were talking near the door to the stable yard. When she got out she noticed both pairs of eyes goggle at Patrick above slight grins.

Darline put on her most patrician air and said, 'Patrick is now to be dressed in this manner and there is to be no undue levity. Is that understood?'

'Yes, madam,' the cook and the groom mumbled.

'You should be usefully occupied. What are you doing here?'

'Madam, I just came out to ask Lucan if he had any fresh rosemary in the garden. I wanted it for a recipe.'

'I see, well get along with you both.' She swept in through the front door with Patrick following. She took him along to her bedroom to beautify him with the cosmetics they had bought. She put a light foundation on his face first, and then heightened his cheek colour with a little rouge. His heart fluttered as she brushed mascara on his long lashes and then darkened his eyelids with some brownish eye shadow. For the final touch she took a vermilion lipstick and painted his lips as carefully as if she were painting a canvas. She said, absently, 'You have such lovely lips. They're quite inviting. As you see, I'm accentuating their shape with this gorgeous bright red stick. It's just like painting with a lovely greasy oil bar.'

When she had finished making him up, she made him stand. 'Now, let's have a look at the entire ensemble. Yes, I think you will do nicely. In fact you will more than do; you look quite ravishing. I want you to feel quite happy and relaxed as a girl. Do you feel different with your hair-free body and your waved hair, your war-paint and your girl's clothes?'

He could tell that she was filled with an exciting sensuousness at his changed appearance and he spoke ecstatically. 'Oh, I feel so utterly different. And from the inside out. My body feels lovely and smooth – like silk or satin. And I'm so happy wearing these clothes. They glide across my soft skin and they're so pretty and colourful. Mistress, I'm so grateful to you for doing this to me.'

'What a lovely thing I have made of you,' said Darline. Then she took his face in her hands and kissed him on the lips.

Later that afternoon, Flavia called Darline, to hear what happened with their experiment. Darline picked up the telephone:

DARLINE: Hello.

FLAVIA: Hello.

DARLINE: Darling, how sweet of you to call.

FLAVIA: And how are you?

DARLINE: Very well, thank you. Actually I feel like I'm flying at a blissful ten thousand metres.

FLAVIA: Tell me about what you have had done to yourself and your boy.

DARLINE: Oh, sweet. I feel fantastic with my hair cropped short. The hairdresser said she had made me look just like a very pretty boy.

FLAVIA: I can scarcely wait to see you.

DARLINE: We should be able to do something about that.

FLAVIA: And what about Patrick?

DARLINE: You should see him. He's really been given the treatment. His body has been depilated until it's as hairless as a snake and a lot lovelier and more exciting. His hair has been cut and waved most delightfully. His blond locks descend to his shoulders like a waterfall. He now has an entirely new wardrobe of exciting little knickers and suspender belts and bras; and the cutest little mini-skirts and dresses. And I bought him the most divine and sexy shoes and sandals.

FLAVIA: Mmm, sounds exciting.

DARLINE: Oh, darling, I must tell you. I bought him a whole range of cosmetics and when I got him home I made him up myself. Foundation, blusher, the lot. And I painted his lips with a lovely shade of vermilion. It all makes me so excited – what I've done to him and what I've done to myself. I can't wait to see you again to show me and my boy off to you. Oh sweetheart, I can think of things I want you to do to me! Do come over this evening.

167

FLAVIA: I must tell you, darling. I've acquired a new maid.

DARLINE: A new maid, really!

FLAVIA: Yes, the Bare Service Bureau sent her along for an interview this morning while you were out shopping.

DARLINE: The ones that sent Patrick to me.

FLAVIA: Yes, and I engaged her. But do you know what? She's Patrick's ex-girlfriend.

DARLINE: Really!

FLAVIA: None other. Her name is Philippina and she's usually called Pina.

DARLINE: The one Patrick liked; the one that whipped him in play.

FLAVIA: At her parents' home and at the older woman's house.

DARLINE: And his parents kicked up such a fuss that he left home.

FLAVIA: The same girl.

DARLINE: Phew! And how do you find her?

FLAVIA: I would like to get to know her better. She seems a pleasant girl; quite content to work as a maid.

DARLINE: And I suppose Sally will be glad to have some help around the place.

FLAVIA: She will indeed. My qualified assistant had been doing quite a lot of housework and what impelled us to look for a permanent maid was that Sally found it much easier for her when Patrick was here.

DARLINE: I should imagine so. Why don't you bring Pina over this evening?

FLAVIA: Do you know, the prospect of bringing them both together is quite intriguing. What I didn't say about Pina is that she seems rather boyish.

DARLINE: How very exciting.

FLAVIA: You know, I think I'll bring her over with me this evening. I'll bring her dressed boyishly, perhaps in jeans and a shirt.

DARLINE: Yes, do.

FLAVIA: We'll see how they react to one another.

DARLINE: So I'll see you this evening; and Patrick will

see Pina. If you could make it about eight-thirty. Until then, bye.

FLAVIA: Bye.

Darline was working late in the studio. She was working on the background of the painting in which Trisha was seated in a chair with Patrick crouching as her footstool, her feet resting on his naked back. She was pleased with the images she had created – lady of hauteur and slave submissive.

Patrick entered with a cool drink on a tray which he placed on a painting table.

'Pat, you do look quite fetching. Your mini-skirt shows your gorgeous smooth thighs to the most exciting advantage. I simply can't wait to arrange you in some more poses with Trisha. And that little bolero top is sweet. Doctor Quayle is coming at about eight-thirty.' She looked at her watch. 'Goodness, they'll be here in a few minutes. Doctor Quayle is bringing her new maid with her. I tell you what, Patsy, take off your bolero, sweet as it is, and put on one of your bikini tops. A black one would go nicely with your black skirt. Just lower it slightly to show your tummy button. That way you'll be revealing your thighs below and your naked back and a lot of your frontage above. Just one thing before you go. I'll answer the door when they ring. You may stay here for a while until I call you. Goodness, I must get out of this smock with its paint smears.'

The doorbell rang and Darline went to answer it. She opened the door and was confronted by Flavia and Pina. The girl was in jeans and a white shirt with a pattern of chequered squares.

Darline saw at once that Flavia's eyes were on her cropped head.

'You look quite divine with your hair short. Let me just look at you. You are a very pretty boy, a very pretty boy-girl. This is Pina.'

Pina bowed and Darline said, 'Hello, Pina, how do you do?'

169

'How do you do?' Pina echoed, and bowed again.

'Come along to the drawing room.'

'Have you been keeping busy with your painting?' asked Flavia.

'And how! I had been working on the background of a most exciting picture featuring Trisha and Patrick – I'll show it to you later – and I was so absorbed in it I didn't realise how the time was slipping away. Fortunately I stripped off my painty painting smock just before you rang the bell. I'll go and bring my boy along to see you both.'

Her excitement was mounting as she went towards the studio. How would the two young people react? Patrick looked a picture, seated on a stool with his legs crossed, revealing his sumptuous thighs to good advantage.

'Patrick, come along to the drawing room. Doctor Quayle and her new maid are waiting there.'

He got up from the stool, the waist of his mini-skirt riding up to reveal some of the taut belly below his tummy button. He followed Darline to the drawing room and they swept in.

Darline and Flavia stood aside as the boy dressed as a girl and the girl dressed as a boy looked at one another.

Darline said, 'Pina, this is Patrick.'

The boy and the girl moved and stood facing one another.

Pina's voice was tremulous. 'Patrick. I almost didn't recognise you and then I saw that you were – you really are Patrick.'

Patrick was blushing a little under his foundation and rouge. 'Yes, I'm Patrick.'

'Oh, Patrick! It's so lovely to see you again.'

The painted boy and the natural-skinned girl clasped one another and kissed. Then they looked at one another enraptured and kissed again. Darline experienced a strange thrill at the sight.

'But why are you dressed and made up like this?'

'It's the wish of Ms Pomeroy and Doctor Quayle. It's for psychological reasons. It's to enable me to experience a different persona, and to identify with my anima.'

'What are your persona and your anima?'

'The persona is the mask we all wear, the self we show to the world. The anima is the feminine personality every male person has within him.' He smiled, self-deprecatingly.

'Whoever is feminine and whoever is masculine, I love you,' she said and threw herself into his arms.

They kissed again.

11

Nudes with Python

Darline's hand danced the graphite over the paper. It was an exciting pose to draw. She had arranged Trisha so that she was stretched out on a mattress on the studio floor, rather like a sinuous snake.

'You have a perfect body,' Darline remarked as she worked. 'You are so slim, so long in proportion to your girth. Your waist is quite as tiny as Patrick's. It's a pleasure to draw you.'

'Thank you,' Trisha responded dreamily.

'Do you know, an idea has been simmering in me for some time, bubbling up from the unconscious. I've been playing around with it for a while. It seems to me that every natural creature, every mammal and bird and reptile, represents something. Some force or archetype. My beloved horses represent energy on every level, from the energy which works the cosmos, down to the energy that drives an aircraft through the sky.' Darline stood back and looked at her drawing.

Trisha murmured, 'I must say you have the most interesting ideas.'

Darline moved back to the drawing. 'Take birds, for example. The image of the bird is a reflection of the thoughts, fantasies and symbols which dwell in the upper regions. Birds are like messengers between man and the cosmos in which he dwells. I feel sure that each bird form has a meaning for us. The carrion crow means one thing; she is the eater of carrion, the picker-over of dead bodies and the scourer of refuse. Then the long-tailed tit has quite another meaning as it undulates and dances acrobatically through the branches like a woodland sprite. I'm sure that the green woodpecker contains a wealth of one kind of significant meaning and the peregrine falcon another.'

'Quite possibly,' Trisha mumbled.

Darline was thinking how very sensuous her model was in the pose.

'Then I suppose one can descend to a lowly creature like the snake, cursed in biblical mythology to crawl in the dust and have its head bruised by the heels of women.'

Trisha noticeably brightened at the mention of the snake. 'You know, many people dislike snakes but I simply love them. I love their reticulated patterns and colours and I like their writhing and bending bodies, so sinuous and so lovely. I know a lady who has a pet python, a magnificent creature at least three metres long. She let me handle him once. She's an amateur sculptress and she occasionally engages me. It was a lovely experience to handle him; his name is Sleek. Snakes are warm and dry, not cold and slimy at all. I'd like to have a snake for a pet myself but the landlady would go bananas if I so much as suggested it.'

'How wonderful that, far from having an aversion for snakes, you actually like them,' Darline said.

'I really do. I love wearing snakeskin things. I get a thrill from wearing snakeskin pants, really tight ones. And I have three snakeskin bikinis in different sizes. The trouble is that I love wearing the briefest one, but then I'm only showing minimal snakeskin. If I wear a larger one I look more snaky but am also more covered – well, I suppose you can't have everything. I certainly get lots of stares when I wear them, whatever the size.

'Do you know, Trisha, my imaginings could be brought forward into the realms of the possible. Do you think your friend might be willing to lend me Sleek for a studio session?'

'I could ask her, but he's quite heavy. I wouldn't be able to carry him here.'

'No, of course not. I would arrange transport. I'm

173

starting to get quite excited at the possibilities of nudes with a snake.'

There was a tap at the door and at Darline's bidding Patrick entered with a tray of tea things. He placed the tray on a painting table and bowed. Darline thought what a titillating sight he made in his mini-dress and sexy sandals, his beautifully made-up face framed by the wealth of blond hair.

'You may come out of the pose now, Trisha.' Darline put down her graphite stick.

Trisha got up from the mattress and, as she turned, she caught sight of Patrick. She looked at Darline as if expecting a word of introduction. When none came she said, 'You have someone new, now, then.'

Darline laughed a little, a teasing laugh. 'No, no one new. Don't you recognise who it is?'

Trisha went towards Patrick, naked as she was. She looked closely into his face. 'Patrick! Good grief, I didn't recognise you. You look simply lovely dressed as a girl. And your make-up; it must have been done by a professional.'

'No, I did it,' Patrick said shyly.

Trisha took him in her arms and kissed him. Darline was thrilled at the sight. How wonderful, she thought. I could pose them with him dressed and her naked. Many possibilities began to flood into her mind.

'Before you two blend into one another, like two colours being mixed, I'd like to put our snake proposal to Pat. We usually call him Pat now. It fits better with his outward presentation.'

Trisha withdrew from Patrick with a little reluctance.

'Pat, Trisha and I have been discussing a most wonderful idea. As you know, I've been painting a series of nudes with horses; and I'd like to extend into the portrayal of nudes with other creatures. It just turns out that Trisha is a snake lover and just loves to handle snakes. Furthermore she knows a lady who owns a splendid great python and she's going to see if she can borrow him for us. Would you be willing to pose with Trisha and a python?'

174

'When you say pose, madam, would I have to touch the python?'

'Well, yes, Pat. We would want to feel free to put yourself and Trisha into many different poses.'

Patrick looked down at the boards of the studio floor.

'Well, what do you think, Pat?' Darline's voice was kind.

Patrick looked up. 'I really don't think I can do it. I'm afraid I don't like snakes. I think it's because they have no legs. They are just a long continuation of muscle all along their length.'

Trisha spoke and her voice was kind, too. 'They are really quite likeable creatures, you know, Patrick. They are not cold or slimy as you might think. And when you hold a snake it feels a rather vulnerable creature which could easily be hurt.'

'Perhaps you could overcome your aversion, Pat. Would you be willing at least to try?' Darline gave her boy a lovely smile.

'Well, I suppose I could try.'

'I could handle him first and show you that there's really nothing to it,' Trisha said coaxingly.

'We're rushing ahead a bit,' Darline said. 'Trisha has yet to see if her friend will lend the great long thing to us.'

'All right,' he acceded. 'I'll try to overcome it.'

'Now, you recall that a triangle is solved when all angles and lengths have been found. We can use Pythagoras's theorem and the trigonometrical ratios to solve right-angled triangles.'

'Yes, I do recall that, ma'am,' Patrick said, vaguely remembering his previous lessons.

Julia was cool in a crisp white blouse and a tight-fitting, short red skirt. She looked at the apparent girl before her. He or she certainly looked most attractive in the yellow mini-dress. His blond hair descended to his bare shoulders. His make-up had been exquisitely executed; a woman could not have done better. Yet she was not quite sure that she entirely liked this innovation of presenting him as a girl. He had been very attractive dressed as a boy; and he had given her urges then. It had been delicious the time she had put him across his desk for six strokes of the cane. That had been during his naked period. How would she go about caning him now if it should prove necessary? Make him lift his dress and take down his knickers? She told herself she mustn't just want to give him the cane. She must cane him only if he deserved it. She was getting a bit confused and, in her mathematical mind, she liked things to be clear; as in the clear beauty of an equation. She wanted to impart some of the clarity of her thinking to him. Suddenly her mind was made up. She would have him sit beside her.

'Come here and we'll go over a problem together, Patrick.' She couldn't somehow yet bring herself to call him Pat, but she felt she wanted to and shortly would. 'Bring your chair over.'

The boy got up and came over to her and sat beside her.

'Now, look; here we have a simple example. I'm not going to do all the work. How would you go about it?'

The boy stared hard at the example in the textbook. He went on staring for some time and Julia found herself looking down at his naked thighs below the mini-dress.

'I'm sorry, I really don't know how to make a start.'

'You must concentrate harder.'

'I know, but I find it very difficult.'

'You mustn't expect it to be easy. It will become easier if you concentrate harder.'

'I know, but . . .'

'Pat, I have no recourse but to punish you. If nothing else will work I shall have to cane it into you.'

'All right.'

'It's far from being all right, Pat. You are quite infuriating with your dullness. Go now and bring some coffee, please. I shall cane you afterwards.'

The boy got up from beside his tutor. He turned at the door and bowed and went out.

The anger was rising in her now. Well, beauty could show a severe face. She wanted to cane him (or her) and there was an excellent pretext for it. How would she do it this time? She would ponder it as she sipped the coffee.

Patrick came in with the tray of coffee and placed it on

176

her desk. She would be pleasant to him until the time came for the strokes.

She sipped her coffee. 'And how are you getting on generally, Pat?'

'Not all that well, I'm afraid. I didn't do very well in my last driving lesson.'

'And what was the outcome?'

'Mrs Riding drove me to Oxshott woods and whipped me.'

'Whipped you!'

'Yes, she made me strip naked, then she tied my wrists and strung me up to the branch of a beech tree and whipped me.'

'How many strokes?'

'Eighteen.'

'A bit severe.'

'It was raining at the time.'

'Whew! And she went on doing it?'

'It was raining before she started.'

'So you had the rain on your bare skin!'

'Yes.'

'Wasn't she bothered about getting wet?'

'She had on a slinky black raincoat and hat.'

'So she was dry.'

'Yes. It was strange being whipped in the rain.'

'Well, today at least you'll have a dry whipping, which should be a comparative luxury.' Julia finished her coffee and stood up. 'I think we'll have you bending over a chair today. Put your chair in the centre of the room. Now bend yourself over it. Support yourself with your hands on the seat of the chair.'

The boy obeyed, the hem of his mini-dress rising to reveal more of his shapely thighs. Julia went to him, cane in hand. She raised the mini-dress high on his arched back which made a lovely curve defined centrally by the ridge of his spine. She took the little frilly knickers and slipped them down to his knees where they made a band of black froth. The shapely buttocks were like luscious fruits.

'Count the strokes.'

177

'Yes, ma'am.'

She raised the cane and brought it down.

'One.'

The fire was in her now as she raised her rod.

'Two.'

The nipples of her breasts were hard like polished metal knobs.

'Three.'

Now she was blazing. She liked doing this and she would do it again.

'Four.'

All caution, all restraint, was cast to the winds. She would cane understanding into him; they had been right to do that in earlier cultures.

'Five.'

She was exploding inwardly, in an intuition of sexual essence. All was illuminated. She was a goddess.

'Six.'

Julia lowered the cane. 'You may adjust your dress.'

The boy drew up his knickers and smoothed his mini-dress and stood there before her.

She smiled, her beautiful face relaxing as she spoke. 'It was for your own benefit. I take it there is no resentment?'

'None at all, ma'am,' he said happily.

'We will now continue with triangles.'

Patrick and Lucan carried the large plastic box up the stairs and into the studio with Darline and Trisha hovering round them like supervising schoolmarms. They put down the box in the centre of the room.

Darline looked at Trisha. 'You're used to handling him. Perhaps you'd better extract him.'

Trisha released the catch and lifted the lid. Darline looked at the patterned coils within.

Trisha said, 'Soo, soo, soo, Sleek. Now you're going to come out and be free.' With one hand under the python's neck she began to raise him.

Darline watched, fascinated, as the snake emerged from the box and coiled itself around Trisha.

The snake was now supported across Trisha's shoulders, its weight making it droop in curves on either side of the naked girl's body. She took him by the neck and tail and moved her hands along the patterned skin which was a reticulation of dark cobalt blue diamonds on his back; and on his belly a streaking of pale cream over green.

'They're such lovely creatures,' Trisha said. 'It's lovely to feel them against you. You can feel their long snaky muscles moving under the skin.' She eased the python so that he wound around her body, his head moving under her left arm, moving slowly around her back and coming up over her right shoulder.

Darline was sketching rapidly. She felt a profound excitement in herself as she watched the coils circling around the naked body.

'You can do anything with them,' Trisha said. 'Once you feel you've gained their confidence and they know you won't do them any harm you can do anything with them.'

The naked girl eased herself down on the floor saying, 'It's much better to be in a reclining pose with them because they're so heavy to support.'

She stretched herself out on the floor on her back and arranged the snake so that his neck was between her thighs. She drew him over her body with his head raised a little over her belly and nestled it between her breasts.

'That's lovely,' Darline exclaimed. 'Can you possibly keep his head between your breasts for a minute or so?'

'I'll try, but unlike a horse or dog you can't entirely control them.' She slipped both hands to either side of the snake's neck and began to talk to him. 'Soo, soo, Sleek, lovely Sleek. The crawler with the lovely long muscles, soo, soo, lovely Sleek.'

'That's good, if you can hold it there. What an image.' She was sketching furiously, finding herself deeply stirred at the sight of the naked body with the snake. 'I find some correspondence between your naked form, so complex and so beautiful in contact with the simpler form of the snake; and there is such a contrast between the patterning of his skin and the lovely, smooth colour of your own skin. Oh,

179

I'm sure this will result in an exciting series. It's fabulous what we can find in something when we begin to work on it. Matisse was right when he said that inspiration comes from doing work; it's never the other way round.'

'I'm afraid he's getting a little restless,' Trisha said. He was, he had opened his jaws and was flickering his tongue dreamily.

'I think he wants to kiss you,' Darline said. 'But that would surely be going too far.'

'I think it would,' Trisha responded. 'The contact of his warm writhing body is pleasant on my skin, but I think I prefer the kiss of my boyfriend, or at any rate one of my own species.'

'A kiss is certainly a sweet gesture,' Darline said absently as she went on with her drawing. 'The kiss of a mother for her child, or the kiss of schoolgirls. In France young girls and young men will kiss one another on meeting, and at Cap d'Agde it was lovely to see them kiss one another in the nude.' She made some final strokes on the paper. 'There, darling. That will do for that one. You can let him move onwards now. Oh! I'm so excited. I'll leave it to you, Trisha, to play with him as you will.'

'Right! Yes, he wants to move on. I can feel the muscle movement in him. It's lovely! You can feel it just under his skin as he draws himself in and then eases himself forward. He eases himself so sleekly, so slitheringly; it's no wonder he's called Sleek. Now, let's give him a little guidance and not leave it all to his own initiative. So, my snakish beauty, over my left shoulder you go and I feel you slithering around me, your body against mine. There you go, under my left arm, I feel you against my boob, my lovely boob, there you go, and over my neck and out again. It's like coiling a living thick rope around you. Now he's going down again and over his own lower body and under my left leg. It really gives you quite a thrill when you feel him moving against you.'

'That's lovely,' Darline said. 'A beautiful body entwined with a beautiful body of another kind. There, I'll work very fast. There's no need to try to hold him still. I'll try to capture something of the sinuousness of his movement and something of the electrifying skin contact.'

As she drew she was wondering how Patrick would take it if asked to pose with Trisha and Sleek. During the poses he had been standing well away from the models. He looked sweet in his mini-skirt and blouse with the dark shape of his bra under the filmy material and his nicely made-up face and his long shingled tresses.

'I think that will do for that one, darling. Rest for a few minutes, now.' She turned to Patrick. 'Would you like to take part in a pose, Pat?'

Patrick cringed visibly. 'I don't really think so, madam.'

'You really do have an aversion for them, don't you?'

'I'm afraid so.'

'Look how natural Trisha is with him; so unconcerned.'

'It really is something you can overcome,' Trisha said kindly.

'Why don't you try, Pat? Just try making contact with him,' Darline urged gently.

'Well, I'll try,' Patrick said timidly.

'I have some emergent desire to do something with two people, male and female, with a snake. Perhaps Adam and Eve. Those ancient myths are powerful and persistent. Anyway, would you like to get your clothes off and we'll take it from there.'

Patrick stripped off the mini-skirt over his head.

'Oh, what sweet underwear,' Trisha gushed. 'Lovely little knickers and bra.'

Patrick unhitched the bra and peeled it off, lowered the knickers and stepped out of them and stood there in sandals with his green-painted toenails.

'You've been depilated,' Trisha exclaimed. 'You look lovely with your body all smooth. You're as hairless as Sleek or one of those Mexican dogs.'

'Models are lovely, with hair or without,' Darline said. 'I've only ever known one lady model to depilate herself entirely and that was at the Wimbledon School. I tutored there for a while,' she explained.

'Just let me bring Sleek into contact with you,' Trisha

181

coaxed. She eased herself along the floor, towards Patrick, moving on all fours with the snake on her back.

A phrase came to Darline: woman carrying a snake. Was there some meaning there? Woman carrying a snake, the one accursed for ever, the despised one doomed to crawl for all time in the dust and through the grass. Trisha was now close to Patrick who wore the look of a hypnotised hare. The girl now rose with the snake round her back, holding it by its two ends.

'There, Patrick.' Trisha's voice was soft, coaxing. Then she moved and touched the snake to Patrick's hand. A look of profound revulsion came over the boy's face. Trisha again touched the hand lightly with the snakeskin. 'There, you see, Patrick, he's a living being like all of us. He's warm-blooded and vulnerable and he can easily be hurt.'

The boy stood there, transfixed. Darline was thinking what a picture he made, naked but for his sexy sandals, and with his smooth body, the genitalia as bare as a plucked partridge. He was gorgeous, depilated. She was glad she had had this done to him. What a thing it was to have a young male in one's power like this! Her nipples stood out like the heads of brass bolts! But there was sadism in her too. She wanted her boy to engage with the snake, wanted to see how he would take it, what effect it would produce. She was deeply intrigued by the effect one thing could produce on another. That had been the guiding premise of her series of nudes with horses.

'Just take his neck in your hand,' Trisha said. 'Feel his warmth and how he's just like any other animal. He can be hurt like any of us.' She took Patrick's hand in hers and guided it to the neck of the snake.

Darline thought again what beautiful hands the boy had. Trisha brought the hand under the creamy yellow-and-green striated neck. Then the reticent hand made contact with the neck. There came about a noticeable change in Patrick, slowly but unmistakably.

The expression on Patrick's face now had a profound serenity. It was not merely a joyful look, as at the promise of a beautiful day, but seemed to display a temporarily uplifted state of mind.

'I'm beginning to feel something I haven't felt before,' Patrick said in a voice of wonder. His free hand moved up and down the snake, along its back, just behind its head. The stroking went on for about a minute, the painter watching fascinated.

'Let me take him,' Patrick said. 'Let me take him and hold him myself.'

Trisha gently eased the weight of the muscled length from her and let the snake writhe around Patrick's shoulders until he was supporting the weight. The boy's face became suffused in a strange profound joy.

'I'm holding him,' Patrick said. 'He's with me, we are both together.' He moved to the centre of the studio floor and stood there as naked and smooth as the snake.

'I want to lie down with him,' Patrick said. He lowered himself to the floor and let the snake glide from his shoulders. He lay back on the floor and guided the snake's length between his thighs, guiding the sinuous muscle between the luscious smooth flesh. Darline was sketching the riveting spectacle before her.

'Now, could you join in, Trisha, so that you are both writhing on the floor with the snake.'

Trisha moved to the centre and got down with the boy and the snake.

'Good, that's good!' Darline exclaimed. 'I tell you what, could you arrange yourselves so that Sleek is encircling you both; the naked Adam and Eve, joined by the snake. The tempter.' Trisha guided the long body through her thighs, so that it was threaded through Patrick's and hers, joining them.

'My God!' Darline exclaimed. 'He's joining you both together as in the myth of Adam and Eve. I don't know if Flavia would accept this, but I suddenly feel that the snake body is a symbol of the phallus and was needed to draw female and male together. So you, Trisha, can feel the long phallus with you and Patrick can feel it also. What a splendid pose! Nudes conjoined by snake. Now, another notion occurs to me; would you both stand and put your arms around one another? That's it. Now drape him around your shoulders – that's very nice. Now see if you can hold it there for a few minutes.' She was drawing with intense concentration now, eyes moving up to the models and down to the paper. The minutes went by and her concentration was held as she drew.

'There, now, you've all three been very good. I think you both deserve a break and we'll have some coffee. Perhaps you'd like to make us some, Pat.'

The two models eased the heavy snake from their shoulders and Trisha arranged him in a coil, gently guiding him into the form of a maze.

Patrick put on his clothes, drawing on the brief black knickers and inserting his small breasts into the cups and hitching the strap at his back. Then he slipped the mini-dress over his head and smoothed it over his hips, arranging it, Darline felt, exactly as a woman does. He bowed and went out.

Darline looked at Trisha. 'Wasn't that just an awesome experience.'

'He quite overcame his aversion.'

'He absolutely accepted contact with the snake,' mused Darline.

'He did. He looks so lovely with his body all smooth. It makes a defined contrast with the abundant hair on his head. What made you decide to have this done?'

'It was Flavia's idea. She thought it might enable him to identify more readily with his feminine side. I suppose because depilation is a thing more typical of the female than the male.'

'He looks very attractive like that. I almost felt I would like to hold him in a sexual embrace.'

'Now, now, I think you'll have to cool your passion and concentrate on the poses – there's a time and place. Yet, come to think of it, there may be possibilities in what you say.'

'Perhaps for one drawing we could simulate the sex act and have the snake in it? Have Sleek in it with us as the tempter.'

'Good Lord! There may be something in that. And we'd be going right back to the biblical myth of Adam and Eve being tempted.'

Trisha looked at Darline. 'How would we do it, then? Would we have actual sex to the point of orgasm? Or would we just simulate it?'

'I don't think I'd want you to have actual sex. No, I think a model should simulate the pose. Rodin's *Thinker* was not really thinking. The model was simulating thinking. As in *Fugit Amor*, the lovers, or the models used for them, were simulating how fleeting love is. So we'll have you both simulating sex.'

'It's exciting,' Trisha said. 'We've done some exciting poses with Patrick and this is the most exciting of all. We've had him being whipped by me, me standing over him with my foot on his neck. And kneeling to offer his back as my footstool. And now we move on to the actual thing.'

Darline was thinking. 'Do you know, I feel inclined to do some of these poses again with the snake. Yes, I've got it. We'll try one or two of them anyway, and see if we can create a series. I feel, now, that the snake is an archetype of the collective unconscious. He is the dark side of the psyche, like the shadow, into which has been consigned all that we don't want to admit and bring out into the daylight. All the dark things are being consigned to the snake, turned loose in the wilderness to carry the sins of the world.'

'It seems rather fearsome,' Trisha said.

'There is a fearsome, dark side to everything,' Darline said thoughtfully. 'But it's the same as having to have night so that there can be day; having to have dark tones and light tones in a picture.'

'Is it the dark side, do you think, when you enjoy sado-masochism? I mean such as we were having with Patrick crouching to offer his back as my footstool, or my whipping him.'

'No, my darling, it's not dark at all. Sado-masochism is not dark or fearsome; it's a great creative force. It makes it a more sensuous and brighter world. All lovers should whip one another sometimes, or at least the dominatrix should whip and the submissive receive. Afterwards they should be tenderly loving, of course. It's absolutely true that being whipped increases one's love for the whipper. One feels that one wants to kneel and kiss the whipper's feet. Yes, whipping and being whipped are exciting and inspiring.'

Patrick entered with a tray of coffee and put it down on a painting table.

'Pat, don't you think that the thrill of spankings and whippings is just lovely?'

Patrick was pouring coffee. 'It is, it's lovely to be spanked or whipped. It's worthwhile being naughty sometimes just to earn a spanking or a whipping. Well, what I mean is that it's lovely to be whipped by a woman. I'd never enjoy being whipped by a man.'

Trisha looked wide-eyed at Patrick. 'Were you ever whipped by a man?'

'Never.'

'I wonder why you find it so pleasant when a woman whips you?' Trisha was smiling curiously.

Patrick smiled, a little self-consciously. 'Well, I adore women. They are so beautiful with their curvaceous bodies and their breasts and nipples like lovely fruits. And when they are dressed they wear such lovely clothes in such beautiful designs and colours, and the fabrics are soft to the touch.'

'What do you think about one woman whipping another?' asked Trisha.

'Oh, I like that, it's lovely. I find it quite thrilling for one lovely woman to whip another. Well – there you have two lovely curvaceous people with lovely fruits and one of them whips the other.'

There was now a certain unmistakable electric charge in the studio and it was flickering between the three people.

Darline finished her coffee. 'Right, darlings. Let's get on with it and see if we can do something.' She rose and took up her sketchbook. 'Now, we were saying that we should repeat some of the poses with the snake. Well, maybe we shouldn't think of ourselves as repeating something but as creating something completely new and fresh and lovely. That's what art is all about. So let's try something new, now, with both your delectable bodies and Sleek's long muscular body. How about trying the one in which Patrick is kneeling as your footstool? See if you can have Sleek encircling you.'

Trisha was aroused now, and Darline could see that Patrick was too. Trisha arranged Sleek so that he encircled them.

'I tell you what – we'll have the one with Pat as footstool and in the pose you can both voice what you feel.'

Trisha seated herself in the crimson upholstered gilt armchair. Patrick stripped and knelt before her, offering his back. Trisha placed her left foot on his back and crossed her legs.

'Oh, darlings, you look so exciting in that pose. Now verbalise it; tell me what you feel.'

'I feel like a goddess with the world under my feet,' Trisha began.

'I am low, with the feet of my goddess on my back,' said Patrick.

'It is so lovely, so daring and so naughty to do this, to have the male under one's feet.'

'What my goddess says is so true and so truly beautiful,' said Patrick. 'As I kneel, feeling her foot on my naked back, I feel such thrills in my belly and in my crotch. This is what I always wanted. This is the fulfilment of my desires. I can ask for nothing better than this; to kneel and be the footstool of my goddess.'

'What my slave says is so flattering and so beautifully naughty. I feel I want to be wicked. I want to do lovely things. I want always to be the mistress of my slaves and be a noble Roman lady. My slave should wear a collar, then I can take him to a party with him on a leash like a dog.' Trisha was now in full flow.

'I'd love to be taken to a party by my mistress with a slave collar on my neck and my noble lady holding me on a leash.'

187

'I'd show him off to my friends,' said Trisha, feeling quite haughty.

'How would you have me dressed for the event?' asked Patrick.

'There are so many possibilities. Let me see, I'm just visualising it. I could take you naked. You'd look lovely all smooth with your depilated body and not even the covering of a mat of pubic hair. Your genitalia would be on bare display, like the body of a plucked partridge.'

'Oh lovely!' enthused the submissive.

'Or let me see, I could make you wear a slave's costume: a breechclout with a band coming up and over one shoulder. But perhaps not. It might give you a little too much coverage, and, of course, I'd want you to feel naked and vulnerable because it's so delicious to be naked and vulnerable or make one's slave naked and vulnerable. Come to think of it, I wouldn't mind being a naked slave myself, taken to the party by my mistress.' Trisha paused then shook her head. She seemed to prefer the idea of being mistress herself. 'How else could I dress or undress my slave? I could make you wear a thin band around your hips with a length of fabric between your crotch, passed through the band and hanging in front and behind.'

By now Patrick was almost swooning with delight. 'Oh, that sounds fabulous.'

'It would be lovely to see the fabric swinging fore and aft and brushing your thighs,' she mused.

'Maybe the material could be leather,' Patrick suggested quickly.

'Yes, beautifully made of leather with an embossed design,' said Trisha.

'What would the design incorporate?' asked Patrick eagerly.

'There are numerous possibilities. Perhaps a vulva, the two lovely curves of a vulva. Or should we make it a phallus? The Greeks and the Romans incorporated phalluses a lot in their art. On your frontal square of leather an upstanding phallus with its top like a helmet and the division into two swellings like tiny breasts in front.'

'I think I prefer the lovely vulva,' said Patrick breathlessly.

'Well, I suppose I could accommodate you there; although you shouldn't expect to be allowed any choice. As a slave you are not a person and you have no legal rights. You are mine to do what I like with. But maybe I'd let you have the vulva.'

Darline put a final stroke to her drawing and stood back. 'I think that will do for that one, darlings. It was so stimulating to hear your dialogue, most exciting. Have a stretch now, after that one.'

She actually felt quite turned on by the talk of her models.

'Right, darlings, I think we'll go to work again. The day is yet young and creative work calls. The muse is murmuring.'

Trisha and Patrick rose from their recumbent postures on a mattress.

'Now, how can we arrange you with your snake? Isn't he good! No trouble at all. Shall we try the one where you're whipping Patrick with one foot on his neck? Can you place your foot on Sleek's neck as if you are grinding him into the dust, and then we'll try one with your foot on Patrick's neck later.'

Trisha went to Sleek and placed a foot on his neck. He began to writhe slowly as if not entirely averse to the attention, although he didn't entirely welcome it.

'I think he'll accept it if I don't press hard on his neck,' Trisha said.

Patrick said, 'Maybe if you take the weight on your heel on something laid beside his neck.' He looked around and his eyes lighted on a block of wood. 'This might do.' He took the block of wood and placed it near Trisha's foot, where it rested lightly on the snake's neck. Trisha arranged her heel on the block to take the weight.

'That's it! Splendid!' Darline exclaimed. Her hand was moving freely over the sketchbook page. 'Isn't that python docile. I declare he's almost as submissive as Patrick. Would you like to tell me what you feel with your foot on the snake, Trish?'

'It feels as if I'm holding down the brute creation; as if

189

I'm high and lovely. I feel very powerful. It's so lovely to feel adored by the brute creation; but it's not as good as being adored by one's slave.'

'I think that's enough of your foot on Sleek's head, Trisha. We'll now try Patrick in the pose. And this time you can have the whip in your hand.'

Trisha took her foot from the snake's neck. She went over to where the whip was lying coiled on the top of a stool. She took it up and slipped her hand along the length of it. 'They're such lovely things, whips,' she said musingly. 'They have quite a snakish feel to them.'

'They're very snakish in their form,' Darline said.

'They truly are, and they work these whips so beautifully in the countries they come from.' She went over to where Patrick stood. 'Now, how shall we arrange ourselves? Would you like to direct us?'

Darline looked at her models. 'Let me see. We have yourself and Pat and the snake. I think we'll try a correlation between the coiled whip and the coiled snake. See if you can arrange Sleek in a coil in front of you. He really is a handsome snake with his lovely dark blue patterning. Pity we can't see his lovely creamy belly with its pale green stripes, but you can't have everything all the time. We'll leave it for another pose.'

Trisha took Sleek and arranged him in a coil with his head in the centre.

'That's it,' Darline said. 'Now, Patrick, if you will go down on your knees beside Sleek and bend your slim body over. That's it. Now, Trisha, put your foot on Patrick's neck. Now go on with your dialogue. Patrick, you start it.'

'I feel servile bending down here. I feel my belly on my thighs and my head almost on the floor.'

'It's glorious to stand over my slave, to feel that I am totally dominant,' said Trisha.

'There is glory in my submission to you. It's naughty and silly and yet I feel great pleasure.'

'You are so right, my slave, my body servant. I want always to play games. The real fulfilment is in playing gloriously silly games.'

190

'It's lovely to be helpless here, to have my body bent and my bare back awaiting lashes,' continued Patrick.

'I am the supreme princess, the goddess, standing here over you. I am naked, and it is how I want to be. Here are my lovely fruits in front of me,' she said, caressing her breasts. 'They are like luscious gourds suspended on a vine, and the nipples are as hard as studs of polished bronze. I am like a beautiful sculpture. And between my thighs is such a feeling of superiority.'

Darline said, 'You are doing very well, darlings.'

In the afternoon Patrick was due to have another driving lesson. Ingrid drove the Fiesta up to the front door where he was waiting for her. She looked at him in his black mini-skirt and yellow blouse which left his arms bare. His black bra was a ghostly outline beneath the filmy yellow.

'I like your outfit,' Ingrid said as she changed seats and Patrick got behind the wheel.

'It's a new idea of Ms Pomeroy and Doctor Quayle.'

'It's certainly striking. You make a lovely girl.'

'The idea is to enable me to identify more with my female side.'

'Mmm, and does it?'

'It does, it gives me a feeling of being quite different.'

'I should imagine it does. I suppose you feel quite feminine.'

'I do, and it's wonderful.'

'Can you tell me how?'

'It makes me feel daring and unique.'

'Well, let's see if your performance is any better. Let me see you start the car.'

Patrick switched on the ignition, engaged first gear, slipped off the handbrake, began to let up the clutch, let it up in two jerks, and the car began to move forward.

'What should you have done before moving forward?'

'I thought I'd done it properly.'

'It was not proper at all; what did you fail to do?'

'I don't know. I'm sorry. I am trying.'

'I don't think you are trying hard enough. You are an

extremely difficult case and I think we should try extreme measures with you. Is there anything that really wakes you up and makes you feel alert?'

'Well, I think one thing that does it is when I take my morning swim in the pond.'

'Ah, yes, you told me about that. You have it when you're halfway through your run.'

'Yes, in the pond on the village green.'

'We'll change seats and I'll drive us there quickly.' Ingrid started the car with exemplary smoothness and drove them quickly to the green where she parked by the spinney. They got out of the car.

Ingrid looked at her pupil. It gave her an inscrutable feeling, seeing him in his brief feminine clothes and make-up.

'Right, you'd better take off all your clothes.' She watched the boy as he stripped, taking off the skirt and blouse, unhitching the bra and lowering the knickers before stepping out of them. He made a profoundly disturbing sight with his depilated skin, shingled head of hair, and powdered face.

'You make yourself up beautifully,' she said. She felt a little sorry at what she was going to do, but the steely surge of arrogance was growing in her.

'Now, I want you to enter the water and swim to the other side and back.'

She watched as he waded in and swam to the opposite side and then turned and swam back and emerged from the water.

'Now, tell me the correct sequence of moving off with a car.'

'Er, adjust the mirror, switch on the ignition, put the car into gear, let the clutch come up, look around before moving off.'

'You couldn't possibly move off like that.'

'I couldn't?'

'No, you couldn't possibly.' Ingrid was steely now. Her nipples and her clitoris hard. It was good and exciting, this. When she spoke her voice was as metallic and hard as the

feeling she had inside her. 'In you go and swim to the other
side and back.'

The boy looked at her, a strange exultation on his face.
He turned and waded back in. She took in the back view
of the slim body; he really was very lovely. He swam his
breast-stroke to the other side and turned and swam back.
He emerged from the water and stood facing his teacher.

'Now, tell me the correct sequence of moving off with a
car.'

'Umm, switch on the ignition, put the car into gear, let
the clutch come up, look around before moving off.'

'You could not move off like that. What did you omit?'

'I thought I'd given it properly.'

'You did not give it properly. There was something
improper about your sequence. Tell me what it was.'

The boy was flustered now, really at a loss. Ingrid could
see that he was racking his brains.

'I'm awfully sorry, I really can't remember it.'

'We shall have to see if we can stimulate you, then. If it
comes to it I shall have to whip it into you.'

'Well, that might be best –'

There was a sudden creaking of saddle leather behind
them and the sound of hooves on the grass. They turned to
see a policewoman mounted on a magnificent black horse.

'It's Mrs Riding, isn't it? Good morning.'

'Good morning, Jocelyn.'

'I saw the Fiesta parked here and turned in this
direction.'

'This is Patrick Lovelace, a pupil. He works for Darline
Pomeroy, the painter. I'm afraid Patrick is not making
good progress and I thought I'd stimulate him with a cold
dip.'

'And have you found it stimulating?'

'It's very stimulating. Ms Pomeroy makes me take a dip
when I go for a run round the green every morning.'

'But he has still not got the sequence correct. He has
been asked to give me the correct sequence for moving off
in a car. He has tried twice and each time got something
wrong. I am very nearly at a loss to know what to do.'

Jocelyn said, 'Is there anything else you find stimulating?'

'Well, Ms Pomeroy sometimes gives me a swishing.'

'A swishing?'

'Yes, a swishing with birch twigs.'

Ingrid could see that Jocelyn was excited. There was a certain look on her face. She was excited herself; the feeling of domination was flooding through her breasts and hardening the small buds. She looked at Jocelyn. 'What do you think?'

'Well, it might be an idea. There's no harm in trying it. They do it in the saunas in Sweden, my friend and I had it in Uppsala last year, and afterwards they have a roll in the snow or a cold plunge.'

Ingrid knew that she and Jocelyn shared a strange excitement. 'Well, I'll try it. Perhaps I should dry him first.'

'They don't in Sweden. The masseuse takes hold of you, puts you over the massage table and swishes you as you are, all steamy and wet.'

'I'll try it then. Where do I find birch twigs? We mustn't take any from the trees.'

'Ms Pomeroy used those brooms they use for beating our fire.'

'They're a bit big and brutal, aren't they? After all, you're not to be punished. It's a therapy to stimulate you.'

'I know,' Jocelyn said. 'They trimmed a birch tree just over there where it was overhanging the path. I'll canter over and pick some up.' She cantered her horse over to the tree, bent easily from the saddle, and came back with a handful of slender birch twigs. She handed them to Ingrid who took them and looked at Patrick.

'How does she go about it, now, Patrick?'

'I go across that fallen tree and she swishes me.'

'Right, would you like to arrange yourself over it?'

Patrick went to the tree and lay on his front along the length of it.

Jocelyn said, 'You won't mind if I stay and watch, will you? As a policewoman I'm always interested in punishment and one learns a lot from the things people do and the effect it has on them.'

194

'Not at all,' Ingrid said. 'You have no objection, do you, Patrick?'

'No,' the boy said, from his position on the tree trunk.

'I suppose they do it on the back, do they, the back and shoulders?'

'Yes, the back and shoulders, right down to the buttocks.'

Ingrid began to swish Patrick with the twigs, starting on his shoulders and slowly working down. She was now feeling splendid as she swished and watched the boy's skin take on a roseate colour as she moved down his back. She knew that Jocelyn was feeling the same strange excitement. It could be felt in the air. A beatific smile appeared on Patrick's face.

'Is it having a good effect, Patrick, do you feel stimulated?'

'Yes, I feel beautifully stimulated. It's having a good effect.'

'Shall I continue a little longer?'

'Yes, please.'

Ingrid swished again, down the length of his back.

'Is your arm getting tired?' Jocelyn asked. 'I'll have a go, if you like.'

'All right, it's very kind of you. I'll hold your horse.'

Jocelyn took the twigs and worked down the length of the boy's back which every second became more rosy.

What a scene! Ingrid was now on a high; the policewoman was swishing the naked boy; and his face was glowing at the treatment.

'I think this will do,' Jocelyn said. 'I'm glad to have been of assistance. It would be interesting to know if it has the desired effect.'

'I can keep you posted if you like,' Ingrid said. 'It was very nice to see you and have your help.'

'No problem,' the policewoman said. 'That's what we're here for.' She dug her heels in, turned the horse and moved away.

Ingrid felt high and proud as she said, 'Right, let's see if the swims and swishings have worked. I think you can get up now, Patrick.' The boy got up.

Ingrid said, 'I have a towel in the car. We'll dry you and you can get dressed.' She went over to the car and came back with a towel and enfolded the wet body in it and started to pat the skin dry, working over the back and then the front.

'There you are, you're dry now,' she said as she held him in her arms and kissed him, his painted lips meeting hers, her lips pouting and exploring his. Then she kissed him on his back and shoulders, her lips lingering on the pink skin.

'I'll be kind now. Yes, I think you deserve it. You'd better get your clothes on.' She watched as he put on his knickers and bra, the skirt and blouse, and slipped his feet into the sandals.

'Let's get into the car.' They got in and she said, 'Now, my darling, can you tell me the correct sequence for moving off?'

'Adjust the mirror, switch on the ignition, put the car into gear, take off the handbrake, look around before moving off,' he said confidently.

'Excellent,' Ingrid said.

12

A Kinky Party

Darline had received an invitation that morning from Melissa, the art student. It went:

> *SPANKING SPANKING SPANKING*
> *The Students' Union request the pleasure of your company at an SM party to be held on 14 June at the KSU Club. SM dress is obligatory unless you are naked but for metal piercings. Do bring your own whips if you wish. Others will be available on the premises.*
> *Ms Darline Pomeroy*
> *Dr Flavia Quayle*
> *By the way: It is perfectly acceptable for you to bring your slaves.*
> *RSVP*

Darline's imagination had run riot. She would take Patrick to the party as her slave. Should he go as a boy? Or should she make him be her slave girl? Both were exciting possibilities. It would be lovely to take him on a leash. But then, of course, Flavia now had a slave girl in Pina. Each slave could be taken as self-sex, or they could be cross-dressed: girl as boy and boy as girl. She would discuss the possibilities with Flavia. But decidedly they should be on leashes with collars round their necks. There were lovely studded collars available or perhaps they could make collars for them, something simulating a slave's metal collar. They would see.

197

Darline turned it over in her mind for days after. The prospect of the forthcoming party was delicious. It flooded in upon her as if from every side of her life, as she rode Lightning Flash or Tempered Steel around the green, or as she stood painting at her easel. Whatever she did, images of the event to come would appear and float before her. She toyed with different ideas as to how Patrick could be presented as her slave. After a while it occurred to her how his training in fashion design might be turned to good account. She reduced his domestic duties and left him free to design an outfit using an array of fabrics she had accumulated for use in studio sets. It was all so exciting. Yet at times there would be intrusive thoughts of her next monthly treatment by Agrippina.

Patrick finally came up with a devastatingly simple outfit. He dispensed altogether with knickers and bra. He devised a belt of black leather and attached to it, in front and behind, squares of leather of a rich brown. Under it he wore a black leather G-string. A black collar with silver studs completed the scant outfit.

When he paraded in his outfit for inspection by Darline she found him an arousing sight. She almost wanted to put him over her lap and raise the back flap and spank him then and there, but she refrained, having no reasonable pretext.

'You look lovely, Patrick. I had an impulse to spank you – but I won't. I sometimes wonder if I should treat you the way I do.'

'But I have no objection. You really are very kind – and I feel that the things you do to me are done out of a kind of love.'

Darline looked at him tenderly. 'You're almost certainly right, there. I am your dominatrix and I beat and humiliate you – yet it's highly likely that I feel a special fondness for you.'

She took him in her arms and kissed him on the lips. She could feel him responding and she stroked his back and kissed him again and held his body close to hers.

* * *

For the party Darline chose to array herself as a Greek noblewoman and from a theatrical costumier she obtained a beautiful chiton. Under this she wore a black G-string and a black bra with silver studs. She and Flavia had decided that they would go as two noble Greek ladies with their slaves. Over her cropped hair she wore a blonde wig arranged in a classical Greek style and this was surmounted by a jewelled coronet. The most beautiful brown leather sandals with gold studs completed the outfit.

They drove to Flavia's house. Patrick was wearing a black cloak she had lent him over his slave's outfit. They were admitted by Sally, who was wearing a black peignoir.

'Hello, do come in. Oh, what a charming and thrilling sight!'

She took them along to the drawing room where Flavia was seated with her slave girl in attendance. She wore a purple peplum of the type worn by noble Greek women. Pina stood beside her in a leopard-skin skirt which barely covered her pubis.

Flavia said, 'Bend over and show them your matching knickers, Pina.' Pina bent herself to reveal the most minute leopard-skin knickers which excitingly left bare the curves of her buttocks.

'She has such sweet buttocks,' Darline said.

'She has. What is Patrick wearing under his loincloth? It's rather like the ones the native Americans used to wear.' The boy bent over. 'Oh, sweet. A backless G-string.'

Darline turned to her lover. 'You do look lovely.'

'You look divine, my love,' Flavia said. They opened their arms and enfolded one another and kissed. Their kiss was long and open-mouthed.

'Oh, my God,' Darline breathed. 'I feel I'd like to go further. I want to feel your skin against mine, now.'

'Oh yes, it would be so beautiful; but we'll have to wait for a while.'

'It will be worth waiting for,' Darline purred.

Darline saw that the slave girl and the slave boy were also kissing, their arms wrapped around one another. She wondered if they should be disciplined but decided not to intervene.

Sally came in, wearing the most startling outfit of all. She wore a black rubber basque-like garment which was the most high-cut that could possibly have been fabricated. It barely masked her shaven pubis and left her sumptuous buttocks bare but for a strap over the division of them. In front there was a circular cut-out which revealed her taut belly and at the sides two more cut-outs showed the slim area between her hips and her rib cage.

'My God! You are a sight to behold,' Darline said.

'You really are,' Flavia added admiringly.

'You are both quite beautiful,' Sally said.

'And what do you think of our slaves?' Flavia asked.

'They are indeed piquant sights in their leopard skin and leather,' Sally said kindly.

'I think we can be on our way,' Flavia said. 'We can all go in my car.'

They made their way out and got into Flavia's Saab. Flavia was driving with Darline beside her, and Sally sat in the back with Pina and Patrick.

At the art school, Flavia parked the car, then she and Darline attached leashes to their slaves' collars. As they went in they were greeted by Melissa.

'How lovely to see you.'

'So kind of you to invite us,' Darline said as they kissed. 'This is my friend, Flavia, and her slave girl, Pina. You already know my slave, Patrick. And this is Sally.'

'Jeez, I like your outfit,' Melissa said in admiration to Darline.

'I like yours,' Darline said. 'And here are the other members of your quartet. Hello, darlings.' She kissed Sarah, Kirstie and Gala.

'It's lovely to see you again,' Gala said.

'It really is,' Kirstie came in.

'It was so kind of you to invite us over and let us see your paintings,' Sarah said.

'And your beautiful horses,' Gala put in.

'And the special treat you gave her,' Melissa said with a

broad smile. She was looking at the slaves on their leashes. 'I like the way you treat your slaves like dogs.'

Darline smiled impishly. 'It was my idea – you said it was that sort of party.'

'And I fell in with it most willingly,' Flavia said. 'By the way, I like your decorations.'

All around the walls there were pictures in flesh tones, red and yellow. They showed every possible kind of spanking and whipping. People were bent over to be spanked, bending over chairs to be spanked, lying on benches to be caned or whipped, strung up on posts or frames to be flogged. In a central position there was one particularly striking picture. It showed a large and heavy looking studio easel. Tied to it with cords was a naked woman, her arms making a wide V shape, her wrists lashed to the easel frame. Another woman, dressed in a black mini-skirt and a black bra with silver studs, was lashing her with a long whip. The artist had caught the moment when the lash of the whip landed on the naked back.

'Wow! What an image that makes!' Darline said in sincere admiration.

'It's very striking,' Flavia said.

'Shall I introduce you to a few people?' Melissa asked. They moved further in among the throng of people, dressed in every manner of imaginative garb.

'Let me introduce you to this lovely person,' Melissa said to Darline, Flavia and Sally. 'This is Sonia.'

Sonia made a beautiful and imposing figure. She was attired in a G-string, encrusted with sparkling gems so that her pubic region glittered with flashes of light. Her tummy button was pierced and displayed a green jewel which flashed an aura of green over the curves of her belly. Above her navel hung the most luscious breasts Darline had ever seen. The nipples were pierced and from each there dangled a string of jewels about twelve centimetres long, in reds, greens, aquamarines and clear crystals. The face was fantastically painted in yellow and red. On her head was a helmet such as that worn by the goddess Athene.

The others had moved on and Darline found herself alone with Sonia.

'You do make a most exciting figure,' Darline said in tones of admiration.

'Thank you,' Sonia responded.

'Did you make this outfit yourself?'

'I did, actually, with quite a lot of help from a fellow student.'

'Between you you certainly achieved a striking result. By the way, this is my slave, Patricius. I suppose he shouldn't really be introduced since he's a mere slave, but I'll stretch a point.'

Patrick bowed as Sonia extended a hand and he took it and kissed the fingers very gently.

'So you are a slave,' Sonia said. 'Isn't it a bit extreme that you should wear a collar and be on a leash?'

Patrick grinned and said, 'I have no objection.'

'What's your line?' Sonia said.

'I'm in service with Ms Pomeroy.'

'Yes, but I mean what's your real line?'

'That is actually my real line. I serve this noble lady.'

'Yes,' Darline interposed. 'Patrick is employed by me. He did actually train in fashion design but he found it difficult to get started in that, and he was sent to me by the Bare Service Bureau.'

'Wow, how marvellous. They're the people who supply people to do housework in the nude, aren't they?'

'The very same.'

'It must be exciting to have someone in your house, doing the chores naked.'

'It is, we tried it with Patrick.'

'You did!'

'Yes, it was the idea of my friend, Flavia. She's a psychiatrist, and is making a study of the effect of reducing the predominance of the ego by stripping away some of the persona.'

'I'm not entirely sure that I understand that.'

'Removing the mask we all present to the world. The front we put on for everyday purposes.'

'Do you know, that's most interesting,' Sonia said. 'I suppose when we play sexual games we throw off our

202

hibitions and become what we really are. Isn't it a wonderful idea!'

'It really is wonderful,' Darline said. 'Do you know, that's what I've started doing in my paintings. In my series of nudes with horses I did that and in my most recent work I'm doing it.'

'What are you working on?'

'We've been trying out some poses of nudes with a python.'

'With a python!'

'Yes, I used a model called Trisha Spear and we had Patrick in the poses as well.'

'Wow! You certainly are daring.'

'Patrick did admirable work. He quite overcame his version for snakes. You may join in the conversation, Patricius.'

'Yes, I must say I did manage to overcome my dislike of snakes completely.'

'My, you are brave. I have an aversion for reptiles and I'm sure I couldn't overcome it; not in a thousand years. How about a drink?'

'That sounds a nice idea.'

'We have red or white wine and we have some devil's brew, a kind of punch which is chilled instead of being hot.'

'I think I'd like a glass of white wine, please,' said Darline.

'How about you, Patrick?' Sonia eyed the boy up and down in his tiny loincloth.

'Well,' Patrick said hesitantly, looking at Darline.

Darline looked at Sonia, with a grin on her face. 'I don't know that slaves are allowed to drink alcohol.'

'Perhaps they might be on a special occasion,' Sonia said coaxingly.

'Well, I suppose they might. Do you think we should let him have a glass on this occasion?'

'I think we should. What would you like, Patrick?'

'The same as my mistress, please, noble lady.'

Sonia went to get the wine and Darline drew Patrick to her on the leash.

203

'There, my boy-slave, my body slave. You are to have a special treat this evening, a glass of wine of the same vintage as your mistress is having.' She touched his cheek gently with her fingertips. 'There, you are sometimes treated rather harshly. But then, you accept it and go along with it willingly and submit to everything. I tell you what, this evening we'll suspend your slavish status to some extent and allow you to join in the conversation. Say whatever you like. How would you like that? And you need not call me madam or noble lady. How's that?'

'All right, madam. Oh, sorry, I said it.'

Darline laughed lightly, 'You must try to remember that you are a Cinderella at the ball. You're allowed to be on the same level as the others for the evening. Flavia and her slave girl and Sally seem to have got involved somewhere else.'

Sonia appeared with glasses of white wine and Darline said, 'You may take one, Patricius.' She raised her glass and said, 'Here's to sado-masochism and its wonderful creative power.'

'To sado-masochism and its creative power,' Sonia said. All three raised their glasses and sipped.

'I awfully admire your outfit,' Darline said.

Patrick sipped his wine and bravely said, 'It really is fabulous.'

'That's right, you can join in the talk,' Darline said.

'I think he should,' Sonia said. 'So you trained in fashion design? How interesting!'

'Yes, I specialised in underwear for ladies and men and I also designed skirts for men.'

'Skirts for men! How very original! What gave you the inspiration?'

'Well, it seemed to me that men's fashions are so dull. One never gets away from the essential concept of trousers and jacket.'

'Yes, how true.'

'Women in our society are so lucky. They can wear anything; skirts of any length, from down to their ankles to halfway up their thighs. They can wear trousers and

204

shorts and culottes and hot pants. And, when you think about it, Arabs wear robes. In the classical world the Romans and the Greeks wore robes and tunics of several styles. Even the slaves wore tunics very like a present day mini-dress.'

'You know, you're quite right,' Sonia exclaimed. Why on earth should men always be stuck with jackets and trousers? What do you think, Darline?'

'I agree with what Patrick says. I don't see why males should be under such restriction.'

'I think it's really an inhibition,' Patrick said.

'And in art there's no place for inhibition,' Darline said. She could see that Patrick was relaxing and joining in; maybe his one glass of wine was having some effect.

'Let's have another drink,' Sonia said. 'Shall we wander over to the bar?'

'What an excellent idea,' Darline said.

They made their way to the bar through the throng of women and men in their fantastic outfits. Darline reflected that they harnessed rather than covered the bodies.

'Look at these wonderful bodies,' Darline exclaimed as they stood at the bar while Sonia called for three more glasses of wine. 'It's glorious to see people as naked as in one's studio; and it's rather nice to see them sometimes with trappings. When I see the body with minimal trappings such as the things they have now in black leather and rubber and plastic it makes the bodies wearing them look as if they are harnessed. I like them naked in my studio or by the swimming pool but I also like to see them harnessed sometimes.'

'I rather like the daring dancing dresses some of the girls are wearing,' said Sonia.

'Yes, they are nice,' Patrick said. 'I like the way they reveal more flesh as the girls dance.'

'Yes, they look very fetching,' Darline said. She could see that the second glass of wine was loosening Patrick's tongue still more. She did not want him to get drunk. She would keep an eye on him. She looked admiringly at Sonia and said, 'Your own outfit is absolutely stunning. You'd stop anyone in their tracks. You look almost like a dancing girl.'

Sonia grinned. 'I really like to be in this sort of get up. The jewelled G-string is just right for me. I like the way it just covers my pussy, and I like the feel of the narrow strap between my backside.'

'I like your tummy-button jewel,' Darline said. She could feel the wine going to her head.

'Yes, I found it in a shop in Kensington High Street and I couldn't resist it.'

'And the pendants dangling from your nipples are fantastic.'

'Yes, they feel quite lovely as they dangle. I can feel the weight of them as they hang and swing there, it makes me more aware of my breasts.'

'I can imagine what it must be like. It must be delicious to feel them hanging there. Somehow they make me want to kiss your breasts. They look like lovely fruits hanging from you as if you're a tree.'

'Really! What a lovely compliment. Why don't you?'

Darline leant forward and kissed Sonia's right breast, feeling the firm texture of the skin, pleasuring in the yielding of the underlying tissue. She drew back and said, 'Aren't we lucky to be free enough to enjoy one another's bodies.'

'You put it so beautifully,' Sonia said. 'I liked the feel of your lips on my breast,' she whispered flirtatiously.

'I love to kiss,' Darline said.

'Me too.'

Suddenly Flavia came into sight, with Pina on the leash. 'It's a lively party, isn't it,' she said. 'This is highly useful material for my research.'

'I should imagine it would be,' Darline said.

'Shall we dance?' Flavia asked.

'I'd love to,' Darline said. 'But what shall we do with these creatures on the leashes?'

'Well, shall we be munificent and turn them loose to run for a while?'

'I suppose we could. It would be a kind thing to do. Would you like to be let off the leashes for a while?'

'Yes, noble lady,' Pina said.

'Yes, noble lady,' Patrick echoed.

'So be it,' Flavia said. 'We shall turn them loose to run.' She grinned.

'Would you excuse me for a while?' Darline said to Sonia.

She and Flavia moved onto the floor and started to dance. They swayed and swirled, moving their bodies in time to the music. They could feel the twirlings of the dancers around them and saw Pina and Patrick among them. Then Darline saw Sonia dancing with a brown-skinned male wearing a leopard-skin skirt. It was obvious that they were superb dancers. They stepped and swayed and swirled, bending their bodies this way and that, dipping low and coming up again. Sonia was a picture with the jewels of her G-string sparkling and the strings of jewels swaying from her breasts. Darline felt jealous of the brown male in the leopard skin. She wanted to hold Sonia in her arms and kiss those breasts again. She wanted to have Sonia in her studio and draw her in an endless succession of poses. She wished she had asked Sonia to dance. Then she began to feel out of breath and said, 'Can we rest for a while, now?'

'Of course, darling. Do you feel tired?'

'I do, a little. Perhaps we can sit for a while.'

'Of course,' said Flavia with concern.

They seated themselves on a bench by the wall.

'I wonder if I'm not on a downward slide.'

'Oh, I think you're being a bit dramatic, darling. It can't be that bad.'

'My God! You can be hard and indifferent.'

'Not hard and indifferent. I merely remain impersonal; as a doctor I must.'

'I don't think I can take any more of what that woman enjoys doing to me; scrubbing a toilet with a toothbrush, making me go on all fours like a cow and having her husband serve me from behind – slave breeding she called it.'

'I still feel that I have to let this take its course and leave you to work through your problem,' soothed Flavia.

Darline turned on her friend: 'Or is your indifference in aid of your research? You bloody hard clinical bitch!'

'You're not yourself just now, but I don't think there's anything amiss in a medical sense.'

'You wouldn't!'

'It most certainly is a scintillating party,' Flavia said, trying to distract her lover. 'Doesn't Sonia make a splendid sight. What a delightfully daring touch to have those strings of jewels suspended from her nipples.'

'It really adds a distinctive touch to her. I'm sorry I called you a bitch.'

'That's all right.' Flavia looked around the hall. 'I wonder where our slaves are.'

'I haven't seen them for a while. Perhaps they've gone off somewhere. I don't suppose they'd dare to run away.'

'I shouldn't have thought so. They really haven't anywhere to go.'

'Perhaps we should stroll around and see if we can spot them. We might meet some interesting people.'

They linked arms and moved around the hall. Around them were dancing couples and kissing couples wearing every variant of leather, rubber and plastic.

'Oh, darling,' Flavia said. 'Let's kiss and hold one another.' She put her arms around Darline and they kissed, the tongue of one snaking around the tongue of the other.

'I do love you, even if you are being hard with me,' Darline said with controlled passion in her voice. 'I feel I want to make love to you at this very moment. I want to feel your skin against mine.'

'I think it would be better to wait until we get home,' Flavia said. 'And perhaps we should savour the sweet punishment of waiting. Let's enjoy the party and have the total contact of our flesh to anticipate.'

'All right, darling, let's wait. We still haven't found our slaves.'

They wandered in the direction of the bar and saw Pina and Patrick. Darline saw at once that Patrick had drunk rather more than she approved of. She saw that Pina had been drinking, too.

'Have you two been drinking all this time?' Darline demanded, her look severe.

Neither Pina nor Patrick replied, but they both looked decidedly guilty.

Flavia said, 'You were not turned loose to indulge yourselves.'

Patrick said sullenly, 'We only had a few drinks. We thought we were allowed to as you freed us for tonight.'

'You were not let off the leash to indulge yourselves in strong drink; and don't speak to your mistress in that tone.' Darline looked at her slave, the complete patrician. 'Get down on your knees this moment and beg my pardon.'

The boy looked blearily at his mistress.

'Get down on your knees at once and beg my pardon,' she commanded.

The boy got down on his knees, put his hands together in the Hindu manner and said, in a rather shaky voice, 'I beg your pardon.'

'I beg your pardon, what?' Darline felt a splendid hauteur.

'I beg your pardon, noble lady.'

'Kiss my foot.'

The boy bent his body and kissed the scarlet painted toenails.

Darline said, 'I think your girl should do likewise.'

Flavia looked at her slave girl. 'Yes, I really think you should.'

Pina went down and kissed Flavia's feet, first the right and then the left. She raised herself and said, 'I beg your pardon, noble lady.'

Darline said, 'I think they should both be punished.'

'I think they most certainly should,' Flavia said with a look of the most aristocratic disdain.

Darline felt, now, that she wanted the slaves to be humiliated publicly. She wanted them to be whipped there and then in the presence of the dancers. It would be a spectacle to remember. She turned to Flavia. 'Don't you think we should do it here?'

'I think we should,' Flavia agreed.

'I wonder if we can find a suitable instrument.'

'I've got it; their leashes will make eminently suitable whips.

'Of course they will. They're fashioned exactly like
whips. If you reverse them and hold the thick end where
the steel clip is, the length of it makes a long and flexible
lash. Let's give them a real flogging.'

Flavia said, 'Let's tan their hides so they'll remember it.

They both grasped the thick ends of their leashes.
Darline could feel how like a phallus the stiff knobbed end
was in her hand.

Flavia said, 'Everybody is doing what they like, so I
think we should just get on with it.'

'Yes, how shall we arrange them? Those benches might
suit.'

'Shall we do them both together or one at a time?' Flavia
asked.

'I have an idea; why not put the two benches side by side
and whip them both at once. The long lashes will span
both backs at once.'

'What a brilliant idea,' Flavia said, kissing her lover.

Melissa came into view.

'Hello, ladies. What's going on here?'

'These wretched slaves are to be punished,' Darline said.

'What was their offence?'

'The boy drank too much.'

'And the girl?'

'She did nothing to dissuade him from drinking.'

'And how are you going to punish them?'

'We're going to lash them with these long whips.'

At that moment Sarah, Kirstie and Gala came up.
Darline could see a certain excited look on Gala's face.

'We're going to make them both go over these benches,
together, to take their strokes. It will then be a mutual
experience for them. They offended together and they will
be whipped together. Now, let's arrange the benches.'
Darline's face had a demanding look. She could feel her
whole body electrified, her nipples throbbing. She said,
'Just give us a hand with these benches.'

The four girls helped to place the two hefty benches side by side, head to foot.

'Now, over the benches you go, next to each other.'

The two slaves arranged their bodies over the benches, side by side.

'I know,' Darline said in a flash of inspiration. 'We can both whip them. You can lay on a stroke and I can lay on a stroke alternately.'

'What a brilliant idea.' Flavia looked admiringly at her lover.

Darline said, 'We can stand at opposite sides and lay them on one after another. First you and then me.'

'How creative you are.'

The two regal ladies stood at opposite sides of their slaves, each with a whip.

'These slaves are hopeless,' Flavia said. 'They have to be told everything. They should have taken off their clothes before lying down.'

'Remove your rags,' Darline ordered. 'Don't keep us waiting.'

The slaves wriggled on their benches, cast off their skimpy garments and lay there naked.

'Now,' Flavia said. 'How many strokes should it be?'

Her lover pondered. 'Perhaps we should show a little mercy.'

'A little, but not too much.'

'No, it is naughty of a slave to imbibe too much alcohol.'

'Shall we make it three times the traditional six strokes?'

'Well,' Darline mused. 'That seems a little severe.'

'So shall we make it a dozen?'

'I think that seems fair enough. Quite fair enough.'

'Let's lay them on, then. Who shall be first?'

'It doesn't make much difference to the slaves. If you give a stroke to Pina, Patrick receives the end of the lash and vice versa. Anyway, let it be you. Girl slave first.'

'All right, I'll lay on first.' Flavia swung the whip in a wide arc and brought it down on Pina's pert buttocks. Patrick received the end of the lash on the small of his back.

Darline saw the girl flinch and squirm a little. She swung her own whip and brought it down on Patrick's backside. 'There, this will teach you a lesson.'

Flavia brought her whip over and lashed the girl. 'That's for your naughtiness in not discouraging your fellow slave.'

Darline could see a crowd gathering around the scene. She brought the lash over on her boy. She thought almost fondly of him as her boy, remembering how she had kissed him.

Flavia lashed her girl. Darline noticed that Gala's eyes were riveted on the spectacle.

Darline brought the lash over and down. She could tell that Gala was envious of the two slaves.

Flavia delivered a stroke. Darline saw that the crowd was moving closer for a better view. She brought the lash over and down. Out of the corner of her eye she could see the ecstatic look on the boy's face.

Flavia swung over and down. The girl's face, too, was glowing.

Darline swung the lash and brought it down. Patrick's skin was now welted, as was that of his partner. It was necessary to teach slaves a lesson. They must learn how to behave in public or accept the consequences.

Flavia laid the lash on. The girl's face now bore an expression of perfect bliss.

Darline laid the final stroke on Patrick and it overlapped on Pina.

The two noble ladies laid down their whips. They looked round at the admiring crowd.

A girl with a mohican haircut appeared. 'Aren't you cruel, in a way, to punish your slaves like that? Yet I must say I admire you for it.'

Darline smiled. 'No, it's not cruel; they know it's for their own good.'

'I suppose it is,' the spiky-haired girl said. 'Do you know, I'm a little shy to say it; but I fancy having it done to me.'

Flavia said, 'It is a quite delectable experience.'

'Why don't you do it to me? Please do it to me, I'm dying to be whipped. I'd love it,' the girl pleaded.

Gala was watching with envious eyes. 'Please can I be first?'

Darline assumed command. 'Now, whoever wants to be whipped, you'll have to form an orderly queue.'

The students began to get into line and in minutes there was a long queue, almost to the door.

'I think we'd better take turns in laying them on,' Flavia said.

'Yes,' Darline agreed. 'Do you think we should make them bow before they receive their punishment?'

'What a sound idea!' Flavia responded.

'Perhaps we should also make them kiss our feet.'

'An excellent suggestion.'

'Let's have the first recipient,' Darline said, in a commanding voice.

Gala came forward eagerly.

'Ah, the lovely masochistic Gala,' Darline said, her face wreathed in a sadistic smile. 'The lovely masochistic Gala. I do quite love you for being so masochistic.'

Flavia came in with, 'This young lady with the mohawk hair is very keen.'

'Excellent,' Darline exclaimed. 'They can be whipped as a twosome just as our slaves were.'

'What is your name?' Flavia enquired of the spiky-haired girl.

The girl licked her lips and said, 'Clorinda.'

'What a lovely name,' Darline said. 'Well, Clorinda, now you are going to have a lovely lashing.' She looked at Flavia. 'Shall we make them beg for it first?'

'I suppose we could but perhaps we shouldn't make them wait too long; the queue is getting longer all the time.'

Darline pursed her lips and said, 'I know, let's just make them go on their knees and kiss our feet and say, "Goddess, please whip me".'

'What a splendid idea!' Flavia exclaimed. 'Let's do just that. I think we'd better address the queue.'

213

Darline turned to the long line of people and announced imperiously, 'It is most gratifying to see you all eagerly waiting to be whipped. I think we'd better organise it efficiently so that we don't have to keep you waiting too long. Pair up into couples, just as you like, two females, two males, or one of each. One go up to Flavia and one to myself. Go on your knees and say, "Goddess, please whip me".'

Gala knelt before Darline and Clorinda knelt before Flavia. They kissed the feet of their mistresses and murmured their plea in reverent tones. Darline was filled with the splendour of feeling herself adored and was sure that Flavia was feeling likewise. Gala and Clorinda went across the benches and bared their backsides. Darline swung the lash across the pairs of buttocks, then drew back the lash as Flavia swung in turn. It went on, lash after lash after lash. She felt herself transported, now, in a seventh heaven of sadism. The one thing she might have enjoyed even more would be to have been on the receiving end.

Gala and Clorinda got up and the next couple laid themselves in position, ready to feel luscious pain. They were a boy with very dark long hair and a girl with her crimson dyed hair cropped like a lamb's back. They went through the ritual of requesting their goddesses for punishment, laid themselves down and bared their backsides. Darline and Flavia started to cut the air with their whips.

Darline felt as if she were floating onto another dimension now. For her, this was the highest thing one could do apart from creating art, drawing, painting and sculpting. She was full of images. She had experienced such wonderful things. Her art was all triggered and controlled by sexual feeling. That was how it should be. All the greyness of melancholy was charmed away by sexual feeling, by sexual love. That was how she wanted it to be. The next couple came and she scarcely heard the litanied plea on their knees. She had an endless supply of flesh to whip and she was in ecstasy over it. Recent scenes raced through her mind. Taking the boy on runs round the green and giving the occasional lash to his lovely bare back. She loved that phrase, 'bare back'. She loved her lover's bare back. She wanted to be lashed again by Flavia, despite her coolness over the Agrippina affair. There was nothing like it, nothing as good as when one went over the flogging block or was strung to the ring in the stable yard. She would love to be strung in the stable yard herself. She savoured the memory of when Lucan had whipped Patrick at her direction and when that fat white creature Lilian had been strung and whipped. Well, she shouldn't have covered the boy's body with bruises. She had richly deserved her punishment. At the same time it had been hugely exciting to make the boy go naked all the time around the house. Couples came up and bowed and pleaded and went down for their sweet whipping. It had been a dear occasion when the four girls had taken the boy's punishment between them. The image wafted before her, going down on the fallen tree and taking down their knickers.

As the whips hissed, the whipped couples were getting down on the floor and behaving in the most lewd ways. They had created a pulsating carpet of bodies all over the floor. After some time she began to feel so aroused that an idea occurred to her. She would make her slave carry on with the whipping and would join the entangled creatures on the floor.

She looked at Flavia. 'My love, I'm going to have my slave take over this chore so that I can join them on the floor. She called Patrick over. 'Here, you slave boy. Take over this lashing for a while and let your noble lady take a rest; take this whip.'

She glimpsed Sonia nearby. She was fiendishly seductive in her jewelled G-string and with the strings of jewels hanging from her nipples. She wanted to hold the lush body in her arms and stroke it all over and feel the sumptuous flesh. She vaguely wondered if Flavia might not appreciate it; but they had agreed in their many conversations that love should be generous and sharing. Perhaps Flavia would like to share Sonia. But no, she would not share Sonia tonight because of Flavia's coolness towards the Agrippina affair. Sonia had not been whipped yet but that could soon be remedied.

'Darling,' she said to Sonia in her most sultry tones. 'I find you exciting and beautiful. I could absolutely kneel down and adore you. I want to kiss your jewelled G-string or take it off and kiss between your legs. You're the loveliest sight I've seen for ages.'

Sonia smiled enigmatically. 'What a lovely thing to say.'

Darline slipped a hand gently round Sonia's waist. 'It's so fortunate that I should meet you here.' She kissed Sonia on her cheek. 'I'm a painter and I think you have one of the most exciting bodies I've seen for some time; I should really love to paint you.'

'What a sweet thing to say.'

'Nearly all my work is figurative, featuring the nude and sometimes even the nude with animals. I have a lovely model whom I've sometimes posed with Patrick.'

'He's a pretty young man and he has such a slender figure. I've rarely seen such a tiny waist even on a girl.'

'He has indeed,' Darline said, again kissing Sonia, gently and with feeling. 'You have such a lovely body, such sumptuous breasts. And those jewels through your nipples set them off to perfection.'

'I thought it would be nice to have my nipples pierced. I like to feel the weight of the strings hanging and one can swing them around a little and feel them pulling.'

'It must be exciting,' Darline cooed. She bent and kissed Sonia's closest breast.

'What connection has Patrick with you? I take it he's not really a slave although I know it's still practised in some parts of the world.' She laughed lightly.

'Your laughter is like the chiming of tiny silver bells.'

'Thank you, another sweet compliment.'

'Well, Patrick is not of course legally a slave. He's a slave artistically and imaginatively; I think I'm beginning to regard him as a friend.'

'How did you acquire him?'

'I wanted a maid in my house, a sort of personal body servant and when I asked the Bare Service Bureau for someone they sent Patrick. There's a growing fashion now to have boy-maids.'

'What had he been doing before?'

'He was at art school, doing fashion design. He specialised in designing underwear for both sexes and he also created skirts for men. He'd been neglected by his indifferent parents and yearned for the security of strictness, so he simply loves to be disciplined by a woman. I must say it is an exciting experience to spank or whip him.'

'Goodness, I feel amazingly turned on. The sight of the whippings going on over there and your talk of spanking Patrick. How do you usually do it?'

'I usually make him bend over something suitable: a bench or a chair. Once I had him strung up and had my groom whip him.'

Sonia put an arm around Darline. 'You make me feel so utterly sexy and terribly naughty. Your voice is hypnotising me and I feel I could quite let you take me over.'

They kissed hotly, their lips meeting, connecting then drawing apart a little and then again meeting. Darline's hand was fondling Sonia's breast and she could feel Sonia's hand curving around her own.

'Your breasts are so full and firm,' breathed Darline. 'I want to roll your nipples around and tug on those beads. Let me kiss your lovely full lips. I feel that our lips say more by contact than by words. I could go on like this and I could even go further.' She plunged her tongue into Sonia's mouth.

'Oh, darling, let us go further,' said Sonia when they broke apart. 'I'll strip myself of my little jewelled G-string and you can strip too and we press our bodies close. Let's lie down together.'

Darline could feel Sonia's lithe body beside her own on the hard floor. The hands of each woman moved closer towards the delta of the other and the slim fingers were exploring, each teasing their respective clitorises. Their bodies merged into landscapes of flesh that rolled like hills and valleys. They explored and pulled, their vulvas moist and ready. And then, as their breathing quickened and became more shallow, their bodies surged in rhythms of excruciating pleasure as their orgasms took them to the point of no return. They lay together holding one another close.

Patrick entered with her breakfast tray and Darline looked up. He knew that she was in some kind of trouble and wanted to ask what it was but he didn't like to.

'Good morning, Patrick.'

'Good morning, madam.' He carefully placed the tray before her. He could see that she was sad and he wanted to help.

'Don't go, Patrick. I'd like to talk to you.'

'Yes, madam?'

'Drop calling me madam from now on.'

'All right.' He wondered what was coming.

'I can find no one else to confide in – and I'm beginning to regard you as a friend. The fact is I'm being coerced into accepting certain treatment at the hands of Agrippina Dunbar.'

'Being coerced!'

'Yes, Agrippina Dunbar has me under duress. You recall the time she came upon us when I was whipping the girls in the spinney, when they took your strokes?'

'Yes.'

'Well, she wrote and invited me to Dunbar Hall and said she would have me charged – you know she is a magistrate?'

'Yes.'

'She said she'd have me charged with – oh God knows what! – gross indecency in a public place, cruelty, assault, actual bodily harm. Unless, that is, I submit to whatever she wants to do to me once a month – all sorts of humiliations and flagellations. When I went she made me clean a lavatory and bidet with a toothbrush. Then she had me tied to a flogging frame and whipped by her maid with a cat-o'-nine-tails. It wasn't the lead-weighted kind they used to use in the Navy, just knotted along the tails, but it was done in hate and contempt. I had no hard feelings towards the maid, Erna, she was charming to me and was just obeying orders. The awful thing is that in a peculiar way I partly enjoyed it. But I don't want to connive in punishment out of hate.'

He could see that Darline was close to tears, then suddenly she broke down and began to sob uncontrollably. He wanted to take her in his arms and comfort her, but she needed to continue her explanation.

'Then she made me go on all fours and made her husband have sex with me from the back. She said we were slaves and she was breeding from us. The terrible thing is that I loathe such things when they are done in hatred.'

Patrick felt himself flooded with compassion. 'There is a simple solution – just call her bluff and go to the police. Mrs Riding's husband is a policeman. If you like I'll arrange something. Next time you go he could accompany you.'

'Goodness, Patrick, I think you're right. You lovely thing. You've come up with a solution when a doctor of psychiatry remained impassive.'

She smiled entreatingly and opened her arms. He went to her and felt her embrace him and then he held her in his own arms and they kissed.

Flavia looked sternly at her lover. 'I can only say that your behaviour last night was utterly appalling. For a woman of your standing to form an attachment with someone you had only met that evening and sink to the floor and have sex in full view of the entire company! Have you no conscience? Have you not the slightest shame?'

Darline said, penitently, 'I am truly sorry, and I am very ashamed of what I did, what I let happen. I can only suggest that you punish me suitably.'

'Down on your knees.' Flavia's voice was like ice. 'Now beg my pardon.'

'I beg your pardon, my noble goddess. I can only say that I adore you and that such a thing will not happen again. Please give me whatever punishment you deem fitting.'

'I think a whipping in the stable yard will meet the case. Afterwards you will be left to meditate on your transgression. I will punish you this evening.'

They went out into the stable yard, Flavia splendid in leopard-skin pants and matching top, Darline naked but for high-heeled jewelled sandals and dangling earrings.

Darline offered her wrists and Flavia tied one end of the rope around them. Slipping the other end through one of the tethering rings she pulled her lover up until she was on tiptoe. Darline felt a strange excitement in herself as she hung there. An owl hooted from the paddock.

Flavia took up the whip and stepped back and to the left of the strung body. 'I shall have compassion on you and give you six strokes only. As I deliver each stroke I want you to say, "I am yours, darling".' She swung the whip and brought it crashing across her lover's back and shoulders.

Darline in receiving the stroke felt her body on fire. The vision of when Melissa and Sarah and Gala and Kirstie had taken the boy's punishment flitted through her mind.

'I am yours, darling.'

Again the lash wrapped itself on and around her back, a little lower.

She thought of Melissa taking down her knickers to reveal the lovely yellow skin of her backside.

'I am yours, darling.'

A nightjar hooted somewhere. Again the lash crashed on her skin, still lower. The vision came of Sarah's roseate skin revealed as her knickers were lowered.

'I am yours, darling.'

An owl flew over low and the wafted air from the wings blew on her shoulders. Gala's skin had been that sexy grey-white when she was whipped.

'I am yours, darling.'

She felt so free in her strung position, the freedom the masochist knows when whipped. Kirstie's tanned buttocks came into view.

220

'I am yours, darling.'

The lash this time crashed on her buttocks. She felt that she loved Flavia more than life itself. Then she felt her lover's lips on her glowing back and heard her say, 'I love you so I lash you, darling.'

'I am yours, darling.'

13

The Reckoning

Paul Riding looked at her with compassion, 'So you've been having a hard time.'

'I have indeed.'

'Ingrid has told me about you and your work. And about your young man, Patrick.'

'About the regime he was subjected to; well, he is a darling, he came up with the right solution.'

'I think he did.' Riding's voice was gentle. 'It's best to face things, however grim they seem to be.'

Darline smiled wanly and put a hand to her forehead. 'I could cry like a child from sheer relief – or laugh for joy. You're so understanding, and you don't condemn me.'

'Mine is a hard line of work, but I think its very hardness has taught me compassion. I see many things, some of them terrible – the kind of things you'd really rather not know about – and what you've told me about your own activities is far from horrific.'

'It's lovely to hear you say that; lovely and healing. It's like the smell of oil paint when I apply it with the zizz of the brush on canvas – or the flowers in my garden – or when I ride in the freshness of the morning.'

'I really mean it.'

'You don't condemn me then? You don't condemn me at all?'

'No, not in the least. You probably know that I am myself a masochist.'

'Ingrid told me something to that effect. I hope I'm not telling on her.'

'No, I don't see it like that, I think it's good for friends, fellows in sado-masochism, to share it with one another.'

'Jung said somewhere that it's a psychic misdemeanour to keep secrets.'

'I think he was right.'

'You don't think I was wicked in the things I did, I mean to Patrick and the four girls?'

'Wicked!' He smiled gently. 'No. A little bit daring perhaps but then I suppose you've heard of some of Ingrid's treatments of Patrick?'

'I've heard about them. She writes me a note as to his progress after each lesson.'

'But you haven't heard of the time she made him swim naked in the spinney pool?'

'No, why did she do that? I used to have him swim there, but I didn't know she did.'

'She's only done it once, so far. It seems she thought he wasn't concentrating hard enough. She asked him what you did to enliven him and he said you made him take a naked swim.'

'Yes.' She was acutely conscious of what Paul Riding might think of her, but she wanted to be explicit. 'And then I swished him with birch twigs.'

'Where did you obtain twigs?'

'There were some besoms they use for fire-fighting nearby. They're rather big, like birch brooms, so I only swished him lightly with them.'

'Yes, well, Ingrid thought she would see how effective this treatment was and she drove him to the spinney and made him swim.'

'Really!'

'Yes, one of my women police constables, Jocelyn Blake, was on horseback patrol and came upon them. I understand she obtained some lighter birch twigs than the ones used in the fire-fighting besoms, and she assisted with the swishing when Ingrid felt tired.'

'Oh, I hadn't heard about that. I am so relieved that you are so understanding, and that you don't condemn me.'

He smiled gently. 'It's not my place to condemn.'

She felt herself close to tears of sheer relief as she said, 'You're quite the nicest policeman I've ever met.'

'It's kind of you to say so; I'm not always complimented. I haven't the slightest objection to flagellation when the recipient is willing, but I take exception to people being forced into it. I think the best course is for me to accompany you on your next visit to the Dunbars. We'll see if we can rationalise the matter without resort to the courts.'

The car scrunched over the gravel in front of Dunbar House and Darline and Paul Riding got out and went up to the front door. They rang and a few moments later Wilkins appeared.

'Good afternoon, madam, her ladyship is expecting you.' He looked quizzically at the policeman.

'I would like to see Lady Dunbar.'

'Have you an appointment, sir?'

'No, I am Superintendent Riding of the Thames Valley Police. I wish to interview Lady Dunbar in connection with this lady's previous visit.'

'Perhaps you would like to come in, sir. I will tell her ladyship you are here.'

Wilkins conducted them to the drawing room and in a few moments Agrippina appeared.

'Good afternoon, Ms Pomeroy.' She turned to Paul Riding. 'I don't think I was expecting you.'

'Superintendent Riding of the Thames Valley Police, ma'am.'

'My butler tells me that you wish to interview me.'

'Yes, ma'am, in connection with Ms Pomeroy's previous visit.'

'Yes, well, do be seated.'

'I understand, ma'am, that you subjected Ms Pomeroy to certain experiences.'

'Well, yes.'

'To certain experiences of a sado-masochistic and sexual nature. I further understand that she was not a willing participant.'

'Well – really! I thought she was.'

224

'My understanding, ma'am, is otherwise.'

'Indeed!'

'Yes, I understand you used a certain kind of coercion to gain your ends.'

'Coercion!'

'Yes, it has a less pleasant connotation.'

'And what might that be?'

'I think we will leave it unsaid.'

'Well, really! I've never heard anything so preposterous. Are you suggesting that Ms Pomeroy came here under duress?'

'That is so, ma'am.'

'This is ridiculous.'

'You don't deny that you invited her here?'

'No, I simply invited her for tea.'

'Yes, ma'am, you invited her for tea and this was followed by certain other activities.'

'Yes, well, I had come upon her whipping four girls on the village green and I thought it might be suitable for her to have a dose of her own medicine.'

'You are a magistrate, are you not, ma'am?'

'I am.'

'Could it be, shall we say, that you were taking the law into your own hands?'

'I don't quite follow you.'

'That you were taking it upon yourself to mete out a punishment.'

'I wouldn't put that interpretation on it. All right, I'll tell you what I feel about it. I witnessed her whipping the four girls on the village green.'

'And they said they were willing.'

'Yes, they did. They said they were taking it for her boy-maid who was wet after a swim. Apparently he was to be punished for not taking his swim on a previous day. I felt, as a magistrate, that she was doing something improper in a public place and that she was causing bodily harm to the girls. All right – if you want to know – I felt that a little of her own medicine might do her good. And, I suppose, even that she might enjoy it.'

225

'Let us hear what Ms Pomeroy has to say about it.' Paul Riding looked expectantly at Darline.

'I can't say that I enjoyed it. I was coerced into submitting to what was done to me. To be utterly honest, there was a strange dark masochistic pleasure in what I felt, but there was emphatically not the all-pervading joy, the liberation, the freeing from care, that a masochist feels in accepting flagellation or humiliation in love, when it is administered in love.'

'Would you relate what actually happened?'

Darline moistened her lips. 'After tea Lady Dunbar summoned her maid, Erna, and instructed her to take me and dress me more suitably for what was to come. Erna took me to a room lined with wardrobes containing all kinds of kinky gear, the kind of things people wear at sado-masochistic and bondage parties, things in leather and plastics and rubber, mostly black. Erna helped me undress, I must say she was most courteous about it, then she dressed me in a slinky garment.'

'Would you describe it in detail?'

'It was in black glistening leather, as if it had been polished. It was rather like a swimsuit but even more revealing. It left my buttocks bare, just a strap over the division of them, there were thin straps over my shoulders and a plunging back left my back bare, there was an oval cut-out in front to leave my belly bare. Then Erna helped me into a black leather mini-skirt, it had a belt encircling my hips and the bottom of it just covered my pubis.' She paused a moment and moistened her lips. 'Black high-heeled shoes completed the outfit.'

'What happened next.'

'Erna left me there and Lady Dunbar came, now dressed in black slinky trousers that fitted her like a second skin and were low cut on her hips, leaving her belly bare. Her breasts were held in place by a kind of strappy bra that left her nipples bare; her nipples were pierced by miniature whips fashioned in white metal. They were like tiny riding switches about nine inches long and they pierced her nipples vertically. Her tummy button was pierced by the

226

haft of a miniature cat-o'-nine-tails, also in silvery metal and fixed with the haft upright and the lashes dangling; the lashes appeared to be of plaited silver wire. On her feet were black shoes with very high heels. Lady Dunbar took me to a bathroom and made me clean a toilet pedestal and bidet with a toothbrush and a tin of tooth powder. She left me for a while and when she came back she had a birch in her hand. She told me to stand up and bow in her presence; then she said my work was not satisfactory, told me to take off the mini-skirt and bend over and touch my toes. Then she flogged me with the birch on my backside. She told me to go to work again and stood over me and every few seconds applied the birch to my bare back. After a while she said a swishing was insufficient and she would have Erna take me to the chastisement chamber and arrange me suitably. Erna took me to a chamber with suffused lighting and sado-masochistic murals on the walls. She peeled the kinky garment from me, leaving on the shoes and then strapped me to what she called a flogging frame. She strapped me at several points: wrists, ankles, waist, thighs, and tied a thong over the division of my buttocks, tied it tightly to the waist strap so that it cut between them – she said it was an artistic touch. Lady Dunbar entered and told Erna to strip to her underwear the better to apply it and give me thirty strokes with a cat-o'-nine-tails. I have to say it was not the brutal kind of weighted cat-o'-nine-tails once used in the Navy but simply with knots along the length of the thongs. I also have to say that she did tell Erna not to flog me within an inch of my skin. Erna commenced laying on the strokes fairly lightly – I say fairly lightly although it still stung me until she had given me twenty; then Lady Dunbar told her to lay the last ten on really hard and she did so until my back and buttocks were on fire and I writhed and strained at my straps.'

Darline paused, licking her lips. She could see that Paul Riding was excited. 'Lady Dunbar said she was now going to use me in an experiment in slave breeding. She sent Erna to fetch her husband and Erna brought him in; he was dressed in a kind of loincloth of what looked like snakeskin, with a piece hanging down in front and behind and held by a snakeskin belt. Lady Dunbar said, "Isn't he the perfect slave in his snakeskin loincloth and G-string – it's real python skin." She lifted the front flap to show the G-string over his genitals. She told Erna to release me from the frame and told me to go on all fours like the animal I was. She said that her husband was a masochist, he was her slave and she was going to use him to serve me as a stallion does a mare or a bull a cow. Then she told Erna to treat her husband suitably and Erna stripped off his G-string and loincloth and applied cream to his penis and unrolled a condom over it. Then she told Erna to treat my thighs and get the cream into my vulva and Erna did so. She told me to hold my thighs together "to offer resistance" and then ordered her husband to mount me and told Erna to lash him to make him harder, which she did. I could feel his hands on my shoulders and his member between my thighs and I held them together and I could feel the end of it on my clitoris. In a short time he ejaculated. I suppose it was premature and Lady Dunbar remarked contemptuously on this and he seemed to take pleasure in her reviling him. Then she said that would be all and Erna was to take me and help me get dressed. I have to say that Erna was kind and courteous throughout and I'm sure she was only obeying orders. That was it; Erna helped me get dressed and took me to the drawing room where she was told to serve sherry. Lord Dunbar was there as well, now fully dressed.'

Paul Riding said gently, 'And how did you feel after this treatment?'

'I felt extreme distaste, not to say revulsion. To be perfectly honest, there may have been some strange dark masochistic feeling but not the sort of feeling I would enjoy.'

Paul Riding looked searchingly at Lady Dunbar.

'This lady is now putting a very different interpretation on the matter. My understanding is that she came willingly and participated willingly,' she said.

Riding glanced at Darline for corroboration.

'I can only say that Lady Dunbar's statements are untrue. She said that as a magistrate she would have me charged for indecency in a public place, assault, actual bodily harm and incitement to indecent exposure.'

Agrippina looked at Paul Riding. 'Well, did she not perpetrate those offences?'

He smiled. 'Well, there is an ancient bye-law which permits nude bathing there – and a moderate swishing with birch twigs might be considered reasonable – it is widely practised in saunas.'

'So why was it wrong for me to engage in something similar in private?'

'I think, ma'am, that you uttered certain threats to your victim.'

'I simply thought as a magistrate it would be kinder to bring a personal touch to her correction; rather than take her through the courts.'

He looked at Darline.

'I can only say that Lady Dunbar is distorting the facts to her own ends. The truth is that she coerced and put me under duress – and she threatened more than having me charged. She said that if I did not comply with her wishes, submit to what she wanted to do to me, she would foreclose the lease on Pomeroy Place. She said that a property developer was interested. My father once owned the property.'

Lady Dunbar came in. 'All I can say is that a light-hearted interpretation is put on it when Ms Pomeroy engages in this activity and a dark interpretation when I engage in it.'

'I wonder, ma'am,' Riding said, 'how your contention would stand up in a court of law.'

'Then I wonder how this lady's contention would stand up.'

'I think, ma'am, that the matter need not be taken as far as the courts.'

'Well, I did not wish to take Ms Pomeroy to court.'

'But it was wrong of you to attempt to take the law into your own hands.'

'If you will persist in putting that interpretation on it.'

'Lady Dunbar, I can see no other. But I put it to you that the matter can be settled amicably. We will go no further with your, shall we say, coercion of Ms Pomeroy. There will be no question of taking the matter to court; and you, on your part, will never again attempt to coerce Ms Pomeroy.'

Agrippina was showing signs of cracking. It was apparent in her face. 'Well, if you put it like that.'

'And, of course, you will go no further in the matter of Pomeroy Place.'

Agrippina was now beaten. 'I don't think I had any real intention of doing anything.'

'I'm glad to hear it.' Riding smiled gently and said, 'It's good to be able to adjust matters without recourse to the courts.' He looked at Agrippina. 'One final observation, ma'am. I should seriously consider your official position.'

'In what way?'

'You're a magistrate, in a position of some trust and some authority, and your behaviour should reflect this. Otherwise I would think you should reflect upon the propriety of continuing its tenure.'

14

Shrink into Slave

'So he sorted the matter out for you?' Flavia felt the tremor in her voice.

Her former lover regarded her coolly. 'Yes, Paul sorted the matter out for me, he was absolutely wonderful.'

'I hope there is no resentment.'

'As to your indifferent attitude, you doubtless mean.'

'I felt I was doing my duty.'

'You inferred that on many occasions.'

'Well, yes, it's true that I did.'

'You maintained that you were keeping to your professional code of practice.'

'Yes, as a doctor and analyst I felt I had to be impersonal – detached.'

'Yes, and you detached yourself.'

'Perhaps "detached" is too harsh a word, perhaps "non-attached" would be better.'

'Are you now playing with words in an attempt to justify your attitude?'

'Honestly – I attempted to express my state of mind in words. I thought that my attitude was not as harsh as detached.'

'Whatever your state of mind I take exception to it. When I was in difficulty you were indifferent. You remained safe at the edge of the arena and were impassive and just made notes for your research. I can only tell you now that I do not wish to know you, and, as far as I am concerned, our relationship is finished.'

'Really! Can you really be serious and mean it? I loved you and I still love you.'

'You were indifferent when I needed you.'

'I know an analyst's attitude can seem hard but won't you try to see? I meant it for the best. My intentions were honourable, I love you.'

Darline was impassive as her former lover came and knelt before her.

Flavia took her hand and kissed it and whispered, 'I love you,' and looked beseechingly up into her face.

'If you can't see what I did as justified, will you not try to find it in your heart to forgive?'

Darline withdrew her hand. 'I shall probably forgive in the course of time, but this does not alter the reality that our relationship is finished.'

Flavia remained on her knees. 'Is there nothing I can do? Let me undergo a penance, think of some fitting punishment for me, only don't banish me from your life.'

Darline found it profoundly strange to see Flavia, the shaman, the doctor and analyst, abasing herself, pleading for forgiveness and asking to be punished.

'Your grovelling will not necessarily get you anywhere but leave me for an hour and I will ponder the matter.'

'Thank you,' Flavia murmured. 'I will not presume to kiss your hand. I will accept whatever you deem fitting.' She got to her feet, made an awkward half-bow and left the room, glancing back before closing the door.

Darline was painting in her studio and she looked up when there was a light knock and Flavia entered.

'What a splendid painting,' Flavia exclaimed.

'Flattery, I think, is out of place.'

'I just thought how masterfully you had handled the paint; how you had rendered the skins of the two models and that of the snake.'

'Thank you, but I can do without your flattery. I've thought over your request, your grovelling plea for penance and I've come to a conclusion.'

'Yes? Do please tell me, I will comply with your wishes.'

'I warn you that it will be harsh, just as you were harsh.'

'Yes, I will accept your harshness, your coolness will be dear to me; if you will only acknowledge my existence.'

'You realise that to undergo your penance will not automatically reinstate you in favour?'

'No, no, I don't aspire to that. I can only hope. I pray to be privileged to kiss your feet.'

'Don't attempt it. Now listen to what I'm about to say. I have decided that your penance will take the form of your becoming a slave on certain occasions.'

'Yes, yes, mistress. I may call you mistress, may I?'

'I suppose you may. I have decided to give salons, functions at which you will serve my guests and myself.'

'Yes.'

'Just as you had the idea of making Patrick serve naked to strip him of some of his persona, so you will now find yourself serving naked. Have you anything to say?'

'Well – only that I am willing, mistress, and that I will serve to the best of my ability.'

Darline smiled at Flavia, a smile decidedly coquettish. 'We shall have you serve us as a naked slave girl. One not even considered a person or a citizen. Now let me see, how shall we prepare you for your slavishness? Naked to begin with, I think, but we'll permit you something on your feet to make you more titillating, and we'll permit you a slave collar. Then I think we'll have your flesh pierced in various places, say your nipples and your belly button. We'll pierce your nipples with some rugged metal studs and put one of those curved bars with jewelled knobs through your navel. Trisha is adorned so and looks very fetching. And so you shall serve. When your piercings have healed we'll see about some arrows through your nipples and a stiletto for your belly. But this won't constitute immediate expiation. We shall repeat your slave treatment on more than one occasion, most likely on many.'

'I am willing, do with me what you will.'

'You appear to have adopted your abased role quite readily, almost with eagerness. Perhaps you will take masochistic pleasure in my piercing your flesh. Now, should we put studs or rings through your nipples? A new body piercing studio has been set up in Kingston. Shall we take you along there to have you suitably pierced?'

'Well, yes. If you wish, if it will give you pleasure.'

'Perhaps you will also find pleasure in it, hardly any pain, but some deep pleasure.'

'I think I might. I'm sure you don't mean to hurt me.'

'We shall see whether you are hurt or not when you assume slave-girl status. Shall we visit the piercing studio tomorrow?'

The body piercing studio was not far from the university. It was a bright and shining salon, splendidly appointed.

They went in and were greeted by a young woman wearing a dark brown leather mini-skirt, a black shirt and a brown leather waistcoat. Her blonde hair was piled high and tied by a plaited leather thong.

'Hi, I'm Astra, how can I help you?'

Flavia looked at her mistress and Darline spoke. 'My friend wants to have her body pierced; her nipples and tummy button.'

'Splendid! How lovely! Let me show you what we can offer.'

Astra took them to the back of the studio and showed them a selection of bars and bells and studs.

'They come in stainless steel or niobium, which is purer than stainless steel, and comes in black in matt or gloss, in eleven colours or rainbow.'

'They're quite beautiful,' Darline mused. She looked at Flavia. 'What do you think?'

'They are beautiful – but I'd like to leave the choice to you.'

'I think we'll make it these lovely studs in carmine red for your nipples – and for your tummy button we'll make it this jewelled barbell.'

'A very good choice,' Astra approved. 'Is there any special reason why this lady is being pierced?'

'The reason is that she's to serve as a slave at a party – and I thought it would be nice for her to serve naked – apart from some diverting embellishments.'

'How lovely.' Astra's grin widened. 'Well, come along to the treatment room and I'll prepare for the piercing. I'm sure you'd like to see your friend being done.'

Astra slipped on a white coat and latex gloves. 'Now if you'll undress to bare your breasts and your tummy.'

Flavia said, 'I suppose it's easiest if I strip to my knickers.'

'I should think so,' Darline assented.

Flavia undressed and Astra said, 'Now, if you'll just lie down on the couch. One thing – would you like an anaesthetic?'

'No, I'll experience what it's like without.'

'She's a masochist,' Darline remarked naughtily to Astra, and Astra smiled.

Astra took a swab and said, 'I'll sterilise your nipples first.' The cool douche stiffened them, then with a cosmetic pencil, she marked points on the nipples and held a mirror. 'Those are the piercing points – are you happy with them?' Flavia smiled agreement. Astra took an instrument from a plastic tube. 'This is what I pierce you with, it's a cannula, a needle shrouded in a PTFE tube. A straw-like part of it remains in the piercing. I'll hold your nipple with this clamp – so – and now I pierce you.'

Flavia felt herself flinch slightly as the metal went through.

'Now for the other nipple.' Astra deftly repeated the operation. 'Now for your tummy button. Again I'll swab you. Now gently with the clamp on your little hill of flesh and so – it's done. Now I'll insert your studs and your lovely jewelled barbell.'

'They'll set off your nakedness very well,' Darline remarked. 'I'm almost inclined to have it done myself.'

Flavia was on a strange high on the first evening of her naked exposure as a slave girl. The guests were arriving and her first duty was to circulate among them offering drinks and delicacies.

'A little champagne, madam.' Julia looked at her and took a glass. 'Thank you, Flavia,' she said, accepting the servant's nakedness with well-bred nonchalance.

'A little champagne, sir.' Paul Riding took a glass and remarked, 'I like your body jewels.'

'Thank you, sir, they were the choice of my mistress.'

'Then she has excellent taste.'

'Girl,' Darline summoned and Flavia moved swiftly to where her former lover stood conversing with Patrick.

'Some wine for this gentleman, dry, well chilled.'

Flavia felt herself wince as she said, 'Yes, noble lady.' She hastened to a table set with bottles, poured a glass of white wine, set it on a tray and returned to where Darline and Patrick stood talking. She bowed before Patrick and offered the wine. He took it and she bowed and was about to go.

'Stay, girl,' Darline commanded. Turning to Patrick she said, 'Look at this slave girl's body jewels, Patrick. I had her body so pierced on a whim, thinking my guests might find it diverting.'

Flavia could see that Patrick was embarrassed and she was grateful that he felt for her in her abasement.

'There.' Darline took hold of one of the nipple studs and shook the breast slightly.

'Were you happy to have it done?' Patrick asked.

'Yes, I was perfectly happy, sir.'

'Enough, girl.' Darline's tone was peremptory. 'Slaves do not converse with their betters. Be about your duties.'

Flavia bowed and moved away. She was not a person in this gathering, just a mere servant, her only *raison d'être* being to serve her superiors. Having served them all drinks she was to circulate with a tray of delicacies. As she moved to the table to collect them, she brushed against Ingrid and said, 'I beg your pardon, madam.'

'That's all right,' Ingrid said and then remarked admiringly, 'I like your outfit.' She laughed slightly. 'Or your lack of it. Your breast and belly jewels are magnificent.'

She felt herself standing there dutifully, slave girl before patrician lady, standing until it was indicated she might depart.

'Patrick has told me about his stay with you,' Ingrid said

knowingly. 'And how you made him go naked.' She smiled at the slave girl.

Flavia inclined her head. 'Yes, madam.'

'Yes, he said it was to disperse some of his persona.'

'Yes, madam.'

'I took him out driving dressed as a woman too, and a very attractive sight he made.'

'I would think so, madam.'

'You play the naked slave very well.'

'You are very kind, madam. If madam will excuse me, I will be about my duties.' She bowed and moved to the food table, where she piled a tray with delicacies and again circulated. She went to where Melissa, Kirstie, Sarah and Gala were chatting to Pina and offered the tray.

'Oh scrumptious,' Kirstie said, taking a morsel.

'What a fab party,' Gala remarked, eyeing the naked slave's body with its jewels. 'Wow! I like your body ornaments.'

'Thank you,' Flavia murmured.

'You're a psychiatrist, aren't you?' Sarah quizzed.

'I am, but not in my present status.'

'We've heard about your experiments with Patrick, about making him go naked when he was staying with you.'

'And now I serve naked myself.'

'Still, perhaps it will yield further material for your research,' Kirstie put in. 'You'll experience it from the receiving end.'

'Yes, as a masochist.' Flavia smiled wanly.

Paul Riding rapped on a table and announced, 'Ladies and gentlemen, our hostess wishes you to appraise something.'

Darline looked around at them. 'Friends, guests, noble people, I am delighted to say that we are now to divert ourselves, engage in play. Girl, come here.'

Flavia went to Darline who took her arm as if to display her to the company. 'There, isn't she a splendidly pierced and jewelled masochistic sight. We are now going to make sport with her, if you'll follow me out to the patio.' Flavia

237

let herself be led out, feeling like a garlanded heifer being taken for sacrifice. Darline led her over to the edge of the swimming pool.

'Now, people, we are going to stand this creature on the edge of the pool on this dais. Get up there,' she ordered 'Isn't she a vulnerable target. Now here is a tub of water containing wet sponges. For a pound a go you can hurl sponges at her. If she moves she pays a forfeit of three strokes of the birch twigs. If you dislodge her from the dais, six strokes. If you knock her into the water, nine strokes. There is no need for compunction – a swishing will warm her bare body. And, I should tell you, all proceeds will go to the Psychic Health Society.'

There was some diffidence at first, some hanging back, then Gala approached and paid for three sponges.

Flavia prepared herself for the first strike. It hit her between her breasts, making them and their studs shake. The second hit her full in the face and she could not help but jerk.

'Excellent,' Darline cried. 'A hit that shook her. I put her down for three strokes.'

Gala drew back her arm and threw her last missile. The sponge hit the target full in the belly, just above the barbell jewel, and she gasped and jerked her body.

'Excellent!' Darline yelled. 'And I assign her another three strokes.'

Ingrid came up and paid for six sponges and Flavia awaited her attack. She could see a familiar look in the aimer's face and she could feel a change in mood and saw that there was now a queue for purchasing missiles.

Ingrid's first sponge landed just under her right breast. She had to steel herself and managed to take it without a tremor. The next sponge was aimed low and struck heavily and wetly right on her pubis but again she managed to remain immobile. She was shivering a little in the evening breeze. She awaited the next cold splashy hit finding a kind of pride in herself as she stood naked and exposed and alone. The next struck dead centre of her belly and there were cries of 'Shot' and 'Excellent shot'. She could see now, that Ingrid was beginning to enjoy it, not caring how she humiliated or disconcerted her victim. She hurled the next sponge and Flavia took it full on the forehead and felt herself teeter and topple backwards. The cold water enveloped her. There were cheers and yelps of joy; they were now like a pack of hounds baying for blood.

'Splendid!' Darline cried joyfully. 'And I sentence her to nine strokes of the stingy twigs.'

Flavia climbed up the steps of the pool, her body streaming. An owl hooted from the paddock and then emitted a raucous 'kik kik kik kik' as if laughing. She flinched as though stabbed by the call. She saw Sally approach Darline and heard her say, 'Don't you think we might show her a little mercy?'

'I don't think it appropriate but we will ask her if she thinks she deserves it.' She went up to Flavia. 'Girl, this lady has suggested that we might have compassion and release you from further target duty. What do you say?'

'Noble lady, I will submit to whatever you deem proper for me.'

'Well said.' She turned to Sally. 'You see, she accepts her slave-girl status, makes no demur. We shall continue with our sport. Get back up there, girl.'

Flavia stepped up, trying to still the shivering of her wet body. There were profound stirrings in her. She would take whatever her former lover now cared to inflict and whatever the noble gathering cared to hurl at her.

'You have another three to throw,' Darline called to Ingrid, who took a sponge which dripped on the paving as she drew back her arm.

Flavia awaited the impact and then it hit her just above her pubic mound. She gasped but did not move. She heard someone say, 'She's brave, she's got guts.' Then another said, 'Let's break her, let's make her really feel her slavishness.' She could feel their mood getting wilder, they were snarling like dogs hoping to tear a fox apart.

'I know,' Darline cried. 'Ingrid can throw her remaining two and then you can all have a go at once.'

Lilian emerged and approached Darline. 'Madam, I

thought I should tell you that dinner is ready and is likely to spoil if left too long.'

'Thank you, Lilian, we shall not be long. Noble people, dinner is soon to be served. We will let Ingrid throw her two remaining sponges and then we will have this girl wait on us. Throw! Ingrid, throw!'

Again Flavia saw Ingrid's arm drawn back, the sponge streaming. Then it struck her in the diaphragm and she teetered, tried to steady herself and then felt herself falling backwards into the embrace of the cold water. She heard the yelps of joy.

'A markswoman!' Darline cried as she joyfully kissed Ingrid. 'I could make love to you, I could ravish you. That earns her a further nine strokes of the twigs, making it twenty-four.'

As she came up the steps of the pool, back onto dry land, the clamour of her tormentors rang in her ears. She saw that Paul Riding took pleasure in Darline's desire for Ingrid. It was apparent in the deeply perverse excitement on his face. Despite her wet abasement she took pleasure in his pleasure. It ran through her mind that sado-masochism can bring together the erotic and the spiritual.

'I think that's enough for the present,' Darline proclaimed. 'This girl will wait on us as we dine and then, if inclined, we can further disport ourselves. But first a swishing on her wet skin.'

'Don't you think we should dry her first?' Sally pleaded.

'I do not; and I'm sure she does not. Have you any objection to being flogged on your wet body, girl?'

'No, noble lady.'

Darline took up a birch rod tied with black leather thongs. 'Bend over and touch your toes.'

Flavia bent her wet shivering body and put her fingertips to her toenails. She could see her flogger's arm raised and then felt the sting as the twigs met her backside. There was the after-burn as the rod was raised and after long moments the impact and the sting. There was silence from the audience. From her bent position she could see the intent faces, some wearing broad grins. Darline thrashed slowly, giving her time to feel the lick and the tingling after each stroke and anticipate the next. As it went on she felt a warm glow and with the twenty-fourth she felt in herself a strange joy.

Patrick approached Darline. 'Don't you think we should dry her?'

'You may if you wish, we don't want her dripping on us.'

Patrick fetched two large towels, tossed one to Pina and they started to dry her shivering body. Patrick attended to her back and Pina her front. The absorbent towelling was comforting on her lashed skin.

'I thought you were very brave,' Pina remarked as she gently patted her breasts. 'There, I'll be careful not to snag your studs in the towel.'

'You were very brave,' Patrick said soothingly as he patted her back.

'Thank you, you are both very kind.'

'It's the least we can do,' Pina said and then asked, 'Don't you mind this treatment? It must be very humiliating for you.'

'It *is* humiliating – but perhaps I will benefit.'

'I thought you and Darline were lovers, that you really loved one another.'

'We were, and I hope we still may be.'

'I suppose lovers can be cruel to one another at times,' said Patrick.

'They *are* cruel to one another.'

'But I suppose cruelty can be a kind of love,' suggested Pina.

'It can be a kind of love, with Darline and myself it certainly was – and maybe still is.'

'Yet I still don't quite see why you accept such treatment so – well – so compliantly, with such humility.'

'Well, Darline accepted spankings and whippings from me, and Patrick accepted those and more from Darline. And from you once.'

'But you're a professor of psychiatry.'

Flavia smiled wanly. 'A professor of psychiatry has the same desires as others. Everybody has these desires.'

They finished patting her dry, now working on her legs and feet and for a few moments there was silence.

Flavia went on, 'Others accepted it from me and now I accept it.' She smiled gently. 'Thank you both for your kindness in drying me. I will now wait on you at table and afterwards you will make further sport of me. You'll make me wet and I'll shiver, then my former lover will swish and sting my wet skin. It's a form of love.'

NEW BOOKS

Coming up from Nexus and Black Lace

Nexus

There are three Nexus titles published in November

A Taste of Amber by Penny Birch
November 1998   Price £5.99   ISBN: 0 352 33293 X

Expelled from school for spanking a mistress, Amber Oakley finds herself in disgrace and is sent to work on a farm. She quickly discovers that her godfather is not the respectable country gentleman he appears to be. Introduced to the delights of pony-girl fantasy, Amber soon decides that she knows what she wants to be – a pony-girl mistress. Unfortunately for her, many of the people she meets would rather she was at the other end of the reins.

The Discipline of Nurse Riding by Yolanda Celbridge
November 1998   Price £5.99   ISBN: 0 352 33291 3

Prudence Riding suddenly finds herself looking for work after the sudden failure of her trust fund. She gets a post as a nurse but finds that her training is rather more severe than expected, involving strict discipline and an education in the application of bizarre and exotic treatments. Nurse Riding's further instruction in the use of medical restraints is interrupted by a hunch that her long-lost twin sister is nearby – can Prudence ever hope to find her? By the author of the acclaimed *Governess* and *Maldona* series.

Rue Marquis de Sade by Morgana Baron
November 1998   Price £5.99   ISBN: 0 352 33093 7

As Charlotte travels to Steinreich – a tiny, self-governing principality of Europe – to claim her share of her father's legacy, her thoughts turn, inevitably, to her stepsister. Veronica is as sadistic and dominant as Charlotte is masochistic and submissive and, having gained a brief insight into Steinreich's bizarre history, laws and customs, Charlotte begins to wonder what she will be forced to endure in order to qualify for her inheritance. This is a new edition of one of our most popular titles.

There are three Nexus titles published in December

Fairground Attractions by Lisette Ashton

December 1998   Price £5.99   ISBN: 0 352 33295 6

Beneath the glamour and excitement of the fairground there is a sinister world, undisclosed to the visiting crowds. Operating outside the restrictions of the towns they entertain, the fairground's owners are used to indulging their lewd appetites whenever and however they please. Georgia and Holly are reluctant recruits to the fairground and they soon discover the pains and pleasures of this barbarous regime, as both women endure a painful lesson in the fairground's rules. It's a lesson they will never forget. By the author of *The Black Room* and *Amazon Slave*.

The Warrior Queen by Kendal Grahame

December 1998   Price £5.99   ISBN: 0 352 33294 8

In the first century AD, the Roman army has invaded Britannia and its soldiers are sating their lusts on helpless Celtic maidens. A revolt is underway, however, led by Boudicca, queen of the Iceni. She loves dominating men as much as the Romans love dominating women, and surrounds herself with submissives who fulfil her every need, no matter how perverted. Seeking advice from a mysterious druid clan, she finds herself for the first time uncomfortably aroused by the idea of submitting to a man. Will she ever be able to satisfy her darkest urges? By the author of *The Training of Fallen Angels*.

Bound to Obey by Amanda Ware

December 1998   Price £5.99   ISBN: 0 352 33058 9

Master Francis and Mistress Lynne have appointed Caroline as their new maid. But this post requires more than the usual amount of submissiveness from the servant, and a far less substantial uniform. At times, Caroline will be expected to wear no more than a silk scarf bound tightly around her wrists. Just as she is beginning to get used to her kinky employers, Caroline finds that there are others with still more deviant proclivities – ones which she is soon to witness at first hand. This is a new edition of one of Nexus's most popular tales of submission.

Nexus

NEXUS BACKLIST

All books are priced £4.99 unless another price is given. If a date is supplied, the book in question will not be available until that month in 1998.

CONTEMPORARY EROTICA

THE ACADEMY	Arabella Knight		
AGONY AUNT	G. C. Scott		
ALLISON'S AWAKENING	Lauren King		
AMAZON SLAVE	Lisette Ashton	£5.99	
THE BLACK GARTER	Lisette Ashton	£5.99	Sept
THE BLACK ROOM	Lisette Ashton		
BOUND TO OBEY	Amanda Ware	£5.99	Dec
BOUND TO SUBMIT	Amanda Ware		
CANDIDA IN PARIS	Virginia Lasalle		
CHAINS OF SHAME	Brigitte Markham	£5.99	July
A CHAMBER OF DELIGHTS	Katrina Young		
DARK DELIGHTS	Maria del Rey	£5.99	Aug
DARLINE DOMINANT	Tania d'Alanis	£5.99	Oct
A DEGREE OF DISCIPLINE	Zoe Templeton		
THE DISCIPLINE OF NURSE RIDING	Yolanda Celbridge	£5.99	Nov
THE DOMINO TATTOO	Cyrian Amberlake		
THE DOMINO QUEEN	Cyrian Amberlake		
EDEN UNVEILED	Maria del Rey		
EDUCATING ELLA	Stephen Ferris		
EMMA'S SECRET DOMINATION	Hilary James		
FAIRGROUND ATTRACTIONS	Lisette Ashton	£5.99	Dec
THE TRAINING OF FALLEN ANGELS	Kendal Grahame		
HEART OF DESIRE	Maria del Rey		

ANCIENT & FANTASY SETTINGS

THE CLOAK OF APHRODITE	Kendal Grahame		
DEMONIA	Kendal Grahame		
THE DUNGEONS OF LIDIR	Aran Ashe		
THE FOREST OF BONDAGE	Aran Ashe		
NYMPHS OF DIONYSUS	Susan Tinoff		
THE WARRIOR QUEEN	Kendal Grahame	£5.99	Dec

EDWARDIAN, VICTORIAN & OLDER EROTICA

ANNIE	Evelyn Culber	£5.99	
ANNIE AND THE COUNTESS	Evelyn Culber	£5.99	
BEATRICE	Anonymous		
THE CORRECTION OF AN ESSEX MAID	Yolanda Celbridge	£5.99	
DEAR FANNY	Michelle Clare		
LYDIA IN THE HAREM	Philippa Masters		
LURE OF THE MANOR	Barbra Baron		
MAN WITH A MAID 3	Anonymous		
MEMOIRS OF A CORNISH GOVERNESS	Yolanda Celbridge		
THE GOVERNESS AT ST AGATHA'S	Yolanda Celbridge		
MISS RATTAN'S LESSON	Yolanda Celbridge	£5.99	Aug
PRIVATE MEMOIRS OF A KENTISH HEADMISTRESS	Yolanda Celbridge		
SISTERS OF SEVERCY	Jean Aveline		

SAMPLERS & COLLECTIONS

EROTICON 3	Various		
EROTICON 4	Various	£5.99	July
THE FIESTA LETTERS	ed. Chris Lloyd		
NEW EROTICA 2	ed. Esme Ombreux		
NEW EROTICA 3	ed. Esme Ombreux		
NEW EROTICA 4	ed. Esme Ombreux	£5.99	Sept

NON-FICTION

- -

Please send me the books I have ticked above.

Name ....

Address ....

....

....

.... Post code........................

Send to: **Cash Sales, Nexus Books, Thames Wharf Studios, Rainville Road, London W6 9HT**

Please enclose a cheque or postal order, made payable to **Nexus Books**, to the value of the books you have ordered plus postage and packing costs as follows:

UK and BFPO – £1.00 for the first book, 50p for the second book and 30p for each subsequent book to a maximum of £3.00;

Overseas (including Republic of Ireland) – £2.00 for the first book, £1.00 for the second book and 50p for each subsequent book.

If you would prefer to pay by VISA or ACCESS/MASTER-CARD, please write your card number and expiry date here:

....

Please allow up to 28 days for delivery.

Signature ....

- -